HOT POT MURDER

MURDER

Jennifer J. Chow

BERKLEY PRIME CRIME
New York

BERKLEY PRIME CRIME
Published by Berkley
An imprint of Penguin Random House LLC
penguinrandomhouse.com

Copyright © 2023 by Jennifer J. Chow

ISBN: 9780593336557

First Edition: June 2023

Printed in the United States of America
1   3   5   7   9   10   8   6   4   2

Book design by Daniel Brount

For Mom Chow / A-Ma,
who made hot pot a family tradition

ONE

ALL HAPPY HOT POT GATHERINGS ARE ALIKE; each unhappy hot pot event is disastrous in its own way. It started off early with the invitation from Nikola Ho. Continuing his trend of irritating me ever since we were middle school academic rivals, Nik had now single-handedly ruined my plans for a quiet Thanksgiving dinner with my nearest and dearest beside me. The holiday was one of the few times that Ba actually shut down his dim sum restaurant, Wing Fat, and focused on family. Even though it'd been quieter in recent years with just the two of us sharing slices of turkey, I'd still appreciated the time spent with my dad. This year, it'd be even livelier with the presence of my cousin, Celine, who'd flown in from Hong Kong last month. Although she and I had two decades of silence between us, we'd mended our ways recently, especially while clearing our shared Yee name from police suspicion when someone had died at the night market where we run our food booth. The murder

and its subsequent resolution had placed the inaugural
Eastwood Village Night Market on the L.A. dining map.
It also ended up creating an exciting food event every
weekend in the planned community of Eastwood Village.

I loved living in the local area. Everything had its
place and order. All essential services were within walking distance of my apartment—and Celine's current
residence while living in the States—at Fountain Vista.
I could stroll to my two favorite spots, the Eastwood Village Public Library and The Literary Narnia, my beloved
bookstore (and previous place of employment, until I'd
rediscovered my passion for cooking).

Nik hadn't bothered to officially invite me to his
Thanksgiving banquet. He didn't send me a card or call
me on my landline (Celine was still trying to convince
me to get a cell phone). To be honest, I wasn't even sure
I'd made it on the list of exclusive attendees. He'd actually asked Ba to come, but added a plus-one option,
which Ba had changed to plus-two. I bet Nik's mother, Ai
Ho, wanted my cousin to show up as the extra guest. She
had rosy-hued dreams of Celine staying in the States and
settling down with Nik.

The Thanksgiving gathering had been billed as a
meeting of the minds for the local Asian restaurant business community. They even had an official title for their
group: Asian American Restaurant Owners Association,
or AAROA.

Nik had called together a group meet-up because of
the dwindling membership of the association. To be fair,
there weren't that many Asian restaurants in West Los
Angeles—many of them stayed in distinct geographic
locations like Chinatown and Thai Town. Others had
branched off to the San Gabriel Valley or even Westmin-
ster, down in Orange County. The ones that stayed in
business in the region either didn't have time to join
AAROA or maybe felt like the restaurant-owner con-

nection wasn't necessary. Nik's mother thought the tie was essential and wanted to promote cooperation among the younger generations of restaurateurs. I half wondered if she'd thought up the original idea of a Thanksgiving meal to promote unity among the business owners.

At the onset of the idea, though, Nik and I had clashed. Once I'd known about the revised Thanksgiving, I offered up Wing Fat as the logical place to gather. We had plenty of space for guests, even though I knew that the group currently numbered only six people. Wing Fat had a whole banquet room, a partitioned space, to fill up with people and food.

Nik declined our offer and said everybody should meet up at his mother's restaurant, Ho's, and he won the argument. I was surprised the Thanksgiving meal wouldn't be at Jeffery Vue's eatery, actually. I figured as the president of AAROA, he'd be ready to jump in with the meeting location. Then again, maybe he didn't want to deal with the cleanup on his day off. Plus, I'd heard from Ba that he was rearranging his priorities and currently focusing on his dating life.

Despite the contentious venue, Celine's ambitious social media influencer inclination to "put a shine" on the event meant that my cousin and I had arrived early on Thanksgiving to decorate the restaurant in advance of the dinner. She stood in front of Ho's, carrying a large cardboard box, while I tapped on the glass door.

Nik came and greeted us with a half-hearted wave. Although it appeared like he'd just woken up, I knew his signature bedhead look took meticulous styling. He'd mastered the effect in high school and then added bleached strands and a goatee to the hair mix post-college.

He pushed the door open to let us in. "If it isn't the deadly Yee duo."

"Very funny," I said, although I hadn't seen any humor in the situation when I'd literally run into a dead body with my food cart during the night market event around Halloween. "Can't believe you wrote that I made 'brutal boba.'" Nik had run a column in his *Eastwood Village Connection* blog about how the night market had turned deadly, perhaps due to my fatal recipe.

"Who are you to complain?" he said. "People were lining up at Canai and Chai last weekend for your signature drink."

I stopped a sigh from escaping my lips. Who knew what would catch people's fancy? Night market–goers did like ordering my grapefruit green tea with boba, those chewy tapioca balls, for the fun of it. Maybe they felt like they were daring death, even though the police had cleared my drink of any suspicion after they'd arrested the real killer.

"Ho's Small Eats didn't do so badly either," I said, referring to the food stand Nik and his mother ran, a neighboring stall to our own. I'd seen a line snaking before them, people eager to eat spiced popcorn chicken and enjoy freezing-cold shaved ice.

Celine dropped her box on the long counter of Ho's, and it landed with a heavy *thump*. "Less talking, more work," she said. "It might take a miracle to transform this place in only one hour."

I studied the restaurant, again reflecting on the fact that a 1950s diner had previously been in this location. Ho's still retained red vinyl booths and checkerboard flooring. They'd even kept the swivel barstools lined up along the counter. "This place has never really screamed 'Taiwanese' to me."

"It's the authentic food cooked in here that draws in our customers," Nik said in an irritated tone. I wasn't sure which hurt him more: that I'd put down his family's restaurant or that I knew the dishes he referred to didn't come from his own hands. Mrs. Ho still didn't trust her son to do more than serve and wipe down the tables.

I leaned toward the kitchen door. In fact, I could hear some banging around in there. Maybe she'd already started preparing. Dad should also be there, and maybe Roy Yamada. All members of AAROA, they'd bonded over their stories about immigrating to America and also the fact that they'd lost their spouses within the past ten years. Mr. Yamada had been widowed the least amount of time. His wife had died last year after a bout with aggressive cancer.

Celine clapped her hands together twice to get Nik's and my attention. "Here's what I'm envisioning," she said. My cousin was a foodstagrammer, and while she loved her food shots on Instagram the most, I could see her creative brain working as she laid out her Thanksgiving design plan. She wanted to decorate the tabletops with scented spice candles, arrange a line of painted pumpkins along the counter, and pin a garland of colorful walnuts against a wall.

"How do you know so much about Thanksgiving anyway?" I said. "Isn't it an American holiday?"

"I live in Hong Kong," she said, "not Antarctica."

"We're not even having turkey per tradition," I said as I shook my head at Nik.

"News flash," he said. "Nobody likes turkey. Usually it comes out too dry."

"*I* like turkey," I said, grabbing a few orange candles and bunching them together on a table. "I'm not sure why we have to do hot pot anyway." I liked veggies and meat simmering away in hot broth as much as the next person, but I had looked forward to the holiday's typical stuffing and candied yams.

"My restaurant, my rules," Nik said, as he lined up a few pumpkins along the counter.

I wanted to make a sharp retort about his mother really owning the place, when the front door swung open. Jeffery Vue, wearing a faded black suit and tie, had arrived.

"Friends, how can I help?" he said, sweeping his hands wide, their huge motion mimicking his booming voice. Jeffery had been president of the Asian restaurant owners' club even back when I'd started helping out after my abbreviated time attending college. I didn't think he ever wanted to leave the position. He was a social man who loved gatherings.

On my dim sum personality assessment scale, I labeled him as *char siu bao*, or barbecued pork bun. He had the same kind of rotund appearance as the steamed treat and overflowed with sweet talk. Jeffery had even snared the woman of his dreams with his honeyed mouth. Although he'd taken his "merry time to do so," according to his internal calendar.

The man was in his forties, about ten years older than me, but I remembered to use a respectful title to greet him. "Hello, Mr. Vue, good to see you," I said. "Did you bring your date?"

I tried to peer behind his broad body to catch a glimpse of her. I didn't know anything about the mysterious lady. No one in the association had met her yet.

"She wasn't free this evening. Family obligations of her own," he said.

"A shame."

"Thank you for showing up early, Mr. Vue," my cousin said. Celine moved toward him in her goldenrod sweater dress with suede boots, which she told me she'd selected to match the autumn season. "You can assist with the garland." She handed him a clear jar full of prepainted walnuts in various colors.

He accepted the container and blinked at its contents. "What am I supposed to do with these?"

"Put holes in them and string them together," Celine said. "The drill and twine are in the box on the counter."

Jeffery had just picked up the tool when the door to Ho's burst open, as though by a strong gust of wind. Derrick Tran barreled through. "I'm here," he said.

"Hello, Veep." Jeffery raised the drill in his hand as greeting.

Derrick flinched at the movement. "I have a first name you can use, Jeffery."

"But it's so much quicker to say Veep," Jeffery replied.

Derrick had been second-in-command in the association almost as long as Jeffery had been number one. I didn't think the titles in the organization mattered much, though, because I couldn't see the difference in their duties. All the members of the group seemed to pitch in to get the word out about local Asian restaurants.

"Maybe I won't be VP anymore in a few months," Derrick said. "Voting is coming around, and new leaders start in January." Worry lines creased his pointy forehead, making him appear like the pot sticker personality I'd dubbed him. He'd always seemed an overdone example of the pan-fried version, too crispy and with abundant sharp folds.

"Don't you worry your remaining hairs about that, Veep," Jeffery said as he powered up the drill and bored a hole in a scarlet unshelled walnut. "Because I'll remain in charge."

Celine stepped between them and said, "I'm sure you can figure out how to work together. In fact, why don't you both assist with the walnut garland? Mr. Vue, you can continue with the drilling. Once he's pierced a few, Mr. Tran, you can begin stringing them together."

"I know my way around a power tool as much as Jeffery," Derrick said, grabbing for the drill. "And who's paying for these decorations anyway? I hope they're not coming out of the AAROA budget."

Celine's attempt at mediation didn't seem to be working, so I abandoned my role crafting the centerpieces. "Why don't I step inside the kitchen and help Mrs. Ho? Then someone can take over my duties."

The two men blinked at me but didn't relinquish their combined hold on the tool. Without waiting for a resolution, I hurried away.

I loved the perfume of a well-kept kitchen. The fragrance of soup and the sound of bubbling broth greeted me in Ho's inner sanctum. Nik's mother stood over a large silver pot, sprinkling in spices. At five feet tall, she almost needed a step stool to cook at the range.

"Smells delicious, Auntie Ai," I said, using the familial term to greet her.

Mrs. Ho turned from the stove. "Yale, come join our little trio. We'll always welcome the next generation and pass down our tricks of the trade. Otherwise we'd be more like AARP than AAROA." She chuckled.

"I can also get Nik in here," I said, but Mrs. Ho waved her oil-spotted hand in the air.

"No need," she said. "Better that he spend extra time with Celine."

I didn't have a response, not wanting to burst her hopes of the two of them getting together. Celine didn't like serious relationships. Besides, she hated being pushed into anything.

Ba called me to his side, and I obeyed. He was bent over a box of tofu at the prep counter.

"Can you help me?" my dad said. "I'm in charge of vegetables. A lot of them. While Ai Jeh"—he'd appended the *jeh*, or "sister," term to her name—"makes the bone broth. Roy, who's coming out of the fridge right now, is going to handle the meats." Ba sometimes used the plural form of a word to talk about it, his one verbal tell of having emigrated from Hong Kong decades ago.

"Hi, Mr. Yamada," I said to the bald man exiting the walk-in fridge. He had plastic trays of meat in his hands, along with a clear bag of raw shrimp, unpeeled and complete with antennae and eyes.

"Yale," he said, squinting at me. "It's been a long time. How was university? You went to your namesake, right?"

"No." I felt my cheeks heat up. "Actually, I stayed local." I didn't tell him that I'd halted my plans to transfer from community college and returned home because my mom had suffered from respiratory issues. Both she and Ba had needed me.

"I wanted her at Wing Fat instead," my dad said before plopping a second box of tofu in front of me. "She got our cooking genes."

Mr. Yamada placed his provisions on the far end away from our vegetables. "The lucky Yee family," he said. "Mother, father, and daughter. All good cooks."

While he wandered away to rinse the shrimp in a colander at the sink, I whispered to my dad under the sound of the rushing water. "Maybe it really is better for us to spend this meal with more than our family. Makes it less lonely for others."

Ba glanced at the back of Mr. Yamada's head. "It's tough to have nobody around. No spouse or child. The holidays can be really rough."

I grabbed a sharp knife and sliced open the package of tofu with a flick of my wrist. "Agreed." This time of the year sometimes draped even us with a veil of sorrow.

Ba and I worked together, side by side, creating tofu cubes on separate cutting boards. I liked the rhythm of cooking together, and unlike my time at Wing Fat, when I'd frozen up over a wok, this felt safe. It didn't feel like usurping my mom's role, but like father and daughter bonding instead.

Mr. Yamada and Mrs. Ho became occupied with their own tasks, and for a while, we had a harmonious arrangement. We made our own special music, with Nik's mom swishing her broth, Mr. Yamada slicing the meat, and we Yees chop-chopping away.

A hot pot meal required a lot of prep work. The ingredients must be washed and then cut into bite-size pieces. These included veggies ranging from enoki mushrooms to napa cabbage to Taiwanese lettuce. As the handler of the meat, Mr. Yamada would cut the beef, pork, and lamb into thin slices. And, of course, the broth added flavor to the mix, enhancing the taste of the boiled items. The fact that Mrs. Ho had used bones to construct her soup would only intensify the deliciousness of the meal.

Anything associated with cooking, even the prep grunt work, pulled me out of my worldly troubles. I couldn't believe I'd resisted the call for so long. I'd stopped cooking because of my guilt over replacing my mom at Wing Fat. That, and because of the tie to my mom's accident; she'd died while driving to pick up a cooking ingredient for me. I still felt shame over the whole incident, but like Celine had told me, my mom's heart attack was from underlying health issues. I needed to remind myself on a regular basis that it wasn't my fault.

The pile of cabbage pieces on my cutting board grew. Soon, I entered a focused cooking zone—before a harsh banging on the back door interrupted the peace.

Since Mr. Yamada was the closest to the exit, he washed his hands and checked on the newcomer. Unlike at Wing Fat, where the screen door to the alleyway remained open while Ba was cooking, releasing both warm air and luscious scents to the outdoors, Mr. Yamada had to unbolt the back door.

On the threshold of Ho's kitchen stood a woman in her thirties with brown skin, her dark hair in a single long braid running down her back. "How dare you lock me out?" she said.

I didn't recognize her, but Mr. Yamada stumbled back. "Ah, Ms. Patil. You're a little early for the dinner."

"The one I wasn't invited to," she said, her hands on her hips.

Mrs. Ho turned down the flame on the range and shuffled over to the doorway. "Oh, Misty," she said. "There must have been a misunderstanding. Maybe the email went to your spam folder."

"This is not the only time emails have been 'lost,'" she said. "I had to learn about this event on a local blog."

I raised an eyebrow at my dad, who shook his head at me. There shouldn't have been any advertising of this private Thanksgiving gathering.

Who could have known about this special meal? I wondered if we'd have more people showing up unannounced. I glanced at the amount of food near us and calculated. Thankfully, we had more than enough for several rounds of hot pot.

Ba wiped his hands against his apron. "Let me introduce you," he whispered to me.

Misty had walked into the kitchen now, and the door shut with a clang behind her. My dad and I strode toward her.

"Good to see you again, Ms. Patil," Ba said. "This is my daughter, Yale. She just joined the cooking ranks."

"Call me Misty," she said as she gave me a sharp look. "It's nice to finally have another young female chef around."

I shook hands with her, and her previous anger seemed to dissipate.

"What else do we need done here?" she asked.

"The food prep is almost finished," I said. "But I'm not sure how the decorating is going in the dining room."

After I uttered those words, I heard the distinct whine of the drill. Then a scream shattered the air.

TWO

I SPRINTED OUT OF THE KITCHEN TO THE DINING area when I heard the scream. An Asian woman around my age, or maybe a few years past thirty, stood in the doorway. She gaped at the whirring drill in Derrick's hand. It did look threatening, especially since he held the drill bit only inches away from her pale face.

"You can't come barging in here, trying to mooch dinner off us," Derrick said. "Who are you anyway?"

The woman gawked at the menacing tool and stammered out her name. "I'm Trisha Kim. And I thought this was a public meeting."

Celine hurried over and gently lowered Derrick's arm. "Sorry, we're using this drill to put together some last-minute decorations."

"Oh." Trisha took in her surroundings, with the lined-up pumpkins and candles at the booths. "It looks really festive in here."

Celine tossed her hair and flashed Trisha a bright

smile. "I know, right? It's my first Thanksgiving celebration, and what's the holiday without a little flair?"

Jeffery laid his half-strung garland down on the counter and joined the group. "Did you say you're here for a meeting?"

"Uh-huh." Trisha tucked a strand of glossy black hair behind one ear. "The post said the Asian American Restaurant Owners Association was meeting for Thanksgiving today. I'm here to join the club."

Derrick raised the drill once more, his eyes narrowing on Trisha's pretty face—she did have a classically beautiful oval face with peach coloring, once she'd recovered from her fright at being threatened with a dangerous tool. "What post?" he asked.

She fluttered her long eyelashes. "On the *Eastwood Village Connection* blog?"

Celine turned her head and trained her gaze on Nik, who looked like he'd been caught breaking and entering.

"It must have gotten posted by accident," he said. "I swore I saved it as a draft."

I stalked toward Nik, who started to slouch behind the counter. "What did you do this time?" I said. He'd already muddied my family name once before with an ill-timed post.

He mussed the top of his bedhead hair, making it no worse for the wear. "Thought I'd write about our gathering and add in some nice photos to highlight Ho's. Make it the go-to venue for other gatherings, more than just the business association."

"But now you've made things awkward. Should Trisha join our private meeting?"

We waited for Jeffery's judgment. As president of the organization, he'd have the final say on the matter.

"Miss Kim," he said, straightening his tie. "Do you own a restaurant nearby?"

"In Koreatown," she said, jerking her neck toward the east. "My parents own an establishment over there."

"Wonderful." Jeffery rubbed his hands together. "It's always good to have new members in our association. Isn't that right, Derrick?" he added in a louder voice.

Derrick harrumphed and returned to drilling holes in the walnuts.

"We're still preparing for dinner, but there's not much to do out here," Jeffery told Trisha. "Plus, I don't trust Derrick with that drill around you. Maybe they need a hand in the kitchen?"

I walked away from the counter and stepped in front of Trisha. After introducing myself, I said, "I'll take you back there. We can see what's left to do."

Trisha and I moved toward the kitchen door, but she paused to run her hand along one of the red vinyl booths in the dining area. "Great furniture," she said. "Retro chic."

"It's been this way for years," I said and shrugged. "Definitely makes for a distinctive place to eat Taiwanese food."

Trisha issued a small gasp of delight as we entered the kitchen. I made the introductions, and the entire crew gathered around her. My dad, Misty, Mrs. Ho, and Mr. Yamada all gave Trisha a warm welcome.

"The broth is ready to go," Mrs. Ho said, "as are the veggies and meat. Maybe you and Yale can set out the platters of raw ingredients."

I ambled over to the sliced meats. Mr. Yamada had outdone himself today. "What's this last dish?" I asked.

"Sliced turkey breast," he said, "in honor of Thanksgiving." Guess I could get my fill of the traditional bird after all.

As I balanced the full plates on two arms, I passed by Trisha, who stood in place, scanning the kitchen. She seemed fixated on the stove and its equipment.

I whistled. "Hey, Trisha. A little help here."

"Oh, sorry." She came out of her trance and grabbed the platter before her, filled with cut vegetables. Trisha bustled out of the kitchen, and I followed in her wake.

We paused before the largest of the red booths in Ho's, but I wondered whether we could fit the platters at one table.

I counted in my head the number of diners. Ten in all. This included Derrick, Jeffery, Misty, Trisha, Ba, Mrs. Ho, Mr. Yamada, Nik, Celine, and me. "We can't fit all the food here," I said, making sure I spoke in a loud voice to let Nik know.

He hurried over and tried to rearrange the centerpiece of candles.

"That's not going to work, Nik. We still have to put the hot plate in the middle. Plus, everybody can't jam into this one booth."

He tugged at his goatee. "Fine. Two booths, then."

"We wouldn't have this problem if you'd gone with Wing Fat as the hosting restaurant," I said. "Our banquet room is meant to hold loads of people."

"You can set down the extra plates over there," he said, pointing at the booth across the way. At least the two groups would be able to speak to each other across the aisle.

Trisha and I managed to divide the meat and vegetable platters between the tables. As we deposited the uncooked ingredients, Ba and Mr. Yamada showed up carrying two burners with their respective stainless steel pots.

They set up the tables. The first booth was positioned near an electric socket, so they could plug in the burner. The second pot, though, would need an extension cord to reach the wall outlet.

"I think we have one in storage," Nik said, his face a deep shade of red as he scurried away from the dining area. The hosting clearly wasn't going as smoothly as he'd planned.

After he disappeared, his mother showed up wielding her huge soup pot. "The broth is already warm, so we don't have to wait long before it gets bubbling." She ladled some of the steaming soup into the two pots, making sure to add liquid to both sections of the partitioned steel containers. The inner section was usually reserved for cooking meat while the outer portion boiled the veggies.

The kitchen door swung open, and Nik stumbled out with a confused look on his face. "I can't find the extension cord in the supplies closet, Ma."

"Ah," she murmured. "I pulled it out earlier today. It's got to be somewhere in the kitchen." She heaved the big pot of soup toward the counter, and Nik sprinted to place a pot holder underneath it.

Derrick jumped up from his seat. "I'll search for it," he said. "Fresh eyes, you know." He clapped a hand on Nik's back, and Nik jolted from the semi-forceful shove.

"Go ahead," Jeffery said, as though giving Derrick permission for the task. "I prefer being the coordinator anyway."

"Don't I know it," Derrick mumbled as he slipped into the kitchen.

As president of AAROA, Jeffery did like to be in charge. I remembered seeing him wear an "I'm the Boss" apron while grilling at past association picnics.

Jeffery motioned to my dad. "Sing, you can put in the raw ingredients."

"Sure." Ba started placing veggies into the outer portion of the hot pot with a pair of tongs. It would take a while for the vegetables to cook, so the thinly sliced meat could wait until later to pop in.

Celine cocked her head at the decorated tabletop. "Are we missing something?"

With a practiced glance, Nik's mother said, "The bowls for eating."

"Of course," Celine said. "I'll help get those. Um, could you tell me where you keep your dishware?"

"Certainly," Mrs. Ho said. "We'll also need chopsticks and soup spoons. You and Nik can work together to get them. You two make a perfect pairing."

Celine bit her bottom lip while Nik shuffled his feet. Mrs. Ho jumped at chances for them to be together in any sort of capacity. It didn't matter to her that Celine would eventually leave for Hong Kong. Of course, Nik's mother was also plotting to reverse my cousin's course of action. Mrs. Ho thought Celine would be the ideal girlfriend for Nik.

As I watched them go behind the counter to retrieve the bowls, I knew something else was missing. "What about the sauce?" I asked.

Even though hot pot broth was flavorful by itself, I still enjoyed having *sacha*, a Chinese barbecue sauce made from dried seafood and chilies, in my bowl.

After pulling out a stack of bowls, Nik piped up. "Agreed, Yale. The Bull Head brand is the best. There's some in the walk-in fridge. And don't forget the eggs."

"I'll get the items and then we can cook the sauce," Misty said. I watched her long braid swing across her back as she entered the kitchen. I didn't have the heart to tell her that the sauce didn't need any cooking. The simple dip was made from sacha mixed with creamy raw egg.

During her absence, Ba put in the raw meat, making sure to use a different pair of tongs so as not to cross-contaminate. Soon enough, the hot pot boiled away and cooked the food items.

"Where's that sauce?" Nik said, as he and Celine arranged the bowls and utensils around the two tabletops.

Misty came out with a carton of eggs and the sacha container. "Sorry, I had a hard time finding the sauce," she said.

"I didn't realize it came in a silver can. Thought it'd be a glass container. But the picture of the bull clued me in."

As people opted in on sauce only, or sauce plus eggs, in their bowls, Jeffery and my dad exchanged a gleeful grin. "Time to eat," they chimed together.

Trisha moved to the kitchen door. "I'll tell Derrick," she said. Maybe she wanted to get on his better side after that drill experience.

She pushed the door open. "Dinner's ready, Derrick," she called out.

Mr. Yamada, who'd been napping at the second booth, without the plugged-in burner, startled at her yelling. He stretched his arms above his head and wandered toward the restrooms.

"Okay." Derrick bustled out, shaking his head. "But I'm not sure where that extension cord got to."

Trisha peeked into the kitchen. "I think we're forgetting one more item. The noodles. I see them on the counter."

Derrick and Trisha swapped places, as he headed toward the dining area and she marched into the kitchen with purpose.

Since it was her establishment, Mrs. Ho arranged our dining spots. She, rather purposefully, designated an elders' table and a "youngsters" booth. She, Ba, Mr. Yamada, Derrick, and Jeffery would share a table. The other one (with the unplugged burner) would have Misty, Trisha, Celine, Nik, and me sitting at it. Mrs. Ho made sure that Nik and Celine sat next to each other before she took her spot at the booth across the way.

When Trisha exited the kitchen with a mound of uncooked noodles, Mrs. Ho said, "Please place that on the counter next to the soup. Noodles are always cooked at the end of the meal." True. This way they would absorb all the flavor of the past cooking. Besides, I wanted to fill up on veggies and meat, not carbs.

Celine made sure to take several photos of the hot pot food as it bubbled away. I knew she'd soon post those pics on Instagram.

The problem with having only one burner to share was that we all crowded around the boiling food to grab tidbits. With our chopsticks diving into the pot for tasty morsels, I wondered if we looked like clamoring seagulls. It also meant that while our elders leisurely sat to enjoy their meal, the rest of us "youngsters" had to pop up out of our booth and dash across the aisle to refill our bowls. It came as no surprise to me that ten mouths to feed meant that round one of hot pot ended quickly.

We all emitted some sort of dissatisfaction at needing to wait for a second helping of veggies and meat to cook before getting to eat again. Misty wrapped the end of her braid around her fingers, Nik tapped an irritating beat on the floor with his shoe, and even Mr. Yamada gazed at the pot with searing intensity, as though willing it to boil faster.

As the time stretched out, Jeffery said, "Maybe I'll look for that extension cord again." He excused himself from the elders' booth.

Within minutes, he came back out holding a long cord. "Found it," he almost sang out. "Right next to the sink." What an odd placement. I wondered if Nik's mother had used it for something else and had just forgotten with the hot pot preparations.

Jeffery connected the plug of the lonely burner on our table with the extension cord. Then he ambled behind the counter. "Remember," he said, "after we have our share of delicious hot pot, we'll discuss the association's path for next year. Including leadership options."

"The faster we eat, the quicker we'll meet," Derrick said. "Plug it in, Jeffery."

"Okay," Jeffery said, squatting below the counter. "Here's the socket. I wonder why this is so w—"

A strange gargle came from Jeffery's location behind the counter. Sharp sizzling and the acrid smell of burnt flesh dirtied the air.

For a moment, we all froze. Then we jolted into action.

"Are you all right, Mr. Vue?" I asked as I sprinted around the corner, afraid of what I'd find.

THREE

I HALTED SEVERAL FEET AWAY FROM JEFFERY, WHO lay on the ground, unmoving. "Mr. Vue . . ." Words stuck in my throat.

The others crowded around and behind me. Trisha squealed next to my ear. "Is the guy even breathing?"

Nik shoved his way toward Jeffery and bent over him. "No, I don't think so. Someone call the paramedics."

Derrick took charge, using his mobile to call 911. It was one of the few times I realized that a cell phone could be quite useful to have. What were the odds of something like this happening, though? I still decided that uncoupling from technology was to my benefit in the long run.

"I know CPR," Misty said and joined Nik near the still Jeffery. "Maybe I can revive him."

As she started her ministrations, a gurgling noise from behind me caught my attention. "The hot pot," I said, gesturing to the elders' booth. "It's going to boil over."

Mr. Yamada made sure to turn off the burner, but he

left the contents sitting in the pot. I doubted if anyone would even have the appetite to eat anymore.

Meanwhile, Celine and Trisha had returned to the second booth. They shook their heads and took in everything with wide eyes.

Mrs. Ho pivoted her head from left to right, tracking the commotion with a huge frown on her face. She then plopped onto one of the stools before the counter and covered her eyes with an oil-spotted hand.

Ba took a seat next to her. "It'll be okay, Ai." I knew he wanted to comfort his friend, but I wondered if everything would really turn out fine.

When the paramedics showed up, we soon realized nothing would be okay. Despite Misty's attempts, she hadn't managed to revive Jeffery. Even when the emergency responders fired up the defibrillator, it couldn't save the situation.

"We're too late," one of the paramedics muttered.

Before we knew it, the police also swarmed in. They wanted to take statements from each person on-site. We had to sit at separate tables in Ho's as they interviewed us in turn.

In the middle of giving our accounts, the door swung open. A familiar figure filled the frame. Detective Greyson Strauss, whom I'd tangled with before.

I recognized his close-cropped dark hair and strong square jaw. He looked businesslike in a dark gray suit paired with a silver tie. His piercing jade eyes spotted me, and he paused for a moment before stepping into the restaurant with confidence.

Celine and I glanced at each other. I wondered if my eyes shone with as much worry as her amber ones did. We'd encountered the homicide detective before, and it hadn't been a pleasant experience, especially since my cousin and I had both been on his radar for murder.

Detective Strauss proceeded to systematically isolate

every single person present and question us again. I recognized the small notepad he carried and the pencil he used to scribble down his notes.

When the detective came around to me, he gestured for me to move farther away from everyone else. We sat in a booth a few spaces down from the original hot pot tables.

He flipped to a clean page in his notebook and jotted down a few lines. "Putting in your name and age," he mumbled.

"Of course, you already know all that," I said. "But I'm not sure why you've been called in, Detective Strauss. No one was next to Jeffery when he died. It was an accident."

The detective raised his eyebrow at me. "Dying alone doesn't necessarily mean it was from natural causes."

I let out a small gasp, but Detective Strauss ignored my shock.

"Tell me more about Jeffery Vue," he said.

I listed the facts I knew of Jeffery: how he was the president of the association, that he was a second-generation Hmong American, and that he was single. "Erm, although he's been seriously dating someone recently." I didn't bother to talk about my char siu bao theory and Jeffery's honeyed mouth.

"What's his significant other's name?" he asked.

"Her name's Michele. Not clear about her last name," I said. "According to Jeffery, she was the woman of his dreams."

Detective Strauss tapped the notepad with the rubber eraser end of his pencil. "Interesting that someone he was so invested in didn't show up tonight for dinner with friends."

I shrugged. "He mentioned that she had family obligations. Thanksgiving, you know." For a moment I wondered about the detective's own personal life. Shouldn't he be elsewhere and not on duty during the holiday?

"Yale," the detective said, "you've got a keen eye. Walk me through everything that happened tonight."

Had the detective just paid me a compliment? I bit my lip to keep a smile from forming. "A few of us came early to decorate and to prep the ingredients for the hot pot," I said, delineating the two groups: the younger generation decorating the front of the restaurant and the older people helping in the kitchen.

"Keep going, Yale. Any detail might be crucial," he said.

I tried to keep the timeline straight, from when we placed candles on the tables to the arrival of Trisha to Jeffery volunteering to retrieve the extension cord.

"Hmm," Detective Strauss said. "This is all very helpful. Thanks for your time. Contact me if anything else comes up." He slid his business card my way, but I shook my head.

"We still have one in our apartment."

"'We'?" he asked.

"Celine and I. She'll be staying through the holidays."

"Okay. Good to know. I'll be questioning her after I talk to Ai Ho."

The detective homed in on Nik's mother, who still sat at the swivel stools near the long counter.

Once they'd gotten deep into conversation, I decided to deliberately pass by their spot on my way to the restroom. I couldn't help it if the shock of Jeffery's demise slowed my steps down so that I happened to catch a snippet of their conversation.

"Let's cut to the chase," Detective Strauss said. "The extension cord. I heard that *you* last touched it."

Mrs. Ho rubbed her forehead. "I thought I pulled it out from the supply closet to use for tonight."

"And left it lying around in the kitchen, right?"

"Uh-huh."

He flipped back a few pages in his notebook. "Where do you remember putting the cord?"

She shook her head with a feeble pivot of her neck. "I'm not sure."

"Perhaps by the sink?"

"I don't think so because water and electricity don't mix."

Detective Strauss leaned in closer to Nik's mother. "The cord near the vic's body was wet."

Mrs. Ho responded in a whisper. "No," she said, rubbing her arms as though chilled.

I tiptoed away from the pair of them and entered the hallway leading to the restrooms. Was the extension cord somehow tampered with? Who would've done such a thing?

I also reflected on the detective's aggressive interrogation. Could he suspect kindhearted Mrs. Ho of something sinister?

Lost in my thoughts, I wandered past the ladies' restroom. However, I realized that the middle of the hall had an unmarked door to my left. Perhaps a closet of some kind. Was this the supply locker Nik had rummaged through to look for the cord?

I opened it up, but it didn't lead to any supplies. Instead, it was a side door that rerouted back to the kitchen. I hurried inside, thinking that I could conduct some snooping to clarify matters in my mind.

In the kitchen, I found what must have been the supply closet, which was more like a freestanding cabinet. Although I was curious about its contents, I figured it'd be best not to touch the handle, which might get dusted for fingerprints.

Since Jeffery had discovered the extension cord near

the industrial sink, I moved over to that area. I checked the countertop, which held a washing sponge and folded kitchen gloves. I also examined the surrounding floor. There didn't seem to be a puddle or any water lying around.

Inside the sink, I noticed water droplets near the drain, along with detached shrimp parts. Creepy long antennae lined the smooth metal along with broken, discarded crustacean feet.

A kitchen generally offered me a place of serenity, even or especially when bustling with activity. For the moment, though, it gave me the shivers, and I snuck out the swinging door to join the others.

Detective Strauss still seemed occupied with Nik's mother. He kept on asking her questions, even as her oil-spotted hands squeezed together, as though she were clenching dough discs to make dumplings.

I edged over to Celine, who sat at the table with the unused burner, the one that had needed the additional extension cord. Sliding into the booth beside her, I said, "How are you doing, cuz?" I hoped my affectionate term would lift her sad mood.

She stared at the pot of broth on the table, cool by now, her full sweep of eyelashes on display as she peered down. "Another murder? I can't believe it."

I glanced back at the detective seated on the stool near Nik's mother. "I think Strauss believes Mrs. Ho is involved."

"You're kidding, right?" Celine asked, her amber eyes peering into mine.

"I wish."

"Auntie Ai is harmless." Celine tapped her manicured nails against the table. "All Nik's mother is guilty of is plotting a future for her son and me."

"At least we're just witnesses this time around," I said.

A clopping sound came from beside me, and I noticed the detective had arrived at the table. "If you don't mind, Yale," he said, "I'd like to speak with Celine alone."

"Of course, Detective Strauss." As I slid out of the booth, I noticed Celine try to subtly finger comb her honey-colored locks.

I spotted Derrick at the opposite end of the restaurant struggling to fix the colored walnut garland on the wall, which kept sliding down. He yanked out a long strip of clear tape from its dispenser but didn't have enough hands to hold the decoration and stick it back on the wall.

Joining him, I asked, "Need some help?"

"Sure, this nutjob won't stay put. And after all the work Jeffery and I put into it."

I held up the sagging end of the garland, and Derrick slammed the tape against the wall. Thank goodness he missed my fingers.

"Is it okay to let go now?" I asked.

"Let's see."

I eased off my fingers, and the garland seemed to hold for the moment. The bright colors appeared out of place at this festive turned fatal event. I said to Derrick, "It's tragic what happened to Jeffery."

Derrick rubbed his sharp chin, another pointy feature of his that reminded me a lot of a pot sticker. "The weird thing is that Jeffery and I were joking about morbid stuff right before. I mean, you know how he calls me Veep for fun?"

I didn't think Derrick thought the label was such a great joke, but I motioned for him to continue.

"I decided to tease him, too," Derrick said. "About his girlfriend ditching him on Thanksgiving. He told me in a spooky voice that it was because of the family curse."

I could imagine Jeffery supplying Derrick with a whopper in his booming voice. "Did he expand on the specifics?" I bet Jeffery could make up quite a tall tale, complete with extravagant hand motions.

"Something about how he'd called up a curse on himself by dating his girlfriend, but he laughed about it."

A *thunk* noise made me glance at the wall. The end we'd just taped in place had slid down.

Derrick's shoulders slumped, and I stared at the crooked garland. I didn't believe in ghosts or curses, but unexplained deaths did scare me.

When Detective Strauss finally bellowed for our attention, I jumped at the sound of his deep voice. "Okay, we're done here, folks. I have all your contact info, and I've given out my business card. Contact me anytime if you have any further info."

Nik's mother, now standing, wobbled a few steps forward and waved her arms in the air. "I'm really sorry for this mess," she said to the group. "Please feel free to take any leftovers home."

Derrick reached for a takeout box, while other people shuffled their feet and avoided her pleading look. I knew I couldn't take her up on her offer. Raw vegetables and meat didn't seem that appetizing at the moment.

Her voice pitched higher. "Also, have a free meal on us. Just come by Ho's Small Eats at the night market on Saturday."

I saw a few people nod at this last statement. Others shrugged.

Misty and Trisha strolled toward the front door in unison. It was amazing how fast the two women had bonded. I guess tragedy does make strong connections.

On the pair's way to the exit, I heard their whispered exchange.

"Callous," Misty said, tugging at the end of her long braid. "I can't believe she's advertising her event at a time like this."

"Small Business Saturday, ya know," Trisha said with a knowing nod.

"Still. It's not always about the bottom line."

The two bustled out the door.

Even though Detective Strauss stood a few feet away from me and probably hadn't heard their conversation, I wondered if his thoughts followed the same track. Would he interpret Mrs. Ho's offer as one of generosity or confirmation of her heartless personality? Nik's mother organized and ran the Eastwood Village Night Market, so what did it mean that she was focused on business right after such a tragic event?

I didn't wish ill on Mrs. Ho since she was one of Ba's good friends. However, I wondered if the fact that a dead body had wound up in her restaurant would taint Mrs. Ho's reputation—and the night market, my new livelihood, by extension.

FOUR

THE NEXT MORNING AFTER BREAKFAST, I GES-tured for my cousin to sit on the settee in the living room with me. Despite the fact that my "apartment home" advertised such modern amenities as sleek hardwood floors and swirled marble countertops, I still liked furnishings that exuded comfort. I wrapped a delphinium-blue knit blanket around me as Celine settled in the adjacent space.

"Do you believe curses are real?" I asked her.

"Ha," she said. "Only if you mean swearing. Why?"

"It was something that Jeffery said to Derrick. A curse he was under because he'd started dating."

"Who was the woman of his dreams again?" she asked, crossing her legs in a fluid motion. She managed to make that move look elegant in her silk dressing gown.

"Her first name's Michele, but I don't know much about her. She's kind of a mystery to me."

"Speaking of mysterious women," Celine said. "What about that Trisha who crashed our hot pot party?"

"All Nik's doing. With his 'saved' blog post gone haywire."

"The *Eastwood Village Connection*," Celine said. "Why am I partnering with him on it again?"

"Because you love taking pictures and posting them," I said, pointing to her cell phone as she whipped it out.

"It's called being an influencer," she told me. "Anyway, let's see the damage that he's done."

My cousin pulled up the blog. It had logged fifty views since yesterday despite being Thanksgiving weekend, when people should have better things to do than read online content. Eastwood Village was an intimate community, and its residents all seemed to want to know about the local happenings. Nik supplied them with entertaining content while Celine added her stellar photography. Except he'd messed up with yesterday's early post.

My cousin groaned. "What a horrible shot of Ho's that Nik took. You can barely make out the restaurant's name in the glare of the sun."

"I'm more interested in what he wrote than his flawed photo, Celine."

"Fine." She held the screen between us so we could read his Thanksgiving post.

I speed-read the article and voiced an amusing adjective out loud. "'The *illustrious* Asian American Restaurant Owners Association'? I don't think anyone knows about us outside of a two-mile radius."

Celine giggled. "What about this? He mentioned that the 'distinguished' Nikola Ho might be next in line to succeed President Vue."

Pointing at the screen, I said, "I can't believe Nik called himself 'the proprietor of Ho's Small Eats at Eastwood Village Night Market.' I mean, his mom's the real chef. All Nik does is stand there and serve her stuff. She's the real culinary star. How she manages both the food stand and Ho's is beyond me."

Celine tucked a strand of hair behind her ear. "Do you think she's doing all right after that Thanksgiving fiasco?"

"Auntie Ai"—I used the familial title—"can handle this. She's made of grit. Plus, she's got Mr. Yamada and Ba by her side."

Celine put away her phone. "Do you think Uncle's doing okay? It must be a shock for him. Seeing someone pass away up close." *Again*, she could've added.

I felt a phantom twinge in my heart and rubbed at it. My mom had died of a previously undiagnosed heart condition. When she'd been found unresponsive in her stalled car, my dad and I had been called in by authorities to identify her.

Nervous, I picked at a hangnail on my thumb. "We should pay Ba a visit at Wing Fat to check up on him."

"Agreed," Celine said. "After I get prettied up, of course."

We arrived at Wing Fat in our respective fashion styles. Celine wore a cashmere turtleneck sweater paired with cropped black pants and heels. I opted for a plaid shirt and trousers with pockets big enough to fit my slim wallet—I didn't do purses.

Ba's restaurant was like a second home to me. After all, I'd practically grown up inside the establishment ever since I was twelve. Over the years, he'd added upgrades to the place until it became an elegant institution for dim sum. I passed by the hostess stand in the front and waved hello to the woman in a sleek cheongsam.

She smiled at me. Although I hadn't managed to remember her name, I knew she went to the nearby college, UCLA.

I didn't find the usual line of people snaking out the door, and customers weren't yet clamoring for a ticketed number to wait to be served. We must have arrived right before the dim sum rush.

Celine and I marched through the dining area, past the partitioned banquet room, and on to the kitchen. Inside Ba's cooking realm, I breathed in the heady scent of soy sauce and dumplings. My cousin and I waved to the kitchen staff: the assistant cook, a prep person, and the dishwasher.

Then we crept over to Ba, who was examining the steaming contents of a bamboo basket.

Sensing our presence, Ba said, "Oh, hello, girls. Nice to see you here. Tell me, how does this *cheung fun* look?"

I examined the flat rice noodle rolls. "Perfect."

Celine nodded. "Worthy of a foodstagram."

He replaced the lid on the steamer basket. "What are you two doing here? Need some food?"

Celine gave him a hopeful look. She enjoyed eating . . . and documenting her culinary conquests on social media.

"We wanted to know how you're holding up," I said. "Because of last night."

He wiped his hands on his cooking apron. "A tragedy. It was supposed to be an extended family gathering of sorts. We've known each other for so long at AAROA."

I nodded and suddenly remembered the piles of plates and ingredients we'd left untouched. "Oh, sorry we forgot to help clean up."

"You couldn't have even if you'd wanted to," Ba said. "The police rushed us all off the premises to gather their evidences." His slipup—using the plural form—appeared again.

Celine crept closer to my dad—or the steamer basket, I wasn't sure which. "Do you know how Auntie Ai is doing?"

"Okay. Given the circumstances. I think she's focusing her energy on the night market to get through this whole mess."

Work. The balm to everything. Ba himself had increased his hours at Wing Fat to seven days a week after Mom died.

He turned toward me and asked, "Speaking of the Eastwood Village Night Market, what recipes will you be showcasing tomorrow?"

"I've got the tried-and-true cold dishes: spicy cucumber salad and soy sauce eggs. But I want to expand the repertoire and add in green scallion pancakes. They're kind of like the *roti canai* flatbread." I offered my cousin a hard stare. She'd changed the food stand name from "Yee Snacks" to "Canai and Chai" during the initial unveiling on a whim without asking me or my dad. Celine had liked the rhyming *ch* sound of the two words being stuck close together.

She ignored my pointed look and focused on my dad's profile.

"What are you doing for beverages?" he asked.

"The boba drinks and aloe vera juice, but I'd like to also do some sort of chai to match our *branding*." I shot out this last word at Celine, who used it often. She'd taken it upon herself to make sure we drew in customers with matching bedazzled chef coats. She also placed our boba drinks in special light bulb glass containers as a marketing ploy.

"You know," Ba said, "I think Misty Patil might serve chai at her place. Why don't you head over there now? India Snack Mart should be open at this hour."

"Where is it located?" Celine asked.

"Right at the edge of Eastwood Village, on Main Street," Ba said and then gave us the exact address.

"Great. That will require a bit of driving." A wide smile spread across Celine's face, and she held out her hand. "Keys, please."

"I'm not so sure your gift of a car was really for *me*," I said, but I still provided her with the key.

"Beggars can't be choosers," she said, but my cousin had actually been over-the-top generous with her present. I had never imagined that the first car I'd own would turn out to be a Porsche Boxster. Although maybe spontaneously purchasing a vehicle might not seem so strange for Celine. Her parents, after all, did run gala events in Hong Kong and had solid ties to the thriving casinos in Macao.

Once we got to the royal blue Boxster, Celine slid into the leather driver's seat and sighed in happiness. "Driving is the best," she said.

"Have at it." I snapped on my seat belt.

"I will." She pulled open the convertible top, and we sped down the road.

Her locks streamed in the breeze while mine tangled up in the wind. Nevertheless, I enjoyed the open air. It helped calm my nerves whenever I was in a car, particularly since I carried a twinge of fear while driving. I knew logically that my mom had died of heart problems while in a stalled car and not from the actual vehicle, but sometimes my mind still played tricks on me.

When Celine pulled up in the empty parking lot before India Snack Mart, her hair looked beach tousled. I stepped out of the car with matted strands. Trying to use the glass front as a mirror, I patted down my unruly hair, to no avail.

"Come on," Celine said as she pushed open the store door. A merry chime greeted us when we entered.

Misty glanced up from the counter she stood behind, and her eyes narrowed. She must have recognized the pair of us, but all she said was "Windy outside, eh?"

Celine dangled the car keys from her hand. "Convertibles, you know."

Meanwhile, I examined the layout of the store. It was a cramped space with narrow aisles. With a single turn of my head, I could survey the area with dried goods (lentils and beans), a display filled with snacks, and a small freezer section. Misty herself stood near an electronic cash register, her long braid tucked to one side and hanging down the front of her tunic. To the left of her was a small hot food buffet area.

I stepped up to the counter and held out my hand for her to shake. "Misty, I know we didn't get off on the right foot. What with seeing me at that ill-fated AAROA dinner and having that same organization shut you out. But we can work on changing the association together."

She ignored my friendly gesture, and I placed my hand back down at my side.

Celine sidled up to me and slung an arm around my shoulder. "This here is my cousin Yale," she said. "The next-generation chef of Wing Fat."

"Er, I wouldn't quite call myself that," I said.

Misty tilted her head and seemed to check me out from head to toe. "I don't remember seeing you at the dim sum restaurant."

"I was cooking there before . . ." Five years ago, but I didn't give out that fact. My sudden breakdown in the restaurant kitchen was still embarrassing. "I took a break and recently returned to the restaurant business."

Celine's voice sang out the next words. "Yale is also the operator of the greatest food stand at Eastwood Village Night Market, Canai and Chai."

Misty arched one stenciled eyebrow at me.

"Heh," I said. "Actually, I'm here because I need some tips for making the chai."

Celine's gaze slid over to the menu above Misty's head. "If you help Yale, I'll buy a plate of curry and a cup of chai."

"It would be really helpful to have your thoughts," I said. "I don't know much about brewing chai."

Misty clucked her tongue. "My recipe is a family secret."

"Really?" I said, taking a step back. Maybe we shouldn't have driven over here on impulse.

"Nah, just joking," she said, "but I'm not sure if I want to give it out."

"No biggie," I said. "It's just that if I do serve chai at the stand, I want it to be authentic."

She gave me a fierce nod, making her braid bob up for a moment.

"I respect that," she said and turned to Celine. "If you double the curry plates and the chai, then it's a deal."

"Sure," Celine said, reaching inside her purse for some money. After handing over a large bill, she said, "Keep the change." My cousin's wealth always seemed to pave an easy way for her in life. It must be nice to have a soft cushion of cash to fall back on.

Misty invited me behind the counter to a kitchenette at the back of the store. She started by taking out some fresh ginger and spices. I looked at the ingredients she'd pulled out.

I would have to stock up before tonight's event. I wondered if Misty's store would have what I needed. "Do you carry cardamom pods and whole cloves here?"

"Of course I do." Misty bustled around the store and placed the dry ingredients on the counter, and I paid for them.

Then she demonstrated how to make chai in the kitchenette. I wrote down the steps on scratch paper and stuffed it into my pocket. Celine also took a few sneak photos, so I could better replicate the process at home. She even asked for Misty's cell phone number in case I needed to ask more questions later on.

After Misty had brewed two cups of chai for us, I asked her, "So, let me get this recipe straight. You just eyeball the amount of milk to use?"

"Yes, the color of the chai should be like liquid caramel."

I'd need to do some trial-and-error work in my kitchen to figure out the exact ratio, then.

"I'll try my best," I said as she packed up our curry dishes to go. "Want to drop by our stall this evening? You're guaranteed a free cup of chai."

"Want me to be there for quality assurance, huh?" Misty said in a teasing tone.

"Thanks again," I said. "I'll definitely put in a good word for you with the association. Make sure you're on the list for all their events in the future."

Misty bagged our takeout containers, placing them on the counter. "Who's in charge of AAROA now, anyway, since Jeffery is gone?"

"I'm not certain." I didn't have the bylaws of the organization memorized. "Derrick Tran probably. He's the VP."

My cousin picked up our food and waved to Misty. "Come on by tonight," she said. "I'll be introducing something interesting and fun at our booth that you won't want to miss."

I wondered what new ploy Celine was turning over in her head, but I didn't have time to question her about it. Besides trusting her creativity, I needed to spend time in the kitchen measuring out ingredients and creating my own version of chai for our stall.

After a quick curry lunch at home, Celine and I parted ways. She sequestered herself in her bedroom while I ventured into the kitchen.

Creating a fresh cup of chai required several ingredients. I had to crush fresh ginger, cardamom pods, and cloves. Then after I brought the water in the pot to a boil, I added in the spices, sugar, tea, and milk. Finally, I strained it through a sieve.

The process sounded simple, but it took me several hours to create a recipe I was satisfied with. I wondered if the many cups of caffeine I drank while chai experimenting would keep me up this evening. Then again, the event did last until two in the morning. This time around, though, I hoped there wouldn't be any dead bodies waiting for me to stumble over.

FIVE

I INSISTED ON WALKING TO THE NIGHT MARKET. From the apartment complex, Celine and I didn't even need to go half a block before we hit The Shops at East-wood Village plaza, where the event would be held.

I'd equipped my utility cart with the prepped foods and necessary supplies. In lieu of the small stack of cookbooks I'd needed the first time I went to the market, I'd placed a portable gas stove on the top shelf. I knew my recipes inside and out and had grown in confidence of my cooking skills.

"Ready to go?" I asked Celine.

She mumbled an affirmative from her room and then barged out with a large cardboard box.

"What's in there?"

"My secret project," she said.

Outside the apartment, we took a quick stroll to the shopping plaza and scurried past the spouting fountain that marked the edge of the property. We ducked under the velvet ropes barring entry into the night market and joined those preparing for the next few hours. I recognized familiar faces in the games area, arts and vendors booths, and even on the main stage. The break-dancer was back, a beanie crammed on his head while he did multiple flips.

At the food section, I nodded and waved to our crew of usual participants in the front row. We'd gotten the prime location for our stands next to the entertainment stage.

Our Canai and Chai booth was tucked next to Ho's Small Eats. Strangely, Nik's mom wasn't found huddled over her stove in the back. She sat in a folding chair, her hands still for once. Nik hovered near his mom but nodded to us as we arrived.

On the other side of us was the booth for La Pupusería de Reyes. Blake Westby Reyes and his grandmother were bustling around getting ready, but Blake took a moment to wink at us in his typical flirting manner. I was sure a few of his customers came by for his serving of good looks: shaved-sides haircut, expressive eyebrows, and a smattering of tattoos crisscrossing his strong arms.

The last of our foodie crew was farther down the aisle. Lindsey Caine owned a silver food truck for Below Freezing, a liquid nitrogen ice cream enterprise. I didn't see her behind the counter, but she might have been in the inner recesses of her vehicle.

In our allotted space, I set up the kitchen area. I placed the drinks and cold foods on a folding table so they'd be easy to grab and serve. A pitcher filled with batter for the green scallion pancakes was ready to go beside the portable stove. I also placed the preassembled baggie of spices I needed for the chai nearby.

When I'd finished getting everything ready, I donned one of the matching chef jackets Celine had purchased for us. I'd gotten used to wearing the bedazzled attire and didn't mind the fancy embroidering, pearl buttons, and glitter on it.

After putting it on, I turned to check Celine's where-abouts. I was surprised to see my cousin outside the booth. She'd constructed an entire backdrop to the left of the stall while I'd been busy overseeing the food and drinks.

A pop-up aluminum frame held a huge ivory canvas, kind of like a fabric movie screen. Lines of colorful fall leaves twined around the metal bar on top. She'd even added some twinkling LED light strings to the mix.

"Ta-da," she said. "It's our own autumn wonderland."

"Pretty." I touched a strand of sparkling lights. "But what does this have to do with our food?"

"It creates a better ambience." Celine placed a few folding chairs in front of the display. "People can sit here—or stand—and post their Gram-worthy pics and hashtag them with our Canai and Chai name."

"Uh, okay." I didn't know the first thing about social media. Maybe people *would* flock to the backdrop, like my cousin envisioned.

"And for technophobes like you"—she dug into the cardboard box near her feet—"I unearthed your Polaroid camera. Maybe a 'brutal boba' purchase can equal one free instant pic."

I shook my head. "I'm never going to get rid of that drink's nickname."

"Why would you want to? It's catchy and makes for great publicity," she said, giving me a luminous smile.

Eleven o'clock rolled around, and people started trickling in. I recognized the initial two customers who approached our booth. The pair of ladies, both in their sixties, appeared almost like twins at first glance. Dawn and Kelly Tanaka owned The Literary Narnia.

When I'd worked at the quaint bookstore, regular customers hadn't been able to tell them apart. I could, but their similar petite builds and bushy silver hair often fooled others.

"So great to see you here, Dawn and Kelly," I said.

Dawn spoke up. "We came by to support you, dear."

"Also, we were hungry," Kelly said.

"The night market is only a hop and skip away from the bookshop," Dawn said.

I turned and glanced across the way and spotted the front of the store. "Don't tell me you're working late again and looking over the finances." I squinted to see if the lights were on in the building.

"Thankfully no," Kelly said. "What my sister won't tell you is that we specifically showed up to see *you*. I know you've been running the stall for about a month, but we just haven't had the time to come until now."

Dawn stifled a yawn. "It's sad how tired I am at night as I get older."

Celine bustled up to them. "We've got some lovely caffeinated drinks that will help in that department."

"For free," I added. "Everything is on the house for you ladies."

Celine mumbled, "Way to make a sale, cuz."

I ignored her and repositioned our whiteboard menu so the Tanaka sisters could see their options better.

"Chai sounds wonderful," Dawn said.

Kelly raised her hand. "Make that two."

"A new recipe I'm trying," I said. "Your order will be right out."

While I worked in the background, Celine took over the conversation. I heard them chatting about the bookstore's recent customers.

Although I appreciated the shop's environment with its towering bookshelves and handmade signs, The Literary Narnia didn't get a ton of traffic. Eastwood Village residents would wander in on occasion, and sometimes the special college discount the sisters offered snagged a few students.

I hoped business was picking up. Dawn sounded positive, saying that the Black Friday sales "were not half bad." She also hoped that the holidays would drive more traffic to their store.

"Knock on wood," Kelly said as she tapped on our front table. Unfortunately, I think it was made of laminate.

I finished with their two beverages and handed the chai over to the ladies but had to call their names to get their attention. They seemed distracted.

"Look over there," Kelly said, peering to the side. "Roy Yamada's visiting the booth next door. I haven't seen that fool in ages."

Dawn giggled. "Not since he placed that whoopee cushion on your seat in class."

"Which was decidedly not funny." She blew on her steaming cup of chai.

"Did you two know Mr. Yamada growing up?" I asked.

"Sure," Dawn said. "We went to elementary school together."

"That one's a prankster," Kelly said. She frowned his way. "He used to hide the teacher's blackboard erasers."

"I'm sure he's more mature now," Dawn said. "I heard he even got married."

"Whoever she was had to have been a saint," Kelly said.

Dawn sipped at her chai. Her eyes grew round. "This is absolutely delicious, Yale."

"Thank you." I felt heat creeping up my cheeks.

Kelly also drank a big gulp and gave me a thumbs-up.

Then they excused themselves to wander around the night market grounds. Kelly set off at a fast pace toward the main stage, where a contortionist was performing. I wondered if she was also trying to escape from Roy Yamada and any negative childhood memories.

After the Tanaka sisters left, we served several more customers. Like Celine had predicted, some did come by to take advantage of the creative display she had designed. People snapped multiple pictures with their cell phones. A few photographers left right after their selfies, though, and didn't order anything. Others waited around and stood in line before our stall. A few even opted for the brutal boba tea and Polaroid combination.

We soon started serving a steady line of customers. I spent a lot of time in the back, flipping scallion pancakes and brewing up chai. While cooking, I hummed, indulging in the joy of creating edible delights from simple ingredients. However, whenever a customer requested one of our cold dishes, I enjoyed the reprieve from the stove and stepped over to deliver their order.

In the middle of serving one such customer a plate of spicy cucumber salad, I heard a commotion coming from next door. At Ho's Small Eats, I heard two angry male voices arguing. Peeking over at the neighboring stand, I spied Derrick and Nik in a heated discussion. Nik's face had turned red, and Derrick pointed one finger in the air and gesticulated emphatically. People who'd been heading toward the booth paused and halted in their steps. Several event-goers even turned around and decided other areas of the night market seemed more appealing at that moment in time. Nik's mother had to rush over and calm the situation with her gentle placating tone.

Celine nudged me in the arm. "I need another order of scallion pancakes," she said.

"Of course." I retreated back to the kitchen, though my mind remained on the argument I'd just witnessed. What had gotten the men so riled up?

I didn't have time to think about it, though, because a flood of customers distracted me. They'd heard about our delicious food or seen our exciting drinks in the hands of the other attendees. A few even noticed the hashtags #EastwoodVillageNightMarket and #CanaiAndChai on their social media feed. At the mention of those, Celine had whispered to me, "See, my idea is working. And trending."

I soon welcomed another familiar face to our booth. Reagan Wood, a UCLA student I'd met the other month, dropped by to order several drinks. I was relieved to hear her call them "tapioca pearls" instead of "brutal boba."

The hours sped by, and near closing time, I spotted Misty Patil heading toward our booth.

"You made it," I said, waving to her. "The chai's been a hit tonight."

"Really?" she said. "Let me have a taste."

I prepared her hot beverage with extra care and then handed her the steaming cup.

She nodded at the brew. "Rich color and heady scent."

I bit the inside of my cheek as I waited for her further verdict.

After several sips, she said, "Not too shabby for your first try."

"I can't thank you enough for sharing your recipe." I hazarded a glance at Ho's Small Eats. "It also took my mind off . . . other things."

She looked toward Nik and his mother. "Ah, the hot pot dinner. Who would've thought Jeffery would go out like that?" She squeezed the bridge of her nose. "I can't seem to get that burnt smell out of my memory."

"Very tragic," I said.

Misty placed her drink on the counter and leaned closer to me. "It's more than a tragedy, you know. There was a reason a homicide detective was called to the scene."

I dropped my gaze from her intense stare.

"There were ten of us," she said. "One person there

ended up killing Jeffery Vue. Maybe we'd all better watch our backs."

She left then, and her chilling words reverberated in my head. I wondered if she'd issued a word of advice, or a warning, to me.

Celine edged around me to reach the photo display. "It's closing time," she said.

I didn't own a watch, but I noticed other vendors breaking down their tables and putting away their supplies. When I assessed the amount of leftover food and drinks, I realized we'd done brisk business. I didn't have much to carry back home with me at all. As I wheeled my cart to meet up with Celine, I noticed her focused on disentangling the leaves from her setup.

"Need any help?" I asked.

"Nah, it'll only take me a few more minutes," Celine said.

Instead of standing and watching her work, I decided to stroll over to Ho's Small Eats. I figured I could offer my assistance there and also ascertain what had happened earlier in the night between Nik and Derrick.

"Hey, Nik," I said as I came up to him. "How was business tonight?"

"Fine," he said. "Could always be better, though."

He lifted a large tablecloth, and I grabbed the other side to help him align the corners.

"What happened with Derrick tonight?"

Nik's hand slipped on the tablecloth, but he caught it again. We folded the two sides together.

"AAROA drama," he said.

"He looked pretty mad."

"Yeah, don't be surprised if there's an emerg—"

Nik's mother raised her voice and called for him. "I need your help cleaning the deep fryer," she said.

I waved to her. "Hi, Mrs. Ho."

She gave me a distracted hello. "Nikola," she repeated, stressing his name.

"Gotta go," Nik said.

Why had Mrs. Ho interrupted our conversation right at that moment? The older lady gripped her back and winced. My doubts vanished. She'd probably just needed Nik's help, given her aching joints.

I rejoined Celine at our food stall, ready to pack up not only our items but all the worries I had experienced throughout the evening. Especially since Celine and I were supposed to go on one of our "sisterly" L.A. outings the next day. I looked forward to a happier time tomorrow.

SIX

WHEN TOURISTS THOUGHT ABOUT VENICE, CAL-ifornia, their attention focused on the well-known beach. I understood the allure of open sands and even the unique weight-lifting area where muscle-bound figures roamed. Nevertheless, I liked the quieter environs of the Venice Canals.

I'd decided to take my cousin there on the "inside Los Angeles" tour she insisted that I give her during her time in the United States.

After breakfast, I asked Celine, "You ready to go?"

"In a minute." She patted down her ensemble, checking to make sure she looked dazzling in her outfit. I thought she looked quite chic in her shearling coat and fitted jeans.

"I'm driving this time, though," I said.

Outside, I again admired the cute Boxster she'd given me. It was a car that fit only two people, but I rather enjoyed the coziness of it. We slid into the car's leather seats and buckled up in unison.

During the drive, I told Celine that the canals in Venice had originated from the creative thinking of tobacco tycoon Abbot Kinney. He'd wanted to provide a little European flair to America. The area featured multiple waterways and bridges spanning paved strolling paths.

I ended up parking the car on a side street, since the whole region consisted of either concrete walkways or an expanse of water.

"Welcome to the Venice of Los Angeles," I told Celine.

"It's gorgeous here," she said, pulling out her cell phone and capturing the alluring sights.

Indeed, residents who lived on the picturesque streets had taken the time to decorate the railings of the bridges with bows and other festive elements.

"Shall we?" I said.

She hooked her arm in mine, and we moseyed along the pavement. At first, we soaked in all the beautiful buildings around us. I couldn't believe people actually lived here, right off the water.

All the homes in the residential area looked catalog ready, as they should, given their multimillion-dollar valuations. Not many of the owners bothered to hide the interiors of their lovely homes from curious passersby. Large glass windows let us view the vast array of elegant furnishings inside, including spiraling staircases and ebony grand pianos. I also spotted several towering fir trees trimmed with intricate ornaments and glittering tinsel.

When we'd quenched our thirst for ogling the homes of the rich and maybe famous, we stood on the arch of a bridge and gazed into the long stretch of water.

"Must be nice to live here," Celine said. "Everyone seems to have their own docks."

She gazed at a bobbing boat with a star painted on its side. Although it was made for single-family use, I wondered if it reminded her of Hong Kong and the Star Ferry transport.

"Do you miss HK?" I asked.

Celine sighed. "I wish my parents were around, even though sometimes we don't get along."

It must have been a huge change for my cousin to switch from living with her folks to moving in with me, someone around her own age. I'd thought about living with Ba after my mom passed away, but my childhood house kept serving up reminders of the past, tainted with loss and sorrow. Still, family was important—which was why I loved being able to call Ba whenever I wanted to and appreciated Celine's current visit. "Would your parents want to make a short trip here to see you?" I said.

My cousin took a while before answering. "I don't know," she said. "De Di and Uncle aren't exactly close."

"I wonder why." I remembered how our two families had only stayed in touch while my mom was alive. The last I'd even seen Celine before this trip was twenty years ago.

My cousin danced her fingertips along the bridge's railing. "Beats me," she said. "De Di would never say anything about it."

"Same here," I said. Ba was quick to give me solutions to my personal problems but never revealed his own issues.

As I mused, I fixated on the dark liquid below me. I'd always been drawn to water the most out of the five Chinese elements, which also included wood, fire, earth, and metal. I usually calmed down by staring into a body of water, but for a moment my mind wandered back to Jeffery's demise.

"Did you know that the extension cord was found wet?" I asked.

Celine latched on to my reference. "You're talking about the hot pot dinner."

"Yeah." I debriefed my cousin on all the snippets I'd overheard from Detective Strauss, along with my own extra snooping discoveries from the kitchen.

My cousin turned to face me, and her eyes locked onto mine. "It must have been done by somebody prepping in the kitchen area. Nobody else would've had access to the cord and sink. Who was in there with you earlier?"

I listed the people who'd worked alongside me while preparing the hot pot ingredients: Ba, Mrs. Ho, and Mr. Yamada. "Plus Misty," I said. "She showed up at the back door, peeved that she hadn't received an official invitation."

"Hmm, were those—" A ding erupted from Celine's phone and cut off her sentence.

She checked her screen while I tapped my foot. What had she been about to say?

A frown flashed on Celine's face before she tucked her cell phone away. She refocused on me. "It's your dad," she said. "We gotta go. There's an emergency association meeting happening at the restaurant."

━━━━━━━━━━

Ba hosted the last-minute gathering in Wing Fat's banquet room. As we slid shut the partition to the rest of the dining area, I beamed at the beautiful space with pride. All my dad's hard work had landed him this lovely expansion. Plentiful round tables were draped in cloth, and each one was equipped with its own lazy Susan.

The association meeting was occurring in the early morning, before Wing Fat opened and the staff came in. I guessed the other restaurants must be closed, or the owners had taken a quick break from their businesses. Everyone who'd been there at the fatal hot pot had shown up for the meeting, even newcomer Trisha Kim.

In a show of hospitality, Ba had laid out baskets of

dim sum on a round table. He'd provided *siu mai* dumplings and rectangular fried turnip cakes.

Celine and I volunteered to serve. She took over providing the attendees with plates and chopsticks, while I poured oolong tea into bright white porcelain cups.

After we'd settled into our seats and started munching or sipping away, Derrick Tran called the meeting to order.

"I know that the transition of leadership is set for January," he said, "but until that time, we need to make sure we have a president in place. As VP, I'm happy to step up in the interim."

Mrs. Ho put her teacup down with a trembling hand. "Wait a minute, Derrick. What do the bylaws say about a situation like this?"

He scratched his head. "I don't have ahold of those documents right now, but we can make this a swift process. I'm the best candidate. You all know how good I am with money."

Someone mumbled, "You mean *stingy*," but I didn't catch who said it.

Mr. Yamada waved his chopsticks around. "We don't need to hold an election at all this year. Everyone knows that Nikola here was next in line to be president. Jeffery made his preference clear many times over."

Misty shook her head. "Nuh-uh. I think we should just hold the elections early instead of waiting for January."

From beside her, Trisha piped up. "I agree. That seems fairer, and I nominate Misty."

No wonder Misty had brought along her new friend.

My dad tried to mediate. "Not so fast, everyone. It sounds like we have three options we could pursue. One, we could have Derrick serve as interim president. Two, we could give the title over to Nikola. And three, we could hold an early election. Why don't we vote on our next steps?"

Mrs. Ho nodded. "And majority rules, as usual per our

votes." She resumed drinking her tea. Her hand didn't wobble anymore.

"Is everyone okay with this?" Ba asked.

Everybody gave signals of affirmation.

"Don't forget," he said. "Only members can vote." His eyes didn't need to flicker over to us, but I knew he meant the sentence for my cousin and me. I'd never applied for membership, and Celine, as a temporary visitor, hadn't even tried.

We made sure to abstain from the vote. When Ba asked for those in favor of Derrick moving up from VP to president, only Derrick raised his hand. Three people voted for Nik to serve as new president: his mother, Nik, and Mr. Yamada. Those who wished to pursue an early election included Misty, Trisha, and Ba.

A stalemate, then. The split vote for the election and Nik as president seemed to stall any forward progress.

"That's too bad," my dad said. "I really wanted to quickly resolve the issue."

Mrs. Ho hit her chopstick against the side of her teacup. "No, we do have a winner," she said. "Trisha isn't an official AAROA member, so her vote doesn't count."

Mr. Yamada appraised Trisha. "That's right. I'm in charge of background checks, and we haven't yet established your ownership of a restaurant."

"Nikola is the clear choice," Mrs. Ho announced with obvious glee.

Derrick blubbered for a moment before saying, "But you can't vote for yourself."

"You did just that very thing," Nik said as he touched his goatee in, perhaps, a victory rub.

"It's decided," Ba said. "Nik will be president."

Derrick stood up. "No way. I'm going to get those bylaws and see what the rules say about this. Jeffery was holding on to the binder with all the official documents and regulations."

Celine whispered to me, "This is why people should store important stuff in the cloud, so they can access it anytime."

"Not now," I said, wanting to avoid a tech benefits lecture from her.

Nik's mother raised her hand in the air to get everyone's attention.

"Speaking of Jeffery," she said, "I'd like to hold a memorial service for him. I don't think that anything official is happening, since he doesn't have relatives nearby. Is everyone in agreement?"

This time around, nobody objected to the idea. Mr. Yamada was even the first to insist that he would host the informal service at his ramen shop.

Derrick closed the meeting, and we all finished eating in a somber mood. Nobody chatted with one another, and my siu mai didn't taste as juicy as usual either.

After I gave up on eating, I approached Nik's mother. "Mrs. Ho, I have a question. Are you sure that Jeffery is not having another memorial of some kind? After all, wouldn't his girlfriend want to commemorate his life?"

"You're right, Yale. I think I have her number in my Rolodex. I'll be sure to contact her." Mrs. Ho finished up her tea in a few sips.

After all the AAROA members (and one almost member) left, Celine and I volunteered to take the dirty dishes into the kitchen. Ba also started picking up the empty steamer baskets, and I lingered at the table so we could walk there together.

"Ba," I said. "What's the deal with this emergency meeting anyway? That's unusual. Couldn't we have waited until January to truly decide?"

"I don't think so, Yale. We usually don't gather frequently, although we do during the holidays. But that's because of our big December charity spotlight."

I'd forgotten about that. Every association member

usually chipped in up to ten percent of their earnings to help out a specific nonprofit every year. "What's the organization for this year?"

"Huh. I'm not sure," Ba said. "We'll have to discuss that, too. The president gets to pick. For the longest time, it's been Order of the Azure Rose . . . which not everyone enjoys contributing to."

We arrived at the kitchen, and I slotted my dirty plates into the dish rack. When it filled up, the tableware would be rinsed and deposited into the industrial machine.

After Celine and I exited the restaurant, I turned to her and asked, "An inquiring mind wants to know. Ever hear of a nonprofit called the Order of the Azure Rose?"

"I will in a minute." She pulled her phone out and searched for it. "The Order of the Azure Rose is an organization that re-creates chivalry and etiquette by using Renaissance-era reenactments."

I could see how not everyone would be on board with that nonprofit. It seemed like such an obscure cause. Besides which, I bet none of the restaurant owners had any ties to European culture and heritage.

We left Wing Fat and headed back to our apartment at Fountain Vista. Both wanting to decompress and needing to prepare for night market anyway, I immersed myself in handling food ingredients. There was something soothing about slicing through crisp cucumbers and creating perfect circles out of them. When I wanted to do it in a rush, I used a mandoline to slice the vegetables. This time, though, I savored the task by using a sharp knife. The afternoon passed as I focused on cucumbers, hard-boiled eggs, and tea leaves in order to replenish the menu for Canai and Chai.

When we opened our stall at the Eastwood Village Night Market that evening, customers swarmed the plaza. Perhaps word had gotten out about the event, or maybe people wanted to finish the last of their Thanksgiving holiday weekend with a fun time. They'd picked a nice night to come, as I spotted a musician drawing a bow across their *erhu*, a two-stringed instrument. Attendees lined up for our snacks and drinks, and I remained busy keeping up with the constant flow of orders.

In the middle of the night, though, I did spot some familiar faces in the food area. Misty walked by with a cup of ice cream, scooping the cold dessert into her mouth. She paused before our booth, giving me a wink as I handed a steaming cup of chai to a customer.

As the hour grew later, the number of customers dwindled. Celine even took a lull to indulge in a bit of gossip with me.

"I see Trisha is definitely checking out something tasty at night market," Celine said, doing a lavish flutter of her long eyelashes.

Peering over at the surrounding food stands, I saw Trisha loitering at the *pupusería* booth. She leaned across the counter, enraptured in a conversation with Blake.

"He's probably giving her his free *pupusa* speech right now," I said with a hint of disgust in my voice.

Blake had pulled the wool over my eyes once before, and I'd been flattered at his initial attention—until I realized that he issued the same invitation for free food at his family's restaurant to all single women. He'd actually asked both my cousin and me to drop by La Pupusería de Reyes at the same time, resulting in an awkward interaction.

"His grandma does make good food," Celine said. She craned her neck. "Wait, is that Detective Strauss making his way over here?"

"Maybe he's here on his time off," I said—but then I noticed his formal attire. The detective wore a blue suit combo, his signature style when on duty.

He marched with purpose toward Ho's Small Eats, where he addressed Nik.

"Too bad we can't hear what they're saying," I whispered to Celine.

A sly smile crossed my cousin's face. "I think this is a great time to tidy up my Instagram display."

She slipped away to our photography setup, which was close to Ho's Small Eats, angling her body toward the detective and Nik.

From where I stood at our booth, I saw Nik cross his arms over his chest during the tense conversation. Then the detective moved into the cooking area in the back and approached Nik's mother. I couldn't see anything happening, but I noticed that Celine had given up all pretense of messing with the backdrop as she eased toward the neighboring booth.

I heard a loud gasp from Ho's Small Eats. Then a flurry of running as Celine pounced toward the food stand. "Are you all right, Auntie Ai?" she asked.

SEVEN

WORRIED ABOUT THE COMMOTION FROM HO'S Small Eats, I sprinted from my booth to check on Mrs. Ho, but Celine intercepted me on the way.

"Auntie Ai told me she's fine and doesn't want to worry any customers. Besides, that one"—she jerked a thumb at Detective Strauss—"looks like he's about to make an announcement."

The detective straightened the lapels of his suit jacket and addressed everyone in the nearby vicinity. "Nothing to see here, folks." He flashed his badge as a symbol of authority. "She just got a bit dizzy. That's all."

Instead of obeying his orders, I moved closer to the scene. Mrs. Ho sat in a folding chair, her face pale. "I'm fine," she said. "Must have been dehydration."

Nik sprang over to a cooler and pulled out a small box of soy milk. He stabbed the straw in and placed the beverage in his mother's hands.

Celine tugged on my arm and motioned toward our booth. We retreated back to Canai and Chai.

"Maybe we'll get the real story after the detective leaves," she said.

"You didn't overhear anything while you were fixing our photo op area?"

She turned her gaze to the booth next door. "I know Detective Strauss showed Auntie Ai a picture of something. That's when she gasped and seemed to lose her balance."

"What could it have been a picture of?" I asked.

"I think—" Celine stopped speaking as Detective Strauss appeared in front of us and gave us a general nod of acknowledgment.

"Celine," he said. "I'd like a favor from you."

My cousin placed one hand on her hip. "Maybe. What do you need?"

"You're an Instagrammer," he said. "I'm sure you took pictures during that hot pot party."

"I got a few good shots and posted one of the boiling food." She shivered all of a sudden. "That was before Jeffery, er, touched the extension cord."

"I need those photos, then," the detective said. "It'd be great if you had shots of both hot pots throughout the night."

"Let's see. Give me a moment to access the camera roll." Celine snuck her phone out of her purse. She held on to her mobile and displayed the relevant pictures to him.

Detective Strauss hummed under his breath as Celine flipped through them. "Can I see those again, but more slowly?" he asked.

Celine complied.

After she'd swiped through about three of them, he stopped her. "Go back one."

"But this photo is only a shot of a hot pot with broth in it," Celine said. "Boring."

"I know, but can you zoom in on the dial?" he asked.

She did so.

"Interesting." Detective Strauss took a notepad and pencil from his pocket and scribbled something down. "If you don't mind sending that photo to my email address, I'd appreciate it. I take it you still have my business card."

"Yeah," she said. "It's at home."

We had one of his cards stuck to our refrigerator with a marbled magnet.

"Sure, send it to me when you get back," he said. "Doesn't matter what time. I know you still have to close up."

Detective Strauss retreated, and I turned to Celine. "Why was he so concerned about the dial?"

"Maybe you can figure that out." She showed me the image on her phone.

It was the hot pot that had been on our table. I knew because the burner plates on the two models were different. I noticed the rich broth still steaming from when Mrs. Ho had slow-cooked the soup in her kitchen. Even through the screen, it made me salivate.

I chided myself and focused my attention on the burner, a model I'd used before. In the picture, I noticed that the dial had been turned to the highest setting. "The hot pot was on," I said. "And it's the kind of knob where you have to deliberately click through to get to the higher temperatures."

"So?" my cousin said.

"That means somebody changed the setting so when Jeffery tried to plug it in, the current went straight through him."

The person who'd wanted to end Jeffery's life must have planned things out in advance. They'd turned on the hot pot, ensuring a domino effect of fatality. I didn't think any of the Thanksgiving meal attendees could have been so coldhearted, but I was obviously wrong.

Celine tapped me on the shoulder. "Hey," she said, "we've got a few more customers."

Closing time soon came upon us. The stragglers at the end of the night market either wanted to eke the maximum out of their tickets or wanted discounts for staying until the very last minute.

I huddled in the kitchen, glad that I didn't have to interact with them while I was cooking or retrieving already prepared food and drinks. I didn't trust myself to act pleasant to strangers while I was mulling over Jeffery's recent death.

We finished with the last customers and then turned our attention to wrapping up for the evening. I focused on putting away the food and equipment while Celine broke down her photo display.

After we'd completed our respective tasks, Celine and I wandered over to Nik and his mother.

"Mrs. Ho," I said. "Are you feeling better?"

"Yes. A-OK," she told me.

"Truly?" I asked. "Because Ba would never forgive me if I didn't make sure you were completely all right." I tossed in the line about filial piety, hoping she'd expand more on her dizzy spell.

"I'm fine," Mrs. Ho said. "Just not a spring chicken anymore. Ha ha."

I didn't give her a pass so easily. "My cousin mentioned that the detective showed you a picture right before you felt ill."

Mrs. Ho snuck a peek at Nik and then fanned herself with her hand. "It was a shocking image. That's why."

Celine moved toward Nik's mother and lowered her voice. "Was it a picture of Jeffery . . . dead?"

"Yes," Mrs. Ho replied, drawing out the word. "May the poor man rest in peace."

I didn't believe Nikola's mother. It seemed like she'd latched on to Celine's explanation out of convenience.

"Speaking of Jeffery," Mrs. Ho said, "we have the memorial set for tomorrow evening at five at Yamada Ramen. Roy is graciously hosting the event."

"That was fast," I said. "Did you contact Michele already? She isn't hosting a more official memorial?"

"I'm afraid not," Mrs. Ho said. "She said she couldn't for family reasons, but she might briefly drop by ours."

"Why should I have expected her to set up a memorial? A girlfriend isn't like a spouse," I said, voicing my train of thought out loud. Of course, I'd never been in a serious relationship, so I didn't know what girlfriend duties consisted of. I'd preferred books over boys my whole life. Admittedly, meeting Darcy in Austen's pages had set a high standard for potential suitors.

"Along those lines . . ." Mrs. Ho said. I wasn't certain if she was referring to girlfriends or the memorial service, but she approached Celine. "You and Nik should work together on that blog to advertise the event to the community at large. We want everyone to have a chance to pay their respects."

Celine dipped her head. "That makes total sense, Auntie."

"In fact," Mrs. Ho said, "since you both are here right now, this is the perfect time for the two of you to work on the blog."

Nik stifled a yawn. "Are you sure, Ma? It's pretty late. Maybe Celine needs her rest, and we can pick this up in the morning."

"The sooner the better, Nikola," his mother said. "If people have lead time, they can adjust their schedules and come to the memorial."

"I guess so." Nik tilted his head at my cousin. "What's your take, Celine?"

"If Auntie thinks it's for the best, then I agree. Besides"—she tossed her luscious locks—"I'm a notorious night owl."

"Excellent," Mrs. Ho said. She retrieved a filled shopping trolley. "In the meantime, Yale and I will leave you two alone for more privacy." She turned to me. "Can you grab that portable deep fryer over there?"

I lifted the unit up and joined Nikola's mother as she ambled away from the food stand.

"I'm parked in the garage," Mrs. Ho said. With the far distance and at our glacial walking speed, we'd give Celine and Nik plenty of time to prepare the blog post. And maybe something more, as Nik's mother probably wanted.

We shuffled in silence for a few minutes before I decided to broach the topic of Jeffery again.

"You know, Mrs. Ho, I can't stop thinking about what happened on Thanksgiving."

"Me neither," she said, shoving the cart along with hard pushes. "It's all my fault, Yale. If only I'd changed to grounded sockets in the restaurant. I told my friends over the years that I would but never got around to it."

She stopped moving and stood at the edge of the parking lot, staring down at the cold concrete beneath our feet.

I touched her arm. "What happened to Jeffery was awful, but it's not your fault. Please don't blame yourself." This morsel of advice was rich coming from me, because I still felt guilty about my mom's death. If only I hadn't mentioned to her that I needed chives for a new recipe, she wouldn't have ventured out that night. Logic dictated that the stalling of her car didn't result in her heart acting up, but sometimes I wondered if the stress of the situation had physically affected her.

"We'd better pack up the car," Mrs. Ho said, withdrawing her arm from my hand.

In the sparsely occupied parking lot, she headed toward a battered Corolla. The car had seen better days, and I noticed a dent on its left rear bumper. Even the lining of the roof inside the vehicle flopped down to reveal sagging foam innards.

She used her key to pop open the trunk, and I placed the deep fryer unit inside. Then I helped Mrs. Ho in unpacking the various boxes and containers from the shopping trolley.

"Did you sell a lot of food tonight?" I asked as I put away a box filled with disposable wooden chopsticks and paper plates.

"Not too bad," she said, "and I hope that those who visit the food stall will also come by Ho's to eat."

"With your cooking, they won't be able to help it."

"Sweet of you to say, Yale. Once we get more business at the main restaurant, maybe I can make all those upgrades I've been dreaming about." She dropped a heavy-looking bag into the trunk with a loud plop.

I heard a cracking noise as she extended herself to reach in and push the bag into the corner. Mrs. Ho gave a soft groan and rubbed at the small of her back.

"Sometimes," she said, "I think I should retire from the restaurant industry."

"If you want to," I said, "I'm certain Nik would do a great job of running Ho's in the future."

"I hope you're right about that."

"Actually, he could help you more around the kitchen even now."

Mrs. Ho frowned at my suggestion, and I wondered if she held on to a belief that men shouldn't cook. Then again, her closest chef friends happened to be male: Mr. Yamada and Ba.

I added, "I'm sure Nik must have wonderful cooking skills. He did major in food science at UC Davis."

"It's exactly that special food science degree that makes me hesitate," Mrs. Ho said. "Ho's might not be fancy enough for Nikola. It needs better equipment before he would want to cook there."

"I don't think Nik thinks of Ho's that way," I said.

Mrs. Ho slammed the trunk lid shut and folded the shopping trolley, depositing it in the back seat.

"Thank you for your help, Yale," she said. "It's about time we got back to Celine and Nikola."

Mrs. Ho and I returned to an exhausted-looking Nik. His eyelids drooped, but he gave us a weary thumbs-up. Celine, on the other hand, still looked fresh and almost radiant in the moonlight.

"Did you manage to get to know each other more?" Mrs. Ho asked the pair of them.

Nik held back a groan. "I mean, we finished the blog post."

"Yes, it's up and running," Celine added.

I grabbed the handle of my laden utility cart, and my cousin got the hint. We bid farewell to Nik and his mother.

Together, Celine and I trudged to the end of the plaza, past the circular fountain. I couldn't wait to slip into bed and sleep off the more intense moments of the night, especially Detective Strauss's invasion of our night market space, when he'd caused Mrs. Ho to almost faint from shock.

Without any help from me, Celine kept up a one-sided conversation. She jabbered on about her beautiful aesthetic Instagram display and the social media frenzy it had created.

"I think," she said, "my creativity must have about tripled our customer base. This weekend probably brought in our highest revenue to date."

"Maybe," I said. "Too bad you can't actually work here on your tourist visa and get paid for your efforts."

"It's not all about the financial reward for us artists." She shook her head a little, making her hair bounce.

I hoped she wasn't rubbing her bachelor's in fine arts degree in my face. Cutting short my higher education still grated on my nerves, even though I stood by my decision to return home. It'd been more important to me to come back after I'd learned about my mom suffering from breathing issues. She'd waved away our concerns, thinking it'd been allergies, but had accepted my assistance at Wing Fat.

Celine's voice pitched high in enthusiasm. "Hey, what if we count all the money from this weekend tonight since we're already up?"

"No, thanks," I said. "Don't you need to sleep? Besides, it's more complicated than just straight sales. We'd have to calculate what it took for all your decorative materials, like the portable stand, canvas backing, and autumn leaves. Plus, the photo alternative for Luddites like me. Those Polaroid prints aren't cheap."

We arrived at the entrance of our apartment building. In the lobby, Celine turned to me. "There's something I want to show you, Yale," my cousin said.

"What?" I asked, peering at the phone she placed near my face.

She spoke with care and precision. "This technological advancement is called a blog. *B-l-o-g.*"

"Very funny," I said. Staying up late didn't improve her sense of humor any, but I still went along and read the latest entry in the *Eastwood Village Connection*. Nik and Celine had created a tasteful post for the memorial. "Wow, you've already got a comment," I said.

"See, not everyone is sleeping at this hour," my cousin said. She glanced at the comment. "Whoa."

I peered at the screen and read the words: Who wants to attend with a murderer in the midst?

"A troll," Celine said, and she shut her phone down.

I wasn't sure about that but didn't want to correct my cousin at this late hour. The commenter didn't seem like a random person hurling a hateful remark. Instead, it had to have been someone with insider information. A person who'd been there at the Thanksgiving hot pot and knew that a homicide investigation was in progress.

EIGHT

After our very late night (or super-early morning, depending on how you counted the time), I decided to cook breakfast for Celine. As a bonus, I'd use up the rest of the leftovers. Crispy scallion pancakes and mugs of spiced chai seemed like an excellent breakfast combo to me. My cousin, deservedly, slept in.

I'd finished cooking and plated everything when an insistent buzzing came from her room. I rushed over to the spare bedroom, where my cousin had taken residence with her loads of accessories and clothes.

Celine lay curled up in bed, snoozing away. She didn't even hear the atrocious noise. I checked her stack of purple suitcases but didn't find any type of alarm clock. Then I pivoted toward the cherrywood bookcase and spied her phone vibrating, right next to my Victorian-style rotary landline with its answering machine.

I grabbed her cell to halt the ringing, but I paused when I noticed a familiar name flashing on the screen. Stepping outside the bedroom, I picked up the call.

"Nik?" I asked. "What's going on?"

"Oh, Yale, it's you. I was trying to get ahold of Celine."

"Blogging stuff?"

"No," he said. "I overslept, and I need help to open up Ho's . . ."

"Why do you need Celine for that? She can't even fry an egg."

"Celine was the first person I thought of." His voice quivered. "I can't find Ma anywhere. She was gone when I woke up. Didn't even leave me a note, and I can't run Ho's alone."

Wow. I hoped everything was okay. Besides his mother's disappearance, I was also bowled over by Nik asking for actual assistance. As his academic rival from middle through high school, I'd noticed his pride in action many times over the years.

"We'll be right over," I said. "But, Nik, you could've called me first. I do have a landline where you can reach me." We were kind of restaurant buddies as well as frenemies. I thought he'd known he could contact me if needed.

He snorted. "Yale, you've never given your number to me."

Oops. Although truth be told, I'd stayed away from reconnecting with previous classmates after I'd returned home from my abbreviated college run. I'd wanted to focus on family only . . . and I suppose I harbored some sort of internal shame.

"I'll punch it into your contacts when we get there," I said. "Hey, do you need my help in the kitchen?"

"It'll be better if you served the customers," he said.

I should've anticipated that response. Nik always touted the authentic food made at both Ho's and its corresponding night market stall. He probably didn't want me to mess with his cooking style. "Sure," I said. "See you soon."

I hung up and rustled my cousin awake. After stretching her arms up, she rushed to pick a suitable outfit while I ate a quick breakfast and packed her food to go. On the ride over, Celine applied makeup in the car while I drove with care, attempting to avoid any potholes.

At Ho's, Nik hurried to push open the door and greet us. "Thank you, both," he said. "We've got half an hour until opening time. Let me give you a quick tour."

I followed Nik, his bedhead hair looking poofier than usual. His steps sounded halting as he made a circuitous route in the old diner, highlighting the cubby for the menus, the trays of extra utensils, and the serving aprons.

At the end of the tour, we returned to the long counter in the front, where Nik demonstrated how to work the cash register. After Celine did a mock ringing up of an imaginary customer to his satisfaction, he disappeared into the kitchen to get food ready. I busied myself making sure to put on a serving apron and stuffed its pockets with an order pad and pen, and a stash of napkins and extra chopsticks.

By the time opening hour came, I felt ready. The customers rolled in, and I was almost crushed by the tidal wave of people pouring into the restaurant. I was glad for the deluge of patrons because last year, Ho's had been in dire straits. Nik had even accused my dad of taking away business from his own family's restaurant by diverting customers to Wing Fat. The arrival and eventual success of the Eastwood Village Night Market must've turned things around for Ho's.

As I worked, the tantalizing scents wafting from the kitchen made me want to ditch my position and sit down at one of the booths. Instead, I seated people, handed out menus, and relayed orders to Nik.

As he cooked each order, I'd emerge from the kitchen with platters of delicious Taiwanese breakfast goodies. I delivered mountains of fried crullers along with steaming bowls of hot soy milk. Sesame bread *shao bing* sandwiches were also favorites among the customers. A few even asked for *fan tuan*, those long sticky rice rolls filled with egg, pork floss, pickled radish, and mustard greens. No doubt about it. Nik's creations definitely rivaled his mother's fare.

I heard one or two patrons even give praise along the lines of "this tastes even better than usual, if that's possible." It seemed like Nik had either added special ingredients or flaunted superb skills in the kitchen.

People continued to enter through the doors of Ho's and pushed at the limits of breakfast time. The Taiwanese morning dishes were supposed to end at noon, but the clock read one before customers stopped arriving for breakfast.

"Whew," I said to Celine when a break occurred. "I finally get to stop moving."

She stretched out her hands. "I didn't know fingers could cramp so much from hitting keys on a cash register."

We'd been really busy, but I'd made sure to look for Nik's mother coming through the front door. Had she gone to the back entrance instead?

I walked into the kitchen and glanced around. "Did your mother show up, Nik?"

"No," he said, standing at the sink and washing his hands. "But I'm going to check my phone right now. Maybe she texted."

He shuffled to the side and retrieved his phone from the supply closet. "Ah, she did send me something."

"Is she okay?"

"Ma had to run errands for the memorial tonight, and now she's finishing up a chat with a friend. She even sent me a pic of their living room." He approached me with his phone facing out so I could see.

I scanned the furnishings of the room. The arrangement of that specific set of furniture set off a warning bell in my head. I recognized the room, from its dove gray love seat to the oil painting of a forest hung on the wall. This was the soft interview room found in the Eastwood Village Police Station.

I didn't want fear to color my voice, so I kept my comment short. "Cozy place."

"Yeah," Nik said. "I wonder why she had to see her friend right this minute. She knows we have a restaurant to run."

I nodded and left the kitchen to speak with Celine. Even though nobody remained in the dining room, I approached my cousin near the cash register and lowered my voice. "I know where Mrs. Ho went. To the police station."

Celine rubbed at her elegant neck. "Are you certain?"

"Nik's mother told him that she went to run errands and stopped by a friend's place. Then Mrs. Ho sent him a pic of that comfy interview room we've been in before, pretending like it's her friend's living room."

"Oh no. Poor Auntie. Did Detective Strauss tell her to go?"

The front door flung open, and Mrs. Ho rushed in. I supposed we could ask her ourselves.

She startled as she spotted us. "What are you two doing here?"

"Helping Nik out," I said while my cousin nodded.

Her eyes crinkled with joy. "You girls are too kind."

"Not a problem, Mrs. Ho," I said.

"My pleasure, Auntie," Celine added.

As Nik's mother started shuffling toward the kitchen, I hopped in front of the swinging door to block her path.

"Wait a moment, Mrs. Ho," I said. "Nik showed me the photo of the room . . . I didn't say anything to him, but I know it's part of the police station. Everything okay?"

Mrs. Ho twisted her oil-spotted hands and took a moment to sort through her thoughts. She probably wasn't sure how much information to give me. "It was purely a misunderstanding. Something about a sharp object that the detective found at the foot of the supply closet."

"What was it?" I asked.

She averted her gaze. "Nothing important to the case, I'm sure."

The kitchen door opened behind me.

"I thought I heard your voice," Nik said, as he scooted around me to give his mother a quick hug. "Ma, you had me worried this morning."

"Sorry, Nikola. I didn't think the errands would take so long."

Nik nodded. "But you could've told me earlier. Or called me."

"Ah yes, I did forget to tell you," she said. "Must have been a senior moment."

I hoped Nik couldn't see right through her lie.

My cousin cracked her knuckles at the counter, and the popping sound made Nik focus on her. "Thanks for all your help, Celine." He turned to me. "You, too, Yale. But now that Ma's back, you're both off duty."

"Anytime you need some extra hands, Nik," I said. "Truly." I pulled the various contents out of my serving apron and put them away.

In the meantime, Nik hurried back into the kitchen.

When I'd finished untying my apron and had folded it into a neat rectangular bundle, Nik came back out. "Swap you," he said, holding out a takeout container. "I put some fan tuan in here for you and Celine."

I accepted the box with gratitude.

"Thanks for the yummy food," Celine said. "And we'll see you both later tonight."

Nik and his mother assented, waving to us as we slipped out of the restaurant. Yes, we'd definitely see them at the memorial service tonight. Before that meet-up, though, I wanted to drop by for a quick chat with Detective Strauss.

I drove to the Eastwood Village Police Station but remained in the parking lot once we got there.

"Let's eat these while they're hot," I said, opening the takeout container from Ho's. The fan tuan were tucked in clear wrap to keep them from getting messy. Beyond making my stomach happy, I wanted to buy myself time before launching into the building and confronting a detective.

Celine followed my lead in getting a snack and murmured her appreciation for the delicious rice roll. When we finished eating, we wiped our hands clean and entered the building.

In the open lobby, our shoes squeaked against the linoleum floor as we approached the glass-partitioned booth. Using the intercom, I asked to speak with Detective Strauss.

"I'm Yale Yee," I said. "He should recognize my name."

The person on duty nodded, dialed a number, and relayed my information. After a moment of listening, he said, "Okay. I'll let her know."

He hung up and turned to me. "Detective Strauss will be right out. Please have a seat in our comfortable waiting area."

Not exactly as he described. The adjective I would've used for the row of hard-backed plastic chairs was "torturous." In fact, both Celine and I, having experienced the seats before, decided to stand to wait for the arrival of the detective.

It didn't take long before Detective Strauss slipped through a connected side door and strode over to us.

"Thanks for emailing me those hot pot photos, Celine," he said. "I don't have too much time to chat, but did you two remember something important from Thanksgiving?"

I answered his question with one of my own. "What's this I hear about a sharp object being found near Jeffery?"

"Word sure spreads quickly," he mumbled. "But it wasn't anywhere near the body."

That's right. I'd misspoken. I now remembered Mrs. Ho having told me it'd been discovered at the foot of the supply closet.

The detective pulled out a phone from his pocket and clicked on it. Then he showed us an image of a Swiss Army knife. "Do you know who this belongs to?"

It looked the same as any pocketknife I'd encountered before, and plenty of people carried those tiny blades around. No wonder Mrs. Ho didn't think the item was related to the case. "Detective Strauss," I said, "no offense, but those Swiss Army knives couldn't hurt a soul."

By my side, Celine tilted her head in thought. "Death by pricks. No way. Although, I've had my share of those kind of men."

I gave her a stern look, but my cousin ignored it and offered me a beatific smile in response.

Detective Strauss checked the leather Timex piece on his wrist. "Were you here just to interrogate me? Well then, your time's up. Or do you have something actually important to tell me?"

Mostly, I'd wanted to question him, but I knew that working with the police required a give-and-take partnership. I needed to provide him with something in return. "I don't know if you've heard, Detective Strauss, but there's an informal memorial for Jeffery Vue. This evening at five." I nudged Celine. "Show him the article."

Celine proceeded to show Detective Strauss the post on the *Eastwood Village Connection* blog.

I pointed at the empty comments section. "There was a strange message posted before. Where'd it go, Celine?"

"I erased it and marked the comment as spam," my cousin said, "but I can pull it up on the back end." She proceeded to log in to the blog's administrative side and shared the screen with the detective.

He read the comment and scratched at his square jaw. "Hmm, interesting."

Celine peered at him, her amber eyes wide. "Will you make it tonight, Detective, to patrol the event?"

He took a step away from her. "Sorry, I can't. Too much paperwork. In fact, I'd better get back to it now."

The detective excused himself from our company. Either he had a legitimate reason for not attending the service or he'd wanted a kinder way of turning down the invitation.

Either way, I thought it'd be better without a homicide detective lurking around the memorial. His presence would make people more on edge and perhaps even disrupt the mourning atmosphere.

We exited the police station, and my thoughts swirled around the pocketknife. How did it fit in with the scenario?

NINE

BACK AT THE APARTMENT, MY HEAD STILL FELT muddled, and I decided to make a steaming mug of chai. That would soothe me after our recent police experience.

Thanks to Misty's addictive recipe, I now turned to the spiced tea for a quick cup of comfort. I made sure to keep my pantry stocked with the necessary ingredients.

As I bustled around the kitchen, my cousin asked, "Need any help?"

I'd already put out the cutting board on the counter along with a bag of cloves and a bottle of cardamom pods. "Yeah, go grab the ginger out of the fridge."

I liked storing the unpeeled root there because it lasted longer. Although I still noticed tiny tendrils growing out of the ginger when Celine brought it over. "Could you get me the peeler, too? Should be in the top drawer over there." I pointed to the spot.

She rummaged in the right location but couldn't find

it. "Oh, uh, I think I used it the other day. Now, where did I put it?" Celine placed her hands on her hips, as though offended by the peeler running off and disappearing on her.

I used to impose my own order on the kitchen. Celine had thrown things off by moving items to different places. But I knew it wasn't malicious, and as she hurried over with a paring knife, I realized it was nice to have company and a cooking assistant.

The paring knife would have to do. I used it to peel the skin off the root; it came off in brown flakes. I also cut off some of the growing tendrils, piling them on the side.

Then I crushed the ginger and spices together, releasing a fragrant scent.

"That's a lot for just yourself," Celine said.

"It'll probably be perfect for the two of us."

She grinned at me. "Aww, thanks."

Huh. I'd included my cousin on autopilot. Actually, it was nice to cook for more than one person after so long—and to have someone who would appreciate my efforts.

"No problem," I said. "Why don't you go boil the water?"

Prepping food was kind of like a culinary dance. After all our time spent together at the food stall, I realized that I enjoyed having Celine as a partner.

While waiting for the water to boil, I scooped up the ginger bark. Then I picked up the pile of tendrils, which looked like wispy wires. My hand slipped. I dropped everything on the floor.

"You okay?" my cousin asked.

"Wire," I said, pointing at the debris on the ground. Then I swiveled to the paring knife. "What if . . . ?"

"Er, that's ginger." Celine moved to a nearby closet and gave me a broom.

I clasped it but didn't sweep while I worked out my thoughts. If I substituted the paring knife for a pocket-knife and the ginger tendrils for actual wires, then I had the perfect cooking parallel to what had happened at the hot pot dinner.

After picking up my mess, I dumped everything into the kitchen trash in one fell swoop. A tidy solution had appeared to me, and I explained my theory to Celine.

She nodded. "So, you're thinking that the knife carved out some of the casing on the cord?"

"Uh-huh. And an exposed wire plus water don't mix well."

Celine raised her eyebrows at me. "Who would've had time to do such a thing at the dinner?"

"That's a good question. We need to nail down the timing."

"It could've been any moment before Jeffery literally got the shock of his life." Celine paused. "The extension cord was in the kitchen. Weren't you in there doing prep work? What did you notice at the beginning of the night?"

I tapped the cutting board before me. "Hmm, I don't remember the cord being near the sink early on, but then again, I wasn't in charge of washing the raw ingredients. When I was helping, I started right in on chopping the veggies."

Ba had rinsed them before my arrival, and he was the only one in the kitchen I knew I could totally trust for an honest answer. Maybe he'd seen the extension cord lying around somewhere.

On the stove, the water in the pot burbled at us. We stopped chatting to add the ingredients. Once the chai was ready, I doled out huge servings. "We'd better fortify ourselves," I said. "We've got some questioning to do at the memorial."

* * *

The somber event was held at Yamada Ramen, a restaurant I'd never been inside before. Even with the black lacquered tables pushed up against the walls, it seemed like a tight space to hold a group event. If the furniture hadn't been moved for the memorial, the pre-existing seating arrangement would probably have had people dining within arm's reach of one another. On the other hand, the close quarters accented with Japanese paper lanterns hanging from the ceiling seemed to broadcast an intimate atmosphere.

Black dining chairs were arranged in several short rows, and about a couple dozen people had shown up for the event. I definitely recognized the older generation of AAROA in attendance. Mr. Yamada, of course, was present, and he formed a tight-knit group with Mrs. Ho and Ba.

Other association members were also around. I saw Derrick carrying a small speaker and microphone up to the impromptu stage area. The sound system looked like it might have been a portable karaoke set.

I also found Nik hovering over the counter on the side. Platters of fried *karaage* chicken and *gyoza* dumplings, along with a pitcher of iced matcha tea, were set out for attendees.

Derrick turned on the microphone and blew into it. The resulting *whoosh* made everyone focus their attention on the stage.

"If everyone could sit down," he said, "we'll get started soon."

People hurried to find seats, most of them opting to sit as near the stage as possible. I wasn't sure if they wanted to hear the eulogies better or physically show their closeness to Jeffery.

The first-generation restaurant owners took over the

front row, close enough to reach out and touch the framed, enlarged photo of Jeffery set up on a wooden easel. A floral wreath surrounded a smiling picture of him holding up a multicolored beverage, as though toasting us in the audience.

Nik settled in the second row, right behind his mother's chair, but Celine and I hung back. We didn't really know Jeffery that well, so we slipped into the seats farthest away at the back.

Derrick raised his hand as though shushing everyone. "Let us take a moment of silence for our dearly departed friend, Jeffery Vue."

We sat through people shifting in their seats and looking at their feet or staring at the framed photo. Then Derrick started his speech.

He droned on about his position as vice president of the association, emphasizing his rock-solid support of Jeffery. Two minutes into his monologue, and he seemed to be praising himself more than expounding on the virtues of Jeffery.

As he continued talking, someone crept through the front door. A feminine figure with a sheer black veil draped over her face perched on the empty seat beside me.

When Derrick finally finished, he asked, "Would anyone else like to offer up their memories?"

Nik sprang up from his seat and shared about how Jeffery had mentored him. He specifically discussed the encouragement he received as a fresh college graduate, uncertain on how to best use his food science degree to its optimal impact. As Nik complimented his mentor, the woman beside me started shaking a little.

I glanced over in concern, but she waved me off.

Once Nik ended his mini speech, a woman walked up to the stage and grabbed the microphone.

She pointed at the wreathed photo. "Jeffery Vue made

one of the best *nab vam* drinks I've ever tasted in my life." The drink was pronounced *naa-va*.

At this confession, the woman beside me burst into tears. Sniffling, she excused herself, and I followed her outside.

Under the awning of Yamada Ramen, I asked her, "Are you all right? Because you're trembling."

"I'll be fine." She opened her purse and pulled out some clean tissues.

Then she shifted her veil, uncovering her face. I had a brief glimpse of sweet-looking delicate features before I looked away to give her some privacy.

She blew her nose and then said, "My crying must have disturbed you. Sorry, you can go back inside now."

"It's understandable you'd be sad," I said. "Jeffery's death was sudden and unexpected."

"Yes, it really was." She tossed her used tissue into the nearby trash receptacle and used a bottle of sanitizer to clean her hands.

"I'm Yale Yee, by the way," I said. "I knew Jeffery through our restaurant connections. How did you know him?"

She replaced the veil over her head. "My name is Michele Yang, and Jeffery—"

"He was your boyfriend," I said.

"You know about me?"

"He couldn't stop talking about you, the 'woman of his dreams.'"

She touched the edge of her gauzy veil. "My parents didn't have such a rosy picture of us, and now I don't have a chance to see him one last time . . ."

It must be hard on a relationship to not have parental support for it.

"I'm going back inside now," Michele said, straightening her shoulders.

She marched back into the ramen shop, and I trailed behind her. We entered right as Derrick spoke some solemn words to close out the service.

After he finished, Mr. Yamada stood up and said, "Thank you for coming, everyone. I've prepared some snacks on the side for you to enjoy."

People rose from their seats and drifted toward the counter filled with food and drinks, except for Michele. She didn't veer toward the snacks but headed straight to the easel. Before the enlarged picture, she lifted her veil for a moment, kissed her palm and then placed it over Jeffery's smiling mouth.

Someone tapped me on the shoulder.

I turned around to find Jeffery's customer, the woman who'd praised his drinks onstage, staring at me.

"You work here, right?" Without waiting for an answer, she continued. "Are there any other beverages being served, like his famous nab vam?"

I could see how she'd mistaken my dark banded-collar shirt and black slacks for a server's uniform. I should've worn a different outfit. "Um, I think iced matcha is the only drink available."

"Too bad." She pointed at the easel, and I turned around. At some point, Michele had slipped away from the photo and disappeared. "That tapioca coconut drink is amazing. Have you ever tried it?"

"No, but it looks almost festive in coloring." The tricolored beverage did appear vibrant, with its white base and splashier fruit and tapioca.

"What I love the most about the drink is the green worm-like *cendols* made with pandan extract. Ah well. I guess the matcha will have to do."

"Sorry about that," I said.

As she wandered back to the counter, I heard her mumble, "Wonder what's going to happen to the food cart."

It sounded like she and perhaps more of Jeffery's customers would be dismayed at the loss of his specialty drinks. I thought about her comment about his food cart.

What *would* happen to all of Jeffery's belongings? He didn't have any family nearby. When his will was read, who would inherit it all? I bet the settling of the estate would open up clues about who could have wanted Jeffery gone.

The only lead to the case that I'd gathered so far had been the position of the cord near the wet sink. This reminded me to question my dad. Despite his stellar memory, it'd be best to ask him as soon as possible, when the facts remained fresh in his mind.

TEN

I SURVEYED THE OPEN AREA OF YAMADA RAMEN and found my dad in a small triad, chatting with Nik and Mrs. Ho.

As I approached, I heard Ba commending Nik's mother for her central role in organizing the memorial event. Wondering how I could snag my dad's attention without appearing rude, I looked around the room for Celine.

She'd just finished pouring herself a glass of iced matcha when our eyes met. I tilted my head toward my dad and mimed talking. She raised her glass at me in acknowledgment.

My cousin wore a dark crepe sheath dress and heels. Nobody would have confused her with the hired help. I paused at the edge of the group and waited for her to make the first move.

She approached my dad and others, holding out a full glass of iced tea to Nik's mother.

"Auntie Ai," Celine said, "I don't think you've had a chance to try this. You must be thirsty."

"How sweet of you," Mrs. Ho said, accepting the glass. Her face brightened with delight. "Nik, isn't Celine so kind?"

"Uh, right." Nik shifted his feet, which were stuffed into scuffed dress shoes instead of his usual sneakers.

While Nik and his mother were focused on my cousin, I tapped on Ba's elbow, and he excused himself for a moment. We stood a few paces away from the rest of them.

"First off, Ba. How are you doing being around all of this?" I gestured at the somber event. The last memorial he'd attended had been for Mom.

He swiveled his head toward the framed photo of Jeffery. "I can't believe he's gone. What a fluke, the electricity going through him like that."

"I'm not sure it's a simple accident, because the police are involved." I moved closer to Ba and lowered my voice to avoid being overheard. "Actually, I found out that the extension cord got wet. You were in the kitchen, Ba. Did you notice the plug lying near the sink?"

"The cord? No." The lines across his forehead deepened. "I was rinsing all those veggies, and it was definitely clear back then."

"When was the last time you went by the sink?"

"Before the hot pot was ready. I remember washing my hands there before eating."

"Were you the last one to leave the kitchen?" I asked.

"Roy and I carried the hot pots and burners to the tables, and Ai was still at the stove."

I remembered Ba and Mr. Yamada setting up the two hot pots and then Mrs. Ho bringing out the broth later. She had been the last person in the kitchen.

Then Nik had tried searching for the extension cord—

in vain. After him, Derrick had volunteered to find it, also to no avail. I wondered when the cord had gone missing and how it had reappeared at the sink.

Everybody had been hungry and distracted at the time. We'd all decided to concentrate on cooking the food on the single working burner. Until Jeffery had gone back in and located the tampered-with cord, eventually to his demise.

Ba placed a warm hand on my arm. "How are you handling everything, Yale? I know it's not your first time discovering . . . um, foul play." I liked his use of the old-fashioned term.

"It was still difficult, especially since I knew Mr. Vue." I'd stumbled on a dead body twice already in my life. On the first occasion, I'd been all alone, in the creepiness of pitch black. This time around, I'd been in a festively decorated restaurant with a group of people surrounding me. I didn't know which was worse, having no one in sight or being within close range of an actual murderer.

I shook my head to clear it of morbid thoughts and focused on the present. All the association members, along with Celine and me, decided to stay and help Mr. Yamada clean up his restaurant.

Ba put away the leftover food while Derrick dealt with the equipment. Celine and I wiped down the counters and chairs with wet rags. Then we offered to help Mr. Yamada move back the furniture.

Celine redistributed the chairs to the side as Mr. Yamada and I lifted a table.

"Thanks for hosting the event," I said as we carried it to a spot Mr. Yamada indicated with a jerk of his head.

"Here will do," he said, and we placed the table down. "I know the restaurant space is very tight, which is why I had to move all the furniture, but offering up Yamada Ramen was the least I could do."

He blinked a few times as though lost in thought.

"You knew Jeffery for a long time, right?" I asked. The man had been president for years, even before I'd left Wing Fat to move on to working at the local bookstore.

"Oh yes." Mr. Yamada wiped his brow for a moment. "He kept the organization running well for many years."

Celine approached us with a stack of chairs, and we moved out of her way.

"Is there a term limit for an AAROA presidency?" I asked after we'd set down another table.

"Nope. A president can run for reelection as long as they want. As long as they're interested. Of course, I know Jeffery wanted to step down this year."

"He did?" I said.

"Jeffery told me so himself. He wanted new blood come January."

We repeated our table-moving efforts.

"He wanted to pass the mantle to Nik, right?" I gestured to where my old classmate and his mother stood before the easel. They were occupied with removing the flowers around the frame and placing the full blossoms into a crystal bowl.

"His mentee was definitely Jeffery's top choice. But he wouldn't have minded any new face. He just wanted to move on."

We put another table back in its original location, while Celine followed us, scooting in chairs.

"But why now?" I asked as we continued to work.

"Michele. He fell in love and wanted marriage, kids, the whole nine yards." Mr. Yamada fumbled with his words and the table.

It must've been lonely being a widower and having no children, only estranged relatives around. We finished up with the rest of the tables in silence, with Mr. Yamada deep in thought.

The quiet made Derrick's booming voice sound even

louder when he spoke up from beside us. "I'm off to open my business."

Celine had reached the last table at this point and pushed in the final chair.

"Which restaurant do you own again, Derrick?" she asked.

"Pho You and Me. Have you heard of it?"

She sucked in her bottom lip. "Don't think so, but I'm visiting from abroad."

"Well, you've got to check out my restaurant before you leave. We're known for our great late-night eats—that's why it's hard for me join the night market more often. I mean, I trust my managers, but . . ."

"It sounds like an amazing spot," Celine said. "And I love taking foodstagrams. Maybe we can drop by to-night?" She glanced over at me, and I nodded.

I hadn't gotten a chance to eat any of the snacks put out, and my stomach let out a low growl at the thought of some Vietnamese fare.

After mapping it out on her phone and double-checking the location with Derrick, my cousin said, "We'll see you there soon."

"*Pho* sure," he said with a hearty laugh as he exited out the front door.

Mrs. Ho carried the crystal bowl of flowers she'd filled up over to the counter and placed them in the center of its wooden surface. "There, looks so beautiful."

"Perfect," Mr. Yamada said. "The customers will appreciate those."

"They'd better," Nik said from his position, staring at the green floral foam embedded in the frame. "Those flowers cost a lot. Especially since we used them only for this occasion."

Mrs. Ho pinched the bridge of her nose. "Nikola doesn't mean that. It was worth the splurge."

Nik proceeded to remove Jeffery's enlarged photo. "And what should we do with this? Is it recyclable?"

Celine marched over to Nik and wagged a finger at him. "Are you trying to toss out his photo? That's disrespectful."

Nik held his hands up. "Fine, take it. But what would you even do with it?"

"I don't know, but trashing it isn't a viable solution."

"Here you go, then." He rolled up the print and strapped a rubber band around the now cylindrical tube of paper.

"Thanks." She took Jeffery's photo. "And now Yale and I are going to dinner."

Either she wanted to try out Derrick's restaurant or to get away from Nik. Whichever her reason, I didn't mind. After we said goodbye to everyone, we matched strides and left Yamada Ramen to visit Derrick's restaurant.

Pho You and Me was housed in a freestanding building. Through its glass windows, we could see various holiday decorations filling up the space. Twinkling lights were draped along the walls, and velvet bows decorated the silver cash register. We even noted a Charlie Brown Christmas tree in one corner.

Inside the restaurant, the atmosphere seemed even more festive as holiday music blasted our ears. A sign near the front entrance read, "Seat Yourself."

We selected a table far away from a speaker. The eatery's furniture all seemed chosen for ease of use. The glass-topped surface meant that spills could be easily wiped. A selection of serve-yourself disposable utensils at the table meant less work for the staff.

Celine and I had been sitting down for about five minutes before we saw Derrick approaching us.

"Great to see you gals again," he said, pulling out a guest check pad. "What can I get for you two?"

Celine ordered a hot pho noodle soup with tripe, while I opted for a cold vermicelli dish topped with egg rolls. Derrick disappeared with our requests, and I glanced around the shop.

"That's nice that he wanted to greet and serve us himself," I said.

"The personalized touch. Works great for customer service." Celine extracted her phone from her purse. Then she clipped a circular light around the camera lens.

"What's that for?" I asked.

"Ring light," she said. "Excellent for nighttime shots that need more illumination."

Derrick soon came by with a piping-hot bowl of soup for Celine and the noodle dish for me. He added a plate of fresh spring rolls, with soft, clear rice paper wrapped around shrimp and vegetables.

"We didn't order that," I said, pointing to the cold appetizer dish.

Meanwhile, Celine had turned on her bright portable light and kept snapping pictures for her Instagram account.

"Don't worry," Derrick said to me. "It's on the house."

"Oh, okay, thanks," I said.

"Enjoy." He retreated to the kitchen.

"That was kind," Celine said, putting away her phone and starting in on the spring rolls.

"Strange, though," I said. "He's usually more vinegar than sugar. Especially when it comes to money."

Had the sudden loss changed Derrick? Maybe he now realized the need for human kindness, although he hadn't seemed that affected by Jeffery's death, even at the memorial service.

"Yum," Celine said, licking her lips. "If only my photos could capture the taste."

I picked up a spring roll and bit into its chewy exterior. "Derrick knows you're on IG. Do you think he's giving us the free spring rolls so you can boost his restaurant on social media?"

"Doesn't matter," Celine said. "I don't doctor my shots, so what you see is what you get. Anyway, this both looks and tastes great. I almost wish I could write about it, not just take photos."

I finished my spring roll before asking, "Do you think he knows you're connected to the *Eastwood Village Connection* blog and wants a good write-up?"

"Nah," she said, breaking open a pair of chopsticks. "We post that stuff anonymously."

I still wasn't sure about the cause behind Derrick's sudden generosity. Sure, a free plate of spring rolls didn't cost much, but he didn't seem like a man inclined to hand out freebies without any expectation behind them.

We'd finished our meal when Derrick returned to our table with the check.

"How was it?" he asked.

"Delicious," Celine said, wiping her mouth with a paper napkin.

"Agreed," I said.

Celine paid for the meal, placing a large bill on the tray. "Keep the change."

"Nah. I don't need it," Derrick said. "Save your money for your Los Angeles sightseeing."

"Excuse me?" Celine said, arching her eyebrow. I wasn't certain if she was offended by him rejecting her generosity or by his possible suggestion that she might need money more than he.

"No offense intended," Derrick said, ducking his head. "It's just that I got an unexpected happy call from an executor."

"Well, congrats, then," Celine said.

Derrick beamed and took away the check.

"Isn't an executor involved in inheritances?"

"I think so," my cousin said.

Derrick had gotten good news about an estate. Who else could have died in his sphere of contacts beyond Jeffery? Besides, Jeffery had been a single, older man; maybe he'd accumulated a lot of wealth over his lifetime. What exactly could he be gifting Derrick, his loyal second-in-command?

Derrick returned, depositing our receipt and change in the center of the table. "Again, thanks for coming."

We nodded at him and murmured more compliments about his food. The smile on his face grew wider before he departed.

Celine pushed the tray of change toward me. "Here you go, lucky lady."

I wouldn't say no to a little extra spending cash. It'd be nice to enjoy some retail therapy after a rough weekend, including an emotion-laden memorial.

ELEVEN

WHENEVER I HAD MONEY TO SPARE, I OPTED TO shop at The Literary Narnia. I loved the local bookstore. Before I set off for the shop, I asked Celine if she wanted to join me.

"No, thanks," she said. "You get stuck in those stacks forever."

"I can't help it, I'm a book addict."

"Go ahead and enjoy yourself," she said. "I'll be busy interacting with my followers online."

With a jaunty wave to her, I headed out of the apartment. The fact that The Literary Narnia was within walking distance made me smile. A quick stroll through the nearby shopping plaza across the street landed me at the strip mall and the bookstore with its adorable brick façade. I hurried inside.

Kelly stood behind the cash register and greeted me. "Off to spend your hard-earned cash?" she said.

"Something like that."

I checked out the new-books display table and glanced

at the cute cover of a cozy mystery with a talking cat. Then I strolled down the aisles, my fingertips dancing along glossy and cloth-bound spines.

Around the corner, I almost bumped into a long stepladder leaning against a bookshelf.

Looking up, I spied a woman climbing the rungs. "Dawn?" I said. "What are you doing up there?"

The other Tanaka sister held out a thick silver strand of tinsel for me to see. "Making the place more cheery," she said.

"Ah. Well, let me hold this for you just in case." I clamped my hands around the base of the ladder to stabilize it.

Dawn had to rise up on her toes to place the garland on top of the tall bookshelf. She had a knack for crafts. After all, she'd made the hand-calligraphed signs advertising the various sections around the store, which were mostly organized by genre.

"I'm so glad you still come by and visit us," Dawn said.

"This is like my second home. I will always be at The Literary Narnia. Well, here and Wing Fat," I said. "Plus, I wanted to buy a book."

"When you worked here, we could never stop you from using almost your entire paycheck on the inventory," she said.

"So many books, so little time. You know how it is."

She finished draping the garland across the bookcase. "That's exactly how I feel. But I'm still so sorry we had to let you go—"

"Water under the bridge," I said. "It's better this way. I got back to cooking, which is pure joy."

"Glad to hear it. By the way, the chai from the night market was delicious, and it was fun to go out at night with my sister."

"You enjoyed the event, then?"

"Yes, dear. The entertainment was particularly exhilarating." Dawn climbed down the stepladder and paused at the bottom rung. "Too bad I'm so short. I had to ask your tall, dark, and handsome neighbor to move so I could see the stage better. Not that he was paying too much attention to the performer. He was too focused on the Asian beauty next to him."

"Who are you talking about?" I asked once she'd placed both her feet down on solid ground.

"The attractive man who runs the pupusa place."

"Oh. Blake." Perhaps he'd taken a quick break from his stall to hang out with this mystery woman. That must mean she'd passed the free-pupusa stage, and he was actually interested in her beyond just meeting up at the restaurant.

"I can handle things from here," Dawn said, pointing at the ladder.

I let her fold it up and take it to the back room. In the meantime, I searched for a specific bookshelf and retrieved a hardcover edition of *Wuthering Heights*. Satisfied with my selection, I met Kelly at the cash register.

She adjusted her wire-rimmed glasses and stared at the title. "Couldn't stay away from another classic?"

"My kryptonite," I said, placing the book down. Then I reached into my pants pocket and pulled out my thick wallet.

"Must have done well at the night market this weekend," she said.

I hedged my answer. "Celine had a great idea of getting more customers by setting up a photography opportunity."

"That was a gorgeous display," Kelly said. "Wish my sister and I had gotten our pictures taken, but I didn't want to stay too long after I noticed Roy."

"You have such bad memories of him?" I said, paying for the novel.

Kelly took my money without counting it. Good, because I'd slipped in more than the cost of the book. She put the cash in the register and shoved the drawer closed.

I felt like I should stick up for the poor man. "You know, Mr. Yamada might have improved a little since you last knew him. He actually volunteered to hold Jeffery Vue's memorial service at his ramen restaurant."

Kelly stared at me without blinking. "Maybe he did it out of obligation. He was always doing stuff to appear more upstanding, like answering the teacher's questions—right before throwing spitballs at the classroom ceiling when her back was turned."

I knew I wouldn't change her mind so soon. "Anyway, thanks for ringing me up."

I called out a goodbye to Dawn before I left.

She bustled out of the back room and said, "Wonderful of you to see us. Also, tell that dear cousin of yours hello."

"Will do," I said.

I found my dear cousin Celine still absorbed in social media when I returned to the apartment.

She lay against the settee, her eyes flicking to me only once when I entered the room. Then she turned back to her screen. "Hmm," she muttered. "You actually came back before lunch."

"And you're still on Instagram, I see."

She scrolled down the screen. "Different platform," she said. "I've moved on to Facebook."

My curiosity was piqued at the mention. "Wait a moment. Are you still friends with Blake on there?"

"Sure. Why?"

"Something Dawn said at the bookshop. She saw him with some Asian woman at night market."

"And you want to know who it was?" Celine tapped at her phone. "Let's find his latest pic. Huh. Is that . . ."

I made my way over to my cousin and peeked at her screen. "That's definitely Trisha Kim."

"I was wondering why she looked so familiar. He didn't actually tag her in his post, though."

"Maybe she's not into Facebook," I said. "Or maybe she's tech-wary like me."

"Perhaps," Celine said, "but she seems like she's a pro at selfies. Check out her pose. The camera is aimed down at her for the best angle."

Trisha did have her face tilted in the shot, looking up at the lens with big brown eyes.

"Is she sucking in her cheeks?" I said.

"I think she's doing fish lips."

"That's a thing?"

"Guess it is for her," my cousin said.

"I do like her lipstick." I'd never attempted to wear such a rich red color. I couldn't imagine doing so, given my aversion to being the center of attention.

"Imagine how much work Blake had cut out for him to wash the lipstick off her glass," Celine said.

Why would he need to wash a glass? I scrutinized the picture and noted the location in the background. They'd taken the shot in front of Blake's family's restaurant. At a cropped corner, I could make out the beginning of the "La Pupusería de Reyes" sign in blue letters.

"Must have been redeeming her free pupusa in that photo," Celine said with a shake of her head. "Which reminds me, what's for lunch, Yale?"

"I can throw together a quick stir-fry."

"Please do," she said, lying down again. "I'm starving."

Maybe showcasing food all the time on her social media resulted in frequent hunger pangs.

I set off to the kitchen and really did toss random ingredients into the skillet. I stir-fried some tofu, snow peas, and canned baby corn. Then I boiled some egg noodles and added them. After mixing everything together, I drizzled oyster sauce over it all.

Celine and I ate lunch together, and then we set off to different areas of the apartment to relax. She retreated to her room to try out a new nail polish she'd bought. I took over the settee and opened up *Wuthering Heights*. Even the physical heft of a book in my hands made me grin.

I put my feet up on the nearby ottoman and lost myself in the atmospheric English setting. I'd really gotten into the detailed description of the moors when an insistent ringing sounded.

Scrambling over to Celine's room, I grabbed the landline phone on top of the bookshelf. Celine didn't even bother to move from her perch on the bed, concentrating on swiping some nail polish on her right pinky.

"Sorry," she said. "It'll mess up my work to pick up the call."

I answered the phone because Ba usually called this number.

I'd guessed correctly, because he said, "Yale. Glad I caught you."

He no longer said that in jest. Prior to Celine's arrival, if I wasn't at The Literary Narnia, it was a sure bet that I'd be at home. Now my cousin and I traipsed all over Los Angeles on an extended tour of the local region.

"Ba," I said. "Isn't this the middle of your lunch rush?"

"It's Derrick," Ba said. "He's asking all the association members for help this afternoon. Most of us are working, but I thought of you and Celine. I think only Trisha Kim has volunteered so far."

"What kind of assistance does Derrick need?" I asked.

"I'm fuzzy on the specifics, but it'll be at his restaurant. Some sort of painting project that starts in half an hour."

Why couldn't Derrick use his newfound money to pay

for that? But maybe his frugal nature had taken over again.

"You can do it, right?" Ba asked. "Represent our family, help out an AAROA member."

I agreed, wanting to please my dad.

"I'll let him know," Ba said. "And make sure to ask Celine, too. She has a great artistic eye."

After we hung up, I turned to Celine. "Hey, cuz. Want to do some painting on a larger canvas than your hands?"

"What do you have in mind?"

"Don't really know, but you can put your fancy arts degree to use."

"Deal," she said. "Just let me blow some cool air on my nails to speed up the drying."

Celine hurried to the bathroom, where I heard the blow dryer turn on.

Once her nails seemed dry enough, we left for Pho You and Me. However, the restaurant was locked up tight when we arrived. We tried knocking on the front glass door, but nobody appeared in its dim interior to let us in.

"Is anyone even in there?" Celine asked.

I called out Derrick's name in a loud voice.

He hurried over to us from around the corner. "Sorry, I forgot to tell Sing," he said. "We're doing the painting in the back."

We followed him to the alleyway in the rear, which was a narrow asphalt-lined space. He led us to what looked like an ice cream pushcart. Basically a trolley, it was previously painted in an egg-white color that appeared stained from use.

"Needs more than a little TLC," Derrick said.

"Couldn't you just wash it?" I asked.

"I did. Also, I want a more eye-catching color for the cart," he said. "And wait until you see this."

He wheeled the pushcart around to show us. A graffiti image marred the entire other side. Someone had sloppily painted a huge magenta heart. It looked like it was bleeding, with its dripping edges.

Celine pointed to the letters framed by the symbol. "Why is there a *V* and a *Y* crossed out inside the heart?"

I peered at the bubble letters. "Maybe someone didn't have time to make the plus sign. Or they messed up while painting it?"

"Well, whatever it means," Derrick said, "I'd like to get rid of it."

He placed a can of mint green paint in front of us. "A nice spring hue for new beginnings."

"Do you have any primer?" Celine asked, glancing at the purplish-red heart and shaking her head.

"Nope," Derrick said. "I only got this one can of paint from the hardware store."

We heard footsteps sprinting our way, and Trisha soon appeared in the alley.

"Sorry I'm late," she said. "I still get lost on these side streets." She wore appropriate painting attire, including a shirt that had seen better days and a grimy baseball cap. I hoped Celine wouldn't complain about any paint splotches that might land on her own pristine denim overalls.

"No problem," Derrick said. "I'm happy you showed up at all. I think it's great that you AAROA members are pitching in and helping me."

Celine, Trisha, and I all looked at one another.

"Actually," I said, "my cousin and I never applied to be in the association."

"And my application is still pending," Trisha said.

"Oh, well, thanks for coming. I can pay you all with free food," he said. Then he frowned at Celine and me. "Then again, maybe not you two. You already got an appetizer from me."

What had changed Derrick's mood from his chipper generosity last night to this dour attitude?

"Okay," Celine said. "Who's going to open the paint?"

I held out my hand to Derrick. "They gave you a tool at the store, right?"

"Um, no, and I forgot to ask them." Derrick squeezed his pointy forehead. "I wish Nik were here. Well, maybe I can find something inside the restaurant."

"A flathead screwdriver should do the trick," Trisha said.

Derrick went inside Pho You and Me, while Celine organized various paint trays and brushes.

"Your membership is still pending?" I asked Trisha, trying to make small talk in the interim.

She shifted the bill of her baseball cap. "Who knew it would take so long? I guess they're still gathering info."

"Are you relocating your restaurant from Koreatown?" I asked.

"Yes, expanding the family business."

"Wow. You must be doing well over there to branch off," I said. "Then again, there's probably a good Asian customer base in that neighborhood."

She blinked her dark brown eyes at me.

Before we could talk further, Derrick came out of the restaurant brandishing a screwdriver. "Found one," he said.

Celine pried open the can and peered inside. "The paint has already settled," she said and frowned. "When did you get this mixed, Derrick?"

"Er," he said, "it was on sale at the store. Discounted. I don't know how long it's been sitting on the shelf."

"All right, then." Celine grabbed a wooden stirrer from nearby. "Who wants to mix it and make sure the texture's even?"

"I will." Trisha stepped forward and grabbed the long wooden stick.

While she applied herself to mixing up the paint, I asked Derrick, "What's the cart for anyway? You gonna sell ice cream now?"

He popped open the lid of the cart and peered into its hollow space. "I'm thinking cold drinks would be nice for my customers."

Celine licked her lips. "Mmm, cold Vietnamese coffee."

"Or maybe sugar cane juice, fresh coconut water, or a soursop smoothie," he said. "I haven't come up with the drinks list yet."

"Those all sound good," I said, wanting to encourage his efforts.

A sudden burst of music filled the air, and Derrick untucked his cell phone from his back pocket.

"Hello?" he said. "Oh yes, come drop it off in the back alley."

A few minutes later, a new visitor showed up to our paint party. She wasn't wearing the black veil that I'd seen her in before, and I got a better opportunity to look at Michele this time around. A sweet smile spread across her face when she noticed me.

"I don't mean to interrupt your gathering," she said, "but I wanted to drop this off as soon as possible."

Michele stepped toward Derrick to hand him a thick three-ring binder. She fumbled the handoff, though, as she got distracted by the ice cream cart. Derrick caught the edge of the binder, so it didn't fall to the ground.

"Oh my," Michele said. She covered her mouth with one hand.

"Yeah." Celine nodded at the drippy-looking heart. "Whoever thought that was art was wrong."

Michele's voice came out breathless. "I should get going now."

She hurried away from us, and Derrick called out his

thanks to her back. "I appreciate you giving me the by-laws," he said.

After Michele's departure, we focused on the painting job. As I slathered mint green across the heart graffiti on the cart, I wondered about her shock.

The letters *V* and *Y* popped out at me. I bet they were initials.

I rolled another layer of color over the bubble letters to make them disappear, although I could still see a faint outline behind the green I'd painted on.

Celine narrowed her eyes and assessed our work. "We're going to need another coat of paint."

"Yes, Captain," I said.

We kept busy for a few more hours, painting our respective parts, letting the paint dry, and then adding another coat.

When we finished, Trisha stretched her arms high above her head. "Who knew painting would be so much work?"

"Haven't you remodeled before? Or watched it being done?" I said. Ba had revamped Wing Fat, and I'd seen the huge effort it took to improve the space.

"Nuh-uh," she said. "The family restaurant was move-in ready when we bought it, complete with the right décor."

"Lucky," I said, but then again, the restaurant had been in Koreatown. Maybe it hadn't needed anything extra before changing ownership.

As Trisha and I chatted, Celine sidled up to Derrick. They took out their cell phones and had a quick whispered conversation.

Then we cleaned up the painting materials and said our goodbyes. Celine and I marched back to our car.

Before I started the engine, I turned and stared at her.

"What?" she said. "Do I have paint on my face or something?"

"No. Tell me about that sneaky convo you had with Derrick."

She splayed her hand out, and I noticed that she hadn't managed to smear her nail polish, even with our long afternoon of labor. "Oh, I was just getting the contact info for Michele."

"Why?"

"Well, she ran off so suddenly. But I wanted to get her number because I thought she might want to keep that blown-up photo of Jeffery."

"That's a great idea, although . . ." I gripped the steering wheel. "I'm not sure how lovey-dovey their relationship really was."

"What do you mean by that?" Celine asked.

"I briefly chatted with her at the memorial service, and her family didn't seem to approve of their relationship. Besides, you saw the dripping heart just now."

Celine swiveled her heard in the direction of the alley. "Are you talking about the ice cream cart?"

"Yep. The letters. At first, I thought they might be initials of first names, but then I wondered . . . Could they represent surnames?"

"Like?"

"For example, Vue and Yang. Plus, didn't you notice they got crossed out? That means a broken relationship."

My cousin tugged at the strap of her overalls. "Why would their names be on something Derrick owns?"

"He's the owner now, but I think it belonged to Jeffery before," I said. "At the memorial, one of his customers told me he sold his drinks from a cart."

I wasn't sure who'd painted the magenta heart, but it was definitely someone unhappy with Jeffery and Michele's relationship. Either a relative or Michele herself had spray-painted the graffiti.

TWELVE

CELINE AND I RETURNED TO FOUNTAIN VISTA, where she changed out of her painting clothes.

"Yuck. I can smell the fumes on them," she said, as she swapped her overalls for a cowlneck sweater dress. "Ahh, much better."

I don't know if she wanted his approval or had just desired to give Ba an update about the volunteering, but she texted him a photo of the repainted cart.

A minute later, and he'd responded to her.

"What did he say?" I asked.

"Good job and . . ." She squinted at the message. "He also invited me to take pictures at a meeting tonight for long-standing members of AAROA. There's supposed to be some sort of exciting announcement happening."

I ran into Celine's bedroom to check my answering machine messages. None from Ba. Why hadn't he bothered to tell me?

Celine called out from the living room, "Hey, you're

also invited," she said. "Looks like it's a last-minute thing that Detective Strauss coordinated."

"Come again?" I stepped out of the bedroom. "Why would the police be involved?"

"Beats me." Celine smoothed out her dress. "Do you think this would be appropriate for tonight?"

"Yes, you look great," I said. "Like always."

She flashed me a shy smile. "Thanks."

I didn't bother to change. In fact, I wasn't so sure about this exciting announcement thing. What did Detective Strauss really have in mind?

When six o'clock rolled around, Celine and I hopped into the Boxster and headed for the police station. The news would be announced in the community room in the very same building.

I'd been in the conference space at Eastwood Village Police Station before, and it seemed as tidy as ever. The large area held rows of gleaming tables and comfortable padded chairs. A large whiteboard took up some space at the front of the room. Detective Strauss stood next to the board, attired in a dark charcoal suit and muted red tie.

He waited while people trickled in. Besides Ba, I noted that Mr. Yamada, Derrick, and Nik had shown up. Somehow these proprietors had managed to hand off their busy restaurant tasks to someone else, or they'd closed up shop for a brief interlude.

At ten minutes past the hour, Detective Strauss cleared his throat for attention. I sat down in the back row, but Celine edged forward, her cell phone poised in her hand to capture the momentous occasion.

"Members of AAROA, hearty congratulations are in order," the detective said, giving us a round of applause. "I've even bought a bottle of Martinelli's to mark the occasion."

Detective Strauss strode over to a side table I hadn't

noticed before. On it sat a bottle of chilled apple cider, along with a stack of clear plastic cups.

The detective broke the seal. "Oh wait," he said. "Anyone have a bottle opener I can use?"

He took his time peering at our small group, pausing on each person's face in turn. Ba stared blankly while Derrick clasped his hands together. Mr. Yamada glanced down at his lap, and Nik reached into his pocket but frowned. I shook my head, and Celine crept closer to the detective and snapped a photo of him.

"Hmm. Fine, then," the detective said. "I'm sure we have one in the building. Excuse me for a moment."

He darted out the door, and a murmuring rose from those gathered. I leaned in to eavesdrop on the conversations. It appeared that nobody really knew the actual purpose of the meeting.

When Detective Strauss returned, everyone quieted down. He opened up the bottle and poured a glass for each of us. Picking up a permanent marker from the table, he said, "Don't forget to write your names on the cups since they all look the same."

We lined up at the table and gathered our drinks, putting our names on the cups as instructed.

Detective Strauss lifted up his apple cider. "A toast to the Asian American Restaurant Owners Association."

"What is this for again?" Nik asked, his cup half-lifted in the air.

"You haven't heard?" the detective said. "Jeffery Vue willed half of his estate to the organization."

Nik's eyes boggled. "Oh wow."

Mr. Yamada made a choking noise while Derrick emitted a low growl. The cup in Ba's hand trembled.

"Yes, congrats," the detective said.

We touched our cups to his and sipped. Celine took pictures of people's reactions to the shocking revelation. Detective Strauss had organized a gathering to let us know about this windfall. Did he want to evaluate people's reactions to nail down a killer?

"Can you talk about the logistics?" I said. "How will the funds get distributed to the association?"

"I believe that AAROA has a business bank account," the detective said, his gaze pivoting to Ba. Why had he singled out my dad?

"Yes," Ba said. "We have a joint one where Jeffery and I are co-owners." My dad was the treasurer of the association.

"Uh-huh," the detective said.

We ended up making small congratulatory remarks to one another, but the excitement was subdued. After all, the reason the organization had more funding was due to the fact that the association president had died.

Detective Strauss broke up the meeting and collected the trash. He held out a plastic bag for us to deposit our used cups in.

Then we filed toward the exit. However, the detective called Nik back. "May I have a quick word with you?"

"Um, sure," Nik said, and let the rest of us leave the community room.

In the police station's lobby, people started chattering.

"I'm nervous about having an influx of money in the account," Ba said. "We should really get another president on board ASAP."

"My thoughts exactly," Mr. Yamada said. Tapping Derrick on the shoulder, he asked, "Did you read those bylaws yet?"

"No, but I will tonight."

"Good," Ba said. "We'll set up a meeting about the presidency tomorrow morning, at an early hour before we need to open our restaurants. We should make sure to invite everyone who's able to vote."

I nodded at my dad's recommendation. We needed to

fill in everyone about the news, and they should all have an opportunity to voice their thoughts. Besides, I knew we were missing a few members at this impromptu announcement session. Nik's mother was probably busy at Ho's, and maybe Misty had been accidentally left out of yet another gathering. Also, Trisha could vote, if her application had gotten approved.

Nik left the community room and joined us. His cheeks looked ruddy.

I grabbed his arm and whispered, "What'd the detective say to you?"

"Nothing," he said, pulling my hand off. "He just had a few questions about the best way to open a bottle of Martinelli's."

His eyes darted away from mine.

Nik raised his voice. "What'd I miss out on here?"

"We're having a meeting tomorrow morning," Mr. Yamada said. "To go over the bylaws and to finally figure out who the new president is."

"Great." Nik stuck his hands in his pockets. "When and where are we holding it?"

After a brief discussion, the long-standing association members agreed on convening at seven in the morning at Wing Fat. Then we departed the police station and went our separate ways.

Back in the car, Celine flipped through the photos she'd taken during the announcement. She cropped and modified them, saying, "I'm going to load these onto the cloud for Uncle to access—your father knows how to retrieve them, right?"

"Probably not. I mean, he uses a flip phone."

"You're one to talk," Celine said.

I ignored the jab. "I'm sure you can walk him through getting it from the cloud, or he can find a friend to help."

"Okay." She scrolled through her shots again and said, "Do you think it's odd that only the men showed up tonight?"

"The others were probably busy," I said.

"Aren't all of the owners?" she said. "Except for Derrick, whose restaurant specializes in late-night eats."

I glanced at the police station building through the windshield. "You think Detective Strauss invited *only* the guys? But why?"

"I don't know, but he was cornering Nik."

It did seem fishy that he'd talked to Nik while the rest of us loitered in the lobby. And when I pressed Nik, he'd avoided answering my question. Nik probably wouldn't have lied straight to my face. And he'd mumbled about bottle openers. Could Nik have been skirting the truth?

I snapped my fingers. "The tool," I said. "Celine, remember when Derrick needed to find something to open the can of paint? He said he wished Nik were there."

"You think Nik carries around some sort of special item?"

"I do," I said, "and I think it's a Swiss Army knife. Something Detective Strauss found close to the scene of the crime and which he thinks plays an important role in the case."

"Interesting," my cousin said. "But I still don't feel like we should rule out the female suspects in our investigation of Jeffery's death."

"Er, when did this turn out to be a case that *we're* pursuing?"

She flipped her hair over her shoulder. "Come on, Yale. You know solving murders is fun."

Our previous investigating had added a certain excitement to my life that had been missing before. It'd also given me a lot of stress.

"Plus," Celine said, "Detective Strauss is shortsighted. Why question only the men? Women can own knives, too."

"We'll see them tomorrow," I said. "Mrs. Ho will be there, though I don't suspect her. And Misty should be invited to vote for a new president. Trisha, though, is a question mark."

"No problem about Trisha." Celine pulled out a compact from her purse and freshened her makeup. "There are other ways to get the lowdown on her. In fact, I'm in the mood for some pupusas right now. My treat, Yale."

"I'm on it," I said, starting up the car engine. We'd seen that incriminating Facebook photo of Blake and Trisha together. I maneuvered the car toward La Pupusería de Reyes.

Celine turned up her charm at the restaurant. The pupusas were good but not so much that they required loud lip smacking and frequent smiles directed at Blake.

We lengthened our meal, taking smaller bites at the end, until we noticed a slowdown of customers coming in for dinner. Once the lull occurred, Celine crooked her finger at Blake and asked him to attend to our table.

"You ladies need something else?" he asked, taking his order pad out.

Celine dabbed her mouth with a napkin. "I saw your last Facebook post. Who's the new girl on your arm?"

"Why do you care?" Blake asked, raising his thick eyebrows.

Celine placed a hand over her heart and gave him a mock pout.

Ever since she'd come to the States, Celine and Blake had traded lighthearted banter. They'd never actually gone on a date, though. Given Blake's unflattering comments about Instagrammers, I could see why Celine hadn't pursued anything beyond talking.

"I saw the pic, too," I said. "She's really pretty."

"Yeah." Blake seemed dazed for a moment, perhaps

pondering Trisha's beauty, before adding, "Plus, she really gets me. Trisha is also devoted to her family and their restaurant."

I leaned forward. "Does she own a place around here?"

"Not yet," he said. "But they'll open a branch here once she finesses the details for the building."

Maybe that was why Trisha hadn't become an official member of AAROA yet, since she didn't have an actual restaurant up and running.

I stroked the handle of the butter knife next to my empty plate. "What interests does Trisha have beyond restaurant stuff? Camping or whittling?" It was a stretch for me ask about those specific hobbies, but I couldn't think of any other way to ask him what I really wanted to know.

Celine gave me a subtle head shake, but I ignored her. I bet Blake already thought of me as the awkward one, so it wouldn't clue him in to our investigating.

Blake rubbed at the stubble on his jaw with a broad hand. "I don't know her well enough to say, but she promised me a home-cooked meal this week, so maybe I'll know more about her interests soon enough."

"Wow," Celine said, crumpling her napkin. "You got her cooking for you?"

"What can I say? Women adore me." Blake faltered at the hard stare my cousin gave him. He added, "Plus, she said that it was only fair since she got free food here from me."

Celine shrugged and asked for the bill. Blake scurried away in response.

I turned to my cousin. "You seem tense. Are you okay with the whole Blake and Trisha thing?"

"Yeah, I'm not bothered by that," she said.

My cousin still stayed quiet in the car, even up to the point when we arrived at Fountain Vista. And she didn't unbuckle once I'd parked.

"What's wrong?" I asked her.

She frowned. "We didn't learn much about Trisha, and how exactly were you thinking about getting intel on Misty? We're both not official members of AAROA, so we won't get invited."

"The meeting will be at Wing Fat, and we've got easy access to it. Ba won't mind us coming in I bet."

She snapped her seat belt buckle off. "Okay, if you say so."

In the comfort of the apartment, Celine got lost streaming music while I read a few more chapters from *Wuthering Heights* as we bided our time before Ba closed his restaurant for the night.

At the stroke of midnight, I called him using my landline. He'd definitely be back home by now.

When he answered, I said, "Ba. I have a brilliant idea. Celine and I can help you tomorrow during the meeting."

"Oh, thanks, but how?" he said.

"The association members will probably want tea and snacks, right?"

"Yes, I already thought of that. I figured I'd go in early to prepare some food."

"You can leave it to me and Celine," I said. "And people might need coffee at that early of an hour. We can come by with a large to-go container of it."

"I forgot about that." Ba didn't carry any coffee in his dim sum restaurant. "Okay, I'll see you both at six in the morning, then."

"Yep. Bright and early," I said. "And, Ba, before I forget, all the members will be there tomorrow, right, including Misty?"

"Of course," Ba said. "It was already a huge mistake to exclude her from the Thanksgiving hot pot."

"And the announcement tonight."

"Well, Detective Strauss managed the invitations for that event," he said.

"Interesting. We'll see you tomorrow, Ba."

"Yes, it'll be nice to have the meeting and settle this already."

I bet Ba was talking about the president role for the organization. However, I was excited to figure out who had really caused Jeffery's death and resolve the open-ended investigation.

THIRTEEN

IN THE EARLY MORNING, CELINE AND I MADE A quick detour to Peet's Coffee before arriving at Wing Fat. She carried the huge cardboard container of medium roast coffee over to the back door of the restaurant. Thankfully, it was already unlocked, and I swung the screen door open for us to enter.

Passing through the empty kitchen, I called out my dad's name.

"Over here," he replied.

We followed his voice to the banquet room, where he stood before a round table. Ba had taken away the lazy Susan and had positioned a gleaming porcelain teacup at each place setting. He took the time now to rest chopsticks on patterned ceramic holders. I wondered if he'd purchased them on purpose, or if he'd unearthed them from the kitchen cabinets in my childhood home.

"Hi, Uncle," Celine said. "Where should I put the coffee?"

Ba waved to another round table, which had a stack of

porcelain plates and foam cups on it. "All the food and drinks will be over there."

He smiled at me. "Do you know what you're making yet, Yale?"

"Not exactly."

"You can take a peek in the fridge for inspiration while Celine and I handle the sugars for the coffee out here."

I nodded and watched Ba move closer to Celine, who had already pulled out a variety of sugar packets from her purse.

"How should we arrange these?" she asked Ba. "In a wreath, maybe, or a fan shape?"

I left them to figure out the aesthetics of the sugar. In the kitchen, I scrounged around the metal shelves of the walk-in refrigerator and its connected freezer. I needed something simple to make, and I leaned toward steaming the food. That way the bamboo basket might keep the items warm right up until the time they had to be served. Plus, I wouldn't have to step near a wok and flame to cook the food.

After ten minutes of inspection, I discovered a few bags of frozen *siu lung bao*, or *xiao long bao*, soup dumplings. Those would be perfect.

I placed the bags on the prep counter and started working on the accompanying ingredients. Grabbing ginger from the fridge, I peeled the roots and sliced them into thin golden slivers. They would pair with the traditional dipping sauce for the dumplings.

Celine appeared in the kitchen. "Need some help, cuz?"

"If you could take the ginger out front, that'd be great. Also, look around for a bottle of soy sauce and black vinegar."

She spotted the nearby plastic bag filled with frozen dumplings. "Ooh, XLB, one of my faves."

I glanced at the wall clock and checked the time. "They won't take long to make."

"Can't wait," she said, proceeding to search for the sauces around the kitchen.

I took a deep breath in and out as I drew in the confidence to cook again at Wing Fat. My cousin's presence helped me to remain calm. No waves of nausea hit me this time around as I started steaming the dumplings.

Celine left the kitchen with the sauce but then came back within minutes. She balanced porcelain plates in her hands.

"I'd better swap these out with bowls," she said. "In case the juice sprays out of the dumplings."

"Good idea. We wouldn't want any injuries by soup."

Celine soon located the bowls and scurried out of the kitchen. I busied myself with making some oolong tea.

When the timer dinged for the dumplings, I carried baskets of them out to the banquet room with a sense of pride. Today I'd taken a small step toward conquering the fears from my past.

I had excellent timing, too, since a knock sounded from the front door only moments after I set down the steamed dumplings. Ba went to unlock the main entrance.

Derrick shuffled into the banquet room with a huge binder in his hands. Once he saw the spread we'd laid out, he placed it down quickly on the food table. He seemed excited about the hot coffee and food.

My dad tapped the three-ring binder with his index finger. "This reminds me. I have something else I need to give the next president."

He darted away and returned with a small checkbook, which he placed on top of the binder.

Then the others started coming in. Nik came with his mother, but Mr. Yamada wandered in alone.

I'd better set out tea for our guests. I hurried into the kitchen and returned with a steel teapot full of strong oolong.

When I came back to the banquet room, every member of the association had arrived. Even Trisha had shown up. I suppose her lease had gone through, and she was now a bona fide owner of a local restaurant.

People made their way over to the table with the place settings, and I remembered my duty. I needed to pour their tea as a sign of respect.

I stood on the side, waiting until they'd all taken a seat. As they sat, I wondered how I could figure out if Misty owned a pocketknife. She'd been slighted many times by the association, and maybe she'd finally taken revenge on the president.

Based on their seating position, I decided to make a loop around the table. I started with pouring the tea to Mr. Yamada and ended up last on Misty. I lingered near her while filling her teacup.

I rehearsed the lie in my head once more before speaking it out loud. Bending close to Misty, I whispered, "Oof. I cracked my nail. Do you happen to have a nail file, like maybe on a Swiss Army knife or something handy?"

She opened her mouth, closed it, and then said, "No, I do not."

Had I surprised her with my question? Misty stared down at her fingers curled around the teacup. I noticed that her nails were bitten and had jagged edges to them. She looked like she hadn't used a file on them in weeks.

Had I offended her in some way? Maybe she'd been embarrassed by the state of her fingernails. She could have thought I'd been giving her a hint about her neglected personal grooming.

I retreated from her so quickly that I bumped into Nik in the process.

He scowled at me.

"Sorry," I said.

"Are you apologizing for your lack of serving manners?"

"Uh, no," I said. "I bumped into you, but I guess it didn't knock that chip off your shoulder."

"Did you realize you served the tea wrong?" Nik said. "It should be from eldest to youngest."

It was true. I'd started with Mr. Yamada, who was older, but had hopped around to different ages because of where people had sat down.

"Easier to go around and pour in a circle," I told Nik, gesturing at the teacups.

"Okay, but can you explain the dumpling mess-up?"

"Mix-up?" I asked.

"Mess-up," he repeated. "Xiao long bao isn't a real dim sum dish. And not typically served at breakfast."

"Whatever," I said. "It's a popular item here at Wing Fat." Although Nik was correct in saying that the dish hadn't originated in Hong Kong. The dumplings were associated with mainland China and often tied to Shanghai cuisine.

"By the way, the Taiwanese version is way better," Nik added. "With more delicate wrappers for the dumplings."

I dipped my head and peered into his coffee. "Do you need extra sugar in your coffee, Nik? To sweeten your tongue?"

Misty must have thought I was serious because she said, "I think there are still sugar packets left. Or Splenda, if you're interested. Let me check for you." She looked over at the adjoining table and gasped.

I followed her line of sight and noticed a puddle under the coffee container. A pool of dark liquid dripped from there to the carpet below.

"Ack." I grabbed cloth napkins from the lacquered cabinet at the side of the room and dropped them on the floor and the table.

Everybody seemed to spring into action then, and

they crowded around to help. Trisha mopped the ground with the napkins. Celine rushed back to the kitchen to wring them out. Mr. Yamada tried to blot the coffee stain on the tablecloth while Ba lifted the cardboard container and examined its underside.

"Do you think there's a puncture?" my dad asked while sloshing the remaining liquid inside.

He placed it on the far side of the table and waited for several moments. Ba lifted it up again. Seeing nothing underneath, he said, "Hmm, not leaking. I wonder what happened."

After a few more minutes of combined cleaning, we got everything under control, although the tablecloth would need to be laundered. Someone would also have to remove the stain from the carpet.

Derrick stood by his teacup and clinked it with a chopstick. "Okay, everyone. Now that we've eaten and gotten something to drink, or tried to . . ." He pointed at the dark coffee stain on the ground. "We should get to voting. Let's go over the rules again."

He marched to the table to retrieve the binder next to the depleted bamboo baskets. I aimed a smug smile Nik's way. Despite his talk about people not eating xiao long baos for breakfast, it seemed like this crew had consumed every single one of them.

My dad raised his voice. "Don't forget the checkbook, Derrick. It's over there, too."

Derrick scanned the tabletop. "Where?"

"It was on top of the binder," Ba said. "Don't you see it?"

"No."

My dad's face turned pale, and he stood up with a slight wobble.

Derrick inspected underneath the table. "Actually, I found it. Must have fallen." He waved the checkbook in the air.

Ba sat back down and took a restorative sip of his tea.

Derrick returned to the association members and read from the notes in the binder. "First off, we need to have the nominations. Anyone in good standing in the organization can run for the position, but members cannot nominate themselves."

Everyone nodded at the logic of this statement and proceeded to put forth names. Of course, both Derrick and Nik were in the mix of contestants. A surprise entry, though, came from Trisha, who added Misty to the list of competitors. An interesting development. I wondered how the voting would fare because of the new nomination.

Derrick raised his hand to get people's attention. "The nominations are all in, and now we'll have a secret ballot." He glanced at Ba. "Do you have something people could write on to privately submit their votes?"

"We've got it covered," I said, sprinting out of the room to secure a guest order pad and a stash of ballpoint pens. I proceeded to hand one slip of paper and pen to each member.

For a few moments, everyone bent over their papers. The sound of scribbling ensued.

When the pen scratching stopped, Derrick spoke up. "Seems like people are done, so it's time to tally the votes." He ran his finger down a page in the binder. "We need someone to count all the votes, and then a second person to double-check the results."

"Yale and I can do it," Celine said in a loud voice. "We're impartial."

Derrick agreed with the suggestion, and my cousin started gathering the slips of paper. I noticed Misty biting one of her fingernails down to the quick. *I'd better step in with something else for her to munch on.*

I took some wrapped fortune cookies and distributed them among the members. The snacking would also keep people occupied as we counted. Plus, more food would help drain the tension from the room.

Even Nik must have been occupied with thinking about the results. He didn't even reprimand me for passing him a fortune cookie, which was definitely a nonauthentic Chinese treat.

After I handed out the goodies, the members started chatting and laughing over their fortunes. Celine and I decided to choose a table far away from them so we could concentrate on the votes. Once we finished counting, we double-checked the votes to make sure we ended up with accurate results.

"Okay, we're done," Celine said. She held up the papers and waited a few beats, perhaps building up the anticipation.

"The race for president was tight," she continued, "but the winner is . . . Nik Ho."

Mrs. Ho grabbed her son and hugged him tight. Misty flipped her braid over her shoulder. Derrick turned an alarming shade of red but shoved the binder and checkbook toward Nik.

Nik accepted the items like trophies and beamed at the others in the room.

"I'm honored to be voted into this position," he said, making sure to look each person in the eye. "The first order of business for AAROA will be the charity donation in December."

"What's that?" Trisha asked.

Nik summarized how everyone in the organization was supposed to chip in money for a combined donation to a nonprofit for the holidays. "Jeffery wanted to contribute to Order of the Azure Rose, but since I'm president now, I can change the cause. And I'm open to suggestions."

People murmured at the table. A few indicated that they didn't care what nonprofit was chosen. However,

Mr. Yamada suggested animal shelters as a better cause. Misty brought up the plight of the unhoused, which some people thought was too political, and Mrs. Ho talked about the needs of the local hospital.

"I'll take all those ideas into consideration," Nik said, "and I'll email everyone my final decision next week." Then he dismissed the meeting, but people continued to chat. Misty conversed with Nik, Derrick talked with Mrs. Ho, and Trisha spoke to Mr. Yamada.

In the meantime, Ba approached my cousin. "Celine, do you have copies of those pictures you took from the special announcement at the police station?"

"Yes, I already gave you a Google Drive link, Uncle."

Ba edged closer to me, as though I'd whisper the definition in his ear. Of course, I was as technologically challenged as him.

"What am I supposed to do with this link? Unchain it?" he said, chuckling.

Derrick edged into our conversation and slapped Ba on the back. "Come on, old-timer, get with the *computing program*."

Ba fished the flip phone from his pocket, and Derrick shook his head in response. "We really need to bring you into the twenty-first century."

"I'm fine the way I am, but I do want to figure out this link. Let me check my schedule, and we'll meet up."

"Do you still use a paper planner?" Derrick said with a wink.

"Of course not," Ba said. "I have a wall calendar."

"You poor soul," Derrick said, although he was smiling.

Celine draped an arm around me. "All this talk about pictures reminds me that I should deliver that photo to Michele Yang."

"You're right," I said. "Having a big print of Jeffery lying around our apartment gives me the shivers."

My cousin pulled out her phone and texted. "There. Sent her a message to see if she's free today."

After the association members trickled out of the restaurant, we cleared the tables. Besides the dirty dishes and utensils, people had tidied up their spaces. I didn't find a single cellophane wrapper or crumpled paper slip from the fortune cookies I'd passed around.

By the time we finished cleaning, Celine had received a reply from Michele, who said she'd be free later this morning.

"Perfect," I said. "We'll give her the photo. And, in return, she might give us a few answers about the graffiti on Jeffery's cart." Because whoever had done the graffiti might have been involved with his murder.

FOURTEEN

MICHELE ASKED US TO BRING THE ENLARGED photo of Jeffery to her place of employment, Scribbles. Not too far from Wing Fat, the store was located in the neighborhood of Mar Vista. When we drove over, we found a tiny storefront overshadowed by the behemoth supermarket next door.

Inside, the cute shop boasted all kinds of stationery. I could find papers of various textures and patterns. The writing implements even came customized for special uses, including brush pens for calligraphy.

Michele stood behind the cash register, waiting for us. Celine deposited the photo on the counter with care. Michele unrolled the picture, and a single tear snaked down from the corner of her eye.

"Sorry again for your loss. He was a great guy," I said. How could I get Michele to talk more about the cart? "You know, I never had a chance to try one of his special drinks before he . . . was gone."

She sniffled. "Jeffery's nab vam was delicious."

"It's sad that someone defaced his food cart," I said.

Michele stiffened and took the photo. "I'd better store this away so it doesn't get ruined." She almost dove into the back room trying to escape from me.

"A little too heavy-handed with the conversation," Celine whispered to me.

The door to the stationery store swung open. An Asian customer wearing light blue scrubs came in. She appeared to already know the store's layout because she marched to a particular aisle, retrieved a pen in several seconds flat, and then stood in line behind us.

Michele had returned to the counter by then and noticed the customer. "Aunt Felicity," she said. "Did you just get off a twelve-hour shift?"

"Yes, and I celebrated it by buying a lucky lotto ticket." Felicity stifled a yawn and turned to us. "Have you already been helped?"

"We're not customers," I said in all honesty. "We were offering our condolences about Michele's ex."

Felicity flared her nostrils.

Celine must have noticed the gesture because my cousin asked, "You know Jeffery Vue?"

"I met the heartless man a few times," Felicity said. "He sold subpar drinks."

Celine lowered her voice. "But did you hear that he died recently? He looked so healthy."

"Well, you can't outrun fate," Felicity said.

Michele made a choking noise from behind the counter.

"What do you mean by that?" I asked Felicity.

"I know why he really died," she said. "From the curse."

Michele raised her voice to get our attention. "You must be exhausted after your long shift, Aunt Felicity. I'll ring up your purchase now."

Felicity skirted around us and placed a gel pen on the counter.

"Pretty color," Michele said before she swiped her aunt's credit card in the reader.

"You know how I love magenta. And this lucky pen will be circling my lotto numbers."

"Good luck," Michele said, handing the pen over.

We bid Felicity goodbye as she exited the store, but I continued to watch her through the glass door. Michele's aunt had expressed her affinity for magenta. Could she have been the one who had spray-painted the food cart in that very same hue?

I turned back to see Celine bending her head close to Michele. "What's this about a curse?"

Michele waved her hand in the air as though brushing away the thought. "It's just superstition. There's an old myth about Vues and Yangs not getting along as families. That's why we're—I mean, they're—not supposed to date."

"Why would your aunt call Jeffery heartless?" I said. In my experience, he was always the first to help in any situation.

Michele bit her lip. "It's just that she thought Jeffery would leave me something in his will." Her voice shook. "But I'd rather have him alive than inherit a million bucks."

I believed in her earnest statement. Her talking about Jeffery's estate, though, reminded me of something. He'd left half his assets to AAROA, but what about the other fifty percent?

Celine and I gave our condolences to Michele once more before we left the stationery store.

I dragged my feet on the pavement outside.

"Our car's over there, slowpoke," Celine said.

"Sorry, got lost in thought."

"What about?" Celine nudged me in the side. "Go on, spill."

"Jeffery Vue's estate. If only we knew where the rest of his estate ended up."

Celine paused before the driver's side of the parked car. "Keys, please. You're too distracted to drive right now." She held an upturned palm out to me. "What if we contact Jeffery's lawyer?"

"I don't know who Jeffery used to draw up his will. Besides, I bet there's some kind of client confidentiality involved." I handed my keys over.

Then I went around to the passenger's door and tugged on it hard. "Another person who might know the entire contents of the will is Detective Strauss." Since he'd announced the new funds to AAROA, he'd probably read the entire document. However, if I badgered him with questions, he might label that as "interference" in his investigation.

We settled into the car, and I drummed my fingers against the glove compartment.

"Who might have inherited the rest of his fortune?" I said. "He's got no relatives, so it has to be one of his friends."

"Or maybe his favorite mentee?" Celine asked, adjusting the rearview mirror.

"Who he might have treated like the son he never had."

"I don't know about you, but I'm in a snacking mood," Celine said. "Popcorn chicken would just about hit the spot."

"Excellent idea," I said, relaxing against the leather seat and pulling my seat belt on.

Nik was tight-lipped about finances, probably to save face, as there had been some lean years in his family restaurant's business in the past. However, if we went in person now, maybe I would notice changes in his behavior if he'd gotten a recent windfall. After all, I'd known Nik since middle school, so I hoped I would spot any clues.

━━━━━━━━━━

At Ho's, we settled into one of the red vinyl booths, and I waved Nik over to serve us. As he approached, I studied his appearance. He definitely wasn't dressing any snazzier than before. In fact, I thought I remembered that same striped shirt from his high school days. His hair also looked as untamed as ever. If he'd gotten any recent money from Jeffery, he hadn't invested it in his personal care.

Nik plopped two menus down before us.

"Don't need one," Celine said. "I'm going to have an order of popcorn chicken."

I opened a menu and scanned the entries. Nik could have used extra funds to enhance the restaurant's food offerings. "Do you have anything new you're trying out in the kitchen? Maybe something you whipped up with your fancy bachelor's degree?"

"Nope." Nik snapped the menu closed. "Ma's back in control of the kitchen, and I'm stuck on serving duty."

"That's too bad," I said. "When we helped you out the other day, I remember customers complimenting everything. Some even thought the food was better than usual. Maybe Ho's got a boost in business from the cooking you did."

I cast my gaze around the restaurant, ready to point out its numerous customers. Instead, I found only one lonesome table of patrons. "Well, it is still early for the lunch crowd."

He ran a hand through his messy hair. "Ever since Jeffery's memorial, business has slowed down for some reason."

Maybe someone had seen Nik's mother at the police station. Rumors would spread quickly after that sighting. The hint of murder might keep people from coming through the door, no matter how good the food.

"So, you gonna order or what?" Nik asked me.

"Sure. I'll have the stinky tofu with dipping sauce."

He gathered up the menus and strode away from our table.

"I didn't realize their business was suffering," I said.

"Yeah." Celine glanced at the kitchen door, which had just swung shut. "Maybe I can use the *Eastwood Village Connection* blog to help with the situation."

I sniffed at the tantalizing scent that had wafted out of the kitchen. "What about a positive restaurant review?"

"Lacks credibility," she said. "I'm not a professional food critic or skilled writer."

"What if you did the post using an image gallery of delicious foodie photos?"

"I'm still not sure that's the right angle, but a picture *is* worth a thousand words." Celine gazed out into the distance, and I could imagine an idea forming in her mind.

I left her alone to think. About five minutes later, Nik returned to our table, carrying our dishes.

Once he placed them down, Celine grabbed his arm. "How'd you like to be a star, Nik?"

His eyes darted to mine, as though asking me to decipher my cousin's words. I shrugged. Who knew what went on in Celine's brain?

My cousin let go of his arm and gestured with her hands. "Picture this. You're the newly elected president of AAROA. I can do a profile about your important position and also share about the quality of Ho's food and the night market stall."

Nik rubbed his goatee. "I like the sound of that."

"I'll be sure to insert an amazing photo of you," Celine said. "Who can resist someone who's tall, handsome, and rich?"

"I'm not rich," Nik said, taking a step backward. "But tall and handsome are true."

"Well, since I have you here, how about a pic right now?" Celine said, reaching for her bag.

"Oh no," he said. "I'd need to change. Interview me some other time."

I had to agree. Up close, the stripes on his shirt looked faded. I also noticed a tiny hole in one of the sleeves.

Celine said, "Okay, text me when you're free."

Nik agreed and sauntered back to the front counter with a livelier spring in his step. Responding to his positive mood, Celine and I smiled and dug into our respective snacks.

"Good work, Celine," I said after we finished eating. She'd not only improved Nik's mood and thought of a way for Ho's to increase their customer base, but she'd gotten the truth out of Nik. He'd given an honest reaction when he'd said he wasn't rich. Nik had an odd habit of literally stepping back when confronted with something shocking.

I paid for the snacks, including leaving a generous tip to help the restaurant in my own small way. As we walked out the door, Celine's phone rang.

She picked up her phone and blinked at the caller ID. "Why is Uncle calling me now?"

What odd timing. The beginning of the dim sum service marked the busiest period of the day for Ba. "Go ahead, answer it," I said.

She clicked the accept button and listened to him speak for a moment. "Yale and I will be right over."

"What is it?" I asked.

"I'm not sure," she said, putting the phone away and picking up her pace toward the parked car. "But Detective Strauss is over there at Wing Fat."

* * *

At the restaurant, we could hear aggrieved voices coming from behind the partitioned banquet room. Celine and I crept inside, where Detective Strauss was waving a rectangular piece of paper in the air.

"How do you explain this?" he asked Ba.

"I really don't know anything about it." My dad slouched in his chair at a table with two filled water glasses.

I placed myself between my dad and the irritated detective. "What's going on here?"

"Your father has survivorship rights and used them today," Detective Strauss said.

"Could you repeat that in layman's terms?" I asked.

"A check was written," he said, "and recently issued by AAROA. I figure it's a test run before writing a bigger check to a personal account."

Celine strolled over to my side. "I don't get it," she said. "People voted Nik in as president this morning. Wouldn't the check need to be cosigned to work?"

The detective placed the check on the table like a winning card in blackjack. "No. Because once Jeffery Vue is out of the picture, one person can write the check by himself. The treasurer."

This must have something to do with the "survivorship rights" the detective had mentioned before.

Detective Strauss continued. "Maybe because of this new election, your father"—he looked at me and then moved his gaze to Celine—"and your uncle, knew a window of opportunity was slipping away and wrote a check as soon as possible."

"That's not even my dad's signature. It's too messy." I turned to my cousin. "Celine, grab me a guest check pad and pen."

She did so, and I let Ba reproduce his name. He topped it off with his usual flourish of a pen stroke.

"See." I tapped the signature on the pad. "Not the same as the one on the check at all."

"It's still suspicious," Detective Strauss said and grabbed one of the glasses on the table. He drank the water down.

As I watched his fingers gripping the cup, I thought back to the announcement at the police station. We'd all celebrated with chilled apple cider back then, using labeled cups, and the detective had collected all our trash afterward.

He must have dusted those cups, hoping for a match to the evidence he'd already discovered on the Swiss Army knife. "You wanted fingerprints," I blurted out. "From the men in AAROA." I remembered that the detective had only invited select individuals to the meeting.

Detective Strauss widened his eyes at my accusation, but he didn't confirm my theory. It wouldn't be aboveboard for him to go and investigate like that. Even if he'd secured a matching set of prints, that kind of evidence couldn't be admissible in court.

Was the detective at Wing Fat even now because he thought the fingerprints he'd discovered belonged to Ba? Loyalty to my dad battled with friendship for Nik.

I glanced over at Ba, pacing around the room. He looked older somehow, more frail. Family won out in the end, and I threw Nik under the bus. "The prints on the Swiss Army knife," I said. "They might belong to Nik. I'm pretty sure he owns a pocketknife."

Detective Strauss studied my face for a moment. "I think you're telling me the truth." He picked up the check and tucked it into his suit pocket. "But money is always a strong motivator."

After what I said about Nik owning a knife, did he

still suspect my sweet dad of wrongdoing? Neither of us knew how to respond to the detective's statement, so Celine and I stayed silent, and Detective Strauss left with a brusque goodbye.

After he'd gone, Ba reached out for the detective's glass of water without looking and almost drank it before Celine jumped in.

"That's the wrong one," she said, offering him the other cup.

"Right," Ba said and took a huge gulp, but he didn't seem any more refreshed after drinking it. In fact, drops of sweat glistened on his forehead.

The assistant cook entered the banquet room with an apologetic look on his face. "Sorry," he said. "Did everything get settled, Sing? We really need you back in the kitchen."

"Of course." My dad gathered up both glasses from the table. "I'm coming now."

As he passed by me, I said, "Ba, please don't worry. I'll take care of this."

He nodded at me, but it seemed more out of politeness than belief, as he followed the assistant cook back to the kitchen.

"Come on," I said to Celine. "I know where to go to get to the bottom of the check situation. The credit union."

FIFTEEN

THE EASTWOOD VILLAGE CREDIT UNION WAS AAROA's banking institution. Ba trusted its staff, and following his guidance, I'd also set up my own account there. Inside the cheery yellow building, I bypassed the teller and went straight to Mr. Miller. He'd known both Ba and me for years, and he treated me like the daughter he'd never had.

I greeted him at his sturdy oak desk and introduced my cousin.

Over the years, his ash-colored hair had receded, but Mr. Miller still maintained his bright smile. "Welcome," he said, "and nice to meet you, Celine. Did you want to open an account?"

We sat down in the two chairs opposite him.

I crossed my legs. "Actually, I'm here about my dad."

"Let me log into the system." Mr. Miller moved to the computer near him.

"It's not about his personal checking, though, but AAROA's account."

"But he hasn't given you permission for that, Yale."

"Please, Mr. Miller." I clasped my hands together. "Someone forged his signature on a check."

"Oh dear. That's serious." Mr. Miller clicked away and hummed under his breath. "I'm not seeing any recent activity."

That's probably because Detective Strauss had stopped an actual transaction from occurring. He'd waved the check around like it'd been a smoking gun.

"It must have been stopped in the nick of time," I said. "Could you make sure that if any other suspicious activity comes up to contact my dad?"

"Certainly."

"As a heads-up, there's a newly elected president for the association. Nik Ho. He'll probably come in with Ba to get added to the account soon."

"I'll make a note of that," he said, reaching for a legal pad on his desk.

After thanking him for his assistance, Celine and I got up from the desk and moved back into the lobby. My cousin paused halfway across the polished floor to the exit.

"What I don't get is how someone could've gotten ahold of a physical check."

I picked at my thumb. "I'm not sure either. Ba had the checkbook tucked away until the election, and then he placed it right on top of the binder meant for the next president."

Celine sucked in her breath. "It must have been the coffee spill. There was never any hole in the container."

I followed her line of thought. "It was staged, a distraction. That's how the checkbook landed on the floor."

"Who would've taken it, if just for a moment?"

I glanced back at Mr. Miller. "If only we'd gotten more info and learned about the recipient of the check." Although I wasn't sure how much the banker would have divulged to me. "And why isn't Detective Strauss going after that person?"

"It wasn't *someone*."

"Excuse me?" I stared at her.

"The check was a written out to a company. The Human Connection, if I recall correctly."

While I'd been examining the scrawl of a signature on the check and pleading Ba's case to the detective, Celine had noticed the payee.

I gave her a brief hug. "You're getting to be an ace at sleuthing."

She tossed her honeyed locks.

"You know, the person who stole the check couldn't have mailed it to the company," I said. "USPS wouldn't have gotten it there fast enough. It must have been dropped off in person."

"Maybe we can find an eyewitness at the place," Celine said, pulling out her phone and searching for The Human Connection. "Bingo. I got the address, and it's only a few blocks east of here."

"That's close by. Can we stroll over instead of driving?" I asked. Now that I had a car, I sometimes missed walking everywhere.

My cousin mock groaned but said, "At least it's bright and sunny today."

I took the lead, and she shuffled behind me.

We found The Human Connection located on Main Street. I almost mistook it for a coffee shop after I entered the premises. The smell of roasted beans floated in the air, and people stood around chatting with one another, cups of steaming beverages in their hands.

A mother and child sat at a tiny table in a corner, hunched over a tattered game of Guess Who? I also noticed a freestanding cluster of mailboxes off to the side, which puzzled me.

A woman approached us. "Haven't seen you two in here before. How can I help?"

I stuck to the truth. "We're following the trail of a check issued by AAROA."

"Who?"

"Sorry, I mean the Asian American Restaurant Owners Association."

Her hazel eyes narrowed at me. "Oh, that. The organization name sounded fake, so I called the police."

The woman directly contacting the cops explained how Detective Strauss had intercepted the check without Mr. Miller at the credit union knowing anything about it.

"Actually," I said, "the association is very real, but that check didn't go through formal channels before being issued."

She raised her eyebrows at me but said, "Figured. What with that chicken scratch of a signature. Besides, we're always underfunded. Why would I expect anything different?"

"Is this, er, a postal office of some kind?" I said, gesturing to the bank of mailboxes.

"No," she said, "we're a hangout center for neighbors in need."

I glanced again at the people milling about and noticed they were all dressed in an astounding number of layers, accompanied by heavy coats and caps.

She continued. "Those without permanent residences can come here to find friendship and a warm cup of coffee during the day."

The woman meant the people who were home insecure. Someone had been talking about giving to a charity like that at the election meeting.

Before I could figure out who had mentioned it, Celine spoke up. "Do you remember what the person looked like? The one who dropped off the check?"

The woman jerked her thumb back at a fancy coffee-maker. "Nope, I was too focused on making the coffee. When the door swung shut, all I saw was the person's back."

"Do you remember the clothes they wore?" Celine asked. Of course she'd ask about the person's fashion choices.

"Not really," the woman said. "I only saw the back of the head and a braid."

"Misty," my cousin and I said at the same time. I remembered now that Misty had indeed been the one to suggest aid to the unhoused for AAROA's December charitable donation focus.

"Thanks for your time," I said to the woman as I ushered Celine out the door. We paused on the pavement.

"Misty stole that check," I said.

"Just so she could give to a worthy cause?"

"It may be like the detective suggested. Start small and then work her way to lining her own coffers. Could she have killed Jeffery for easy access to the account?" I said.

"It's a stretch, but maybe we should share our thoughts with Detective Strauss." Celine reached for her phone, but it had already started ringing.

She almost fumbled the phone before she answered the call. "Ma Mi," she said, "is everything okay?"

Celine listened and nodded while her mother spoke. Finally, she said, "I understand. See you later then."

My cousin stared at the phone's blank screen after she'd hung up.

"What do you mean by 'see you'?" I said. "Are you going to do a video chat with her?"

"More like a face-to-face conversation," she said. "My parents are flying out tonight. Staying through the weekend, if not longer."

"Now?" I said, wondering about the spontaneous trip.

"Yep." Celine trudged forward, and I moved in step with her.

At this rate, it'd take us a while to return to the parking lot of the credit union.

"They must be missing you," I said.

"Unlikely. Their calendars are always booked up. They barely have time to think about me." Celine kicked at the sidewalk with the toe of her boot.

"Then they're coming because . . ."

"Of your father."

"Really?" Ba hadn't reached out to his brother in decades.

"That's what Ma Mi told me."

"Hmm, I think we need to drop by Wing Fat for dinner and try to suss out the situation."

"Okay," my cousin said.

We picked up the pace and speed-walked to the credit union. Just as the building came into sight, a text sounded on Celine's phone.

She checked it. "Nik," my cousin said. "He's game for his profile piece and waiting for us at Ho's."

"Okay, pit stop," I said. It'd be nice to occupy our time with something as simple as interviewing Nik, instead of stewing about our parents.

Nik greeted us in front of his family's restaurant. "Tell me, how do I look?" He struck a pose.

He'd put his signature bedhead hair on full display, but he seemed to have at least combed his goatee. Also, the striped shirt had gone by the wayside, replaced by a tan suit, although the sleeves were slightly too short for his arms.

Celine gave him a thumbs-up while I said, "Did you pull out an old interview suit?"

He ignored my teasing and focused on my cousin. "I figured you'd need to highlight the restaurant in your article, so we can take photos out here first. Then we can move to the dining area and finally to the kitchen. Sadly, there are no customers around to get in the way."

No wonder Nik had agreed to the interview right now. The restaurant was empty. I wondered how long it'd been since the last customer had hobbled in. Perhaps that's how Nik had had enough time to pick up and change into a suit before texting Celine.

I followed my cousin along as she took pictures of Nik outside the restaurant, making sure to capture the Ho's name within the shot. Then we all moved indoors, and I sat down in a booth, while Nik posed at the cash register, standing at the counter with a stack of menus, and then at the doorway to the kitchen.

When they moved into the inner sanctum of the restaurant, I didn't bother to follow them. I bet Mrs. Ho would be delighted to see the pair in the kitchen. She'd probably drop hints about the two of them dating all through the photo shoot.

Nik and Celine didn't take long before returning to the dining area, where they joined me at my table. My cousin opened an app on her phone and aimed it Nik's way.

"Journalism time," she said. "This is being recorded. First off, how do you feel about being elected president of the Asian American Restaurant Owners Association?"

Nik straightened up in the booth and said in a loud and clear voice, "I'm proud to lead such a fine organization."

"How do you feel in general about being an Asian American in the culinary world? What is your take on being an Asian American restaurant owner?"

He messed with the lapel of his suit. "It's a difficult road to travel to make it in the restaurant industry, but I absolutely believe in sharing diverse cuisines."

"Of course," Celine murmured.

"I also strive to cook authentic food at my restaurant, unlike other more fusion places." He waggled his eyebrows at me.

I rolled my eyes at him.

Celine continued. "And you run which restaurant?"

"I'm the co-owner of Ho's with my mom, Ai Ho. We also run a food stall at the Eastwood Village Night Market, Ho's Small Eats. Both places offer true Taiwanese fare."

"Tell me what specialties you've single-handedly created at Ho's."

He tugged at his goatee, ruining the neat combed look. "None," he said. "Would it kill her if she gave me more time in the kitchen?"

"Um . . ." Celine paused the recording.

"Can you erase that last bit?" Nik said.

"Yeah, I'll cut it out," she said. "Let me rephrase the question."

My cousin now asked him about the dishes offered at Ho's without referring to Nik's specific contribution to them. I tuned out the rest of the interview and speculated on his recent turn of phrase. Surely, he'd meant it in jest, but could he actually have been involved in a killing—Jeffery's? I'd almost said as much to the detective. And Nik did own a pocketknife.

All of a sudden, Nik's face hovered near mine. "Why are you looking at me like that, Yale?"

"Huh. Nothing," I said. "Just lost in thought."

"Negative ones," he said. "You were scowling at me."

I dismissed his comment with a vague mumble. When Celine and I left Ho's, I knew I needed a mental break. When had my thoughts become so jumbled that I'd allowed myself to accuse Nik, even if only while my mind wandered?

Shaking my head, I said to my cousin, "Let's get that dinner at Wing Fat. I really need some home cooking tonight."

SIXTEEN

AT WING FAT, CELINE BLATHERED ON ABOUT HER
profile article. She showed me numerous photos of
Nik in various poses. I admitted that a few of them didn't
look half-bad. Even his messy hair looked artistic in certain lighting.

I'd ordered comfort dishes for dinner. I salivated at
the thought of the crispy chicken with its crunchy fried
skin. It'd surely be surrounded by colorful shrimp-
flavored chips, looking like so many edible pastel sea-
shells. The baby bok choy with shiitake mushrooms
would also make for a great complementary vegetable
dish. Along with the other items, I'd also asked for plain
white rice per tradition.

A few bites into the meal, though, I discovered something very wrong with the food. Almost every single dish
tasted off. The chicken had soggy skin, and the vegetables appeared raw. The only decent food on the table was
the steaming white rice, which was pretty hard to get

wrong. My dad must be feeling troubled and had transferred his stress to his cooking.

Concerned about my dad's mood, I only partially listened to Celine while she went on about the profile article on the blog. The other half of my attention strayed to the tables around me.

My cousin had just mentioned that she'd put her byline on the article to finally get credit for both her words and her pictures when I noticed that all the customers had received their food. This would be a great time to speak with my dad. I offered Celine tepid congratulations about the article and excused myself to go to the kitchen.

His cooking activities had wound down, so Ba stood at a steel counter with his back to me. He was downing a glass of water as though he lived in the desert. The kitchen staff greeted me by name, and I waved to all of them. I supposed that I'd become a familiar sight at Wing Fat now, something I'd never have dreamed of, even a year ago, because of my previous bumpy history with the restaurant.

Ba turned around at the mention of my name. "Yale," he said. "I didn't realize you were eating here tonight."

I heard a thread of embarrassment lace his voice, maybe at his subpar dishes. "Uh-huh," I said. "Celine and I are at table ten. But we're really here tonight because of a call Celine got from her parents."

"What did they say?" Ba took another huge gulp of water.

"They're flying to the U.S. tonight."

He choked on his drink for a moment but soon recovered. "I told them not to come. It's really not a big deal."

The reduced quality of his cooking attested otherwise. "What were you talking to them about?"

He didn't look me in the eye as he said, "Oh, this and that. You know, the restaurant business. My chat with a cop."

Detective Strauss must have really gotten under Ba's skin for him to share about that. It'd been years since my dad had made direct contact with his brother. They'd only kept in touch when my mom had been alive, so to extend an olive branch now meant that Ba was scared. He never liked being on the wrong side of the law and felt ashamed of even getting a speeding ticket.

"Sounds like they want to support you," I said.

Ba placed his water glass down. *Thunk*. "They're so spontaneous," he said. "Now I'll have to repay their kindness with food. Whip up something delicious . . ." His voice faltered, and I remembered his issues with cooking tonight.

As if I'd spoken my thoughts out loud, my dad snuck a glance toward the dining area. "Or instead of cooking, I could order takeouts for them."

That wouldn't express the same appreciation and hospitality, especially after they hadn't seen each other in so long. I wanted him to save face in front of his family and said, "I'll do it, Ba. I can cook them something nice."

He nodded at me in thanks. "We'll make it a dinner, so you'll have more time to prepare for the meal."

Could I handle this huge responsibility? I'd have to. I squared my shoulders. "Don't worry about a thing, Ba. I'll ask Celine about what simple dishes they enjoy eating. It might be easier for me that way, less pressure."

"Okay," he said. "Go for it."

"Um, Ba, can we hold the dinner here . . . instead of at the house?"

He looked at me with kindness in his brown eyes. "Yes, Yale, and I do understand. We can have dinner here."

I squeaked out my thanks. Ever since my mom's death, I hadn't darkened the doorway of my childhood home. I didn't know when I'd ever get comfortable dealing with the memories still stuck there.

Ba touched me on the arm. "I'll close the restaurant

early and reserve the time for the dinner. I'll say it's for a private function."

I nodded and returned to the dining room to share the info about the meal, along with my speculations, with my cousin.

Sitting back in my chair, I told her, "I'm pretty sure Ba is afraid. He must have unloaded to your dad. That's why your parents are on their way here all of a sudden."

She glanced down at the table and seemed to focus on a sauce splotch on the cloth. "I think you're right. They're only coming here to check on Uncle's well-being."

For a moment, her quiet voice transported me to a memory of a younger Celine at Disneyland, when she'd been a girl who'd tagged behind her parents in adoration. When she looked up again at me, any trace of a vulnerable child had disappeared. "It's odd that De Di would be the first person Uncle would call, isn't it?" she said. "I thought they weren't close."

"They're not," I said, thinking about the years of silence between the two brothers. "But a detective showing up at the restaurant . . . the potential threat of being behind bars, that could have shifted the balance."

"Did Uncle ever tell you why they stopped talking?"

"No." I put my napkin on my plate, giving up on eating. "I thought it was because of the long distance. Did your dad ever hint at a reason?"

Celine shook her head. "Not really. I figured it was a guy thing."

"Well, we'll see how everything goes between them soon enough. Ba's planning a private dinner for them."

"Oh, will it be at Uncle's house? I could decorate the whole place beforehand." Celine's eyes sparkled, and maybe she had visions of mood lighting and fancy table centerpieces floating in her head.

I destroyed her fantasy by saying, "No, Celine. It'll be right here at Wing Fat."

"Yeah," she said, "that makes sense. All the high-quality restaurant cookware is kept in this kitchen."

I didn't provide her with the real reason for holding the meal here. "Anyway, I volunteered to cook dinner. I'm figuring I could make a few simple dishes for your folks. What are their favorites?"

"Ones that are easy to make?" She tapped a polished fingernail against her bottom lip. "How about *choy sum* veggies in oyster sauce, chicken chow mein, and scrambled eggs with chives?"

Chives. I couldn't help but shiver.

My mother's stalled car and her oh-so-still body flashed in my mind. I placed a glass of ice water against my forehead.

"Are you all right?" Celine said. "You look pale."

"Maybe dehydrated," I lied, removing the glass from my forehead and drinking some of the cool liquid.

I focused my thoughts on the upcoming dinner and steeled myself with positive internal self-talk. I'd gotten my cooking groove back, ever since this past fall. I could handle these easy dishes. "Well, I'm done with dinner. Do you want to go back home?"

"I can drive if you want," Celine said. I knew she offered out of concern for me this time and not because she wanted to get behind the wheel again.

"I'm okay to drive," I said. Besides, if I focused on the road before me, I could stay in the present and not be tugged into the past.

In the car, I made sure to roll the windows down before we started along the road. The breeze cooled my body and my nerves as I drove. While I concentrated on steering the car, Celine peeked at her phone.

"Are you looking at social media?" I asked. I'd gotten used to my cousin being fixated on her screen at random times to check for new comments and followers.

"No," she said. "Actually, I'm going to make a call."

"Will wonders never cease?" I said.

"We forgot to tell Detective Strauss earlier about Misty Patil," my cousin said.

If the detective followed Misty's trail, maybe he'd ease up his focus on Ba. I hoped to get some immediate reassurance from him, but since Celine kept the phone next to her ear and continued waiting, I realized we wouldn't get the chance at a quick response.

"Voicemail," Celine mouthed to me.

I wondered if the detective had taken a break from investigative work for once. Or perhaps we'd contacted him while he'd been eating dinner or fielding an important call.

My cousin pressed the speakerphone icon and said, "Celine and Yale Yee here. Detective Strauss, we figured out who wrote that fake check."

"And it wasn't my dad," I shouted from the driver's seat.

"We found an eyewitness at The Human Connection," Celine said. "They identified the person who dropped off the check as a woman with a braid. It must have been Misty Patil. She always wears her hair like that."

"And she basically told AAROA to write a check to help the unhoused, so you're very welcome, Detective Strauss," I said before Celine hung up.

My cousin raised her eyebrows at me.

"What?" I said. "We're basically doing his job for him."

"Someone's in a bad mood."

"Yeah, well, I'm worried. About this check and the detective's insinuations." Plus, the food I'd need to make at the restaurant tomorrow to welcome Celine's parents to a well-overdue family reunion.

"I wonder if the detective will call us back soon," my cousin said.

When we got back to the apartment, though, we still

hadn't received a response from Detective Strauss. I wasn't sure if he hadn't called back because he hadn't checked his messages or if he wanted to ignore our claim. Maybe he'd dismissed our opinion outright. Perhaps the tie to Misty wasn't strong enough. Or maybe he'd already checked out that lead.

I turned to Celine, who was putting away her purse. "Do you think the fake check and Jeffery's murder are really connected? What if they're not?"

"You're not sure anymore? Let's go and think things through and see where it lands us." She held up her phone. "I'll use my app to take down notes."

"And I'll grab some pen and paper for myself," I said.

"What about snacks?" Celine said. "I often think better with food."

I agreed with Celine. Besides, I hadn't eaten too much at dinner.

To improve our brain power, I made a quick pot of ginger green tea and opened a packet of roasted green peas.

We settled around the dining table with its scalloped lace cloth.

"Who could have killed Jeffery?" I asked.

We went through the list and quickly ruled out Mrs. Ho, who wouldn't hurt anyone, and especially not on her own property. We also crossed out Ba for obvious reasons.

"What about Mr. Yamada?" Celine asked.

"I don't know. Honestly, I can't really see it," I said, sipping my tea. "What would be his motive?"

My cousin shrugged. "Fine. Misty's still a good suspect, then," my cousin said, grabbing a few roasted peas and crunching them in her mouth.

"Yes, because of the charity angle. To make the funds go to the nonprofit of her choice. And maybe to eventually pad her own bank account."

"Wonder if she finally got sick of being overlooked. I get that," Celine said.

"Or she could have another motive, like issues with her personal finances."

Celine blinked at me like she didn't understand while I wrote down our theories.

"How about Trisha?" Celine said.

"A newcomer," I said. "She couldn't have any problems with Jeffery."

"Derrick did though," Celine said. "There was the trash talk, but could there have been more between him and Jeffery?"

"Derrick has always wanted to be president of AAROA, but Jeffery would never give up the position," I said.

"And Detective Strauss *was* looking for a male culprit," my cousin added. "Remember his weird meeting with just the men?"

"He was trying to get their fingerprints," I said. "Let's keep Derrick on the list." I paused before saying, "And maybe Nik, too. He definitely owned the knife, and he's been waiting for a long time for a chance to cook at the family restaurant. Maybe he only meant for a minor accident to happen at Ho's. A small spark, something to literally shed light on how stuck he was."

"Wow, Yale. Do you really suspect Nik?" Celine placed both hands around her teacup, as though extracting its warmth. "I know you weren't the closest of friends when you were younger, but even you have to admit, the guy grows on you. Plus, I've already written this glowing profile of him, which I'll be posting tonight."

I munched on a few green peas. "You're putting it up tonight? Will people even read a post at this hour?"

"It's not that late," Celine said, "especially for night owls like me."

I drank more tea, and it started to make me feel sleepy with its cozy warmth. "I'll leave you to it, then," I said and yawned. I felt exhausted from the demands of the day, especially after dealing with a certain accusatory detective.

"I'll wash all of this when I'm done," Celine said, indicating the bowl, teapot, and cups.

I said good night to my cousin, wondering if the real reason she was staying up was to work on the blog and fulfill her obligation. Or maybe she just wanted to distract herself from lying in bed, worrying about the upcoming visit from her parents.

SEVENTEEN

CELINE MUST HAVE BEEN RIGHT ABOUT THE NIGHT owl readers because she boasted about it in the morning over breakfast. We sat at our dining table again, this time in the early sunshine, with bowls of piping-hot *jook* rice porridge before us. I'd also brought out a platter of dried pork floss and chopped scallions to add as toppings.

I blew on a spoonful of porridge and watched the steam curl in the air. "Okay, Miss Popular," I said. "Why don't you summarize the many comments for me?"

"Of course there were glowing praises about my photography—and also my writing." My cousin's bowl of jook lay untouched before her, so absorbed was she in recounting the reactions to the blog.

"You're getting such good comments you should be paid for it. Pursue journalism or something," I said and proceeded to slurp my porridge.

Her forehead crinkled as she checked her phone again. "Ugh. A new comment. And it's the troll again."

"No." I stopped eating. "What did they say this time?"

"That Nik shouldn't be president. Maybe he'd make a better veep instead."

"Interesting word choice." I moved over to my cousin and read the comment on her phone. "The person called him Nik? But you never used his nickname in the post."

She turned to me with wide eyes. "This must be someone from the inner circle of AAROA."

"And the fact that they used 'veep,' I'm thinking it has to be—"

"Derrick," Celine said.

I recalled how he'd jumped to help Ba out with the photos Celine had stored in the cloud. "Derrick seems tech-savvy enough to do it." I pushed my porridge away from me. "Do you think he could also be knowledgeable about, say, electricity?"

"Maybe you should lure Derrick in and get him to open up," my cousin said. "You could ask him for some computer help."

"But don't I have you around to give me guidance on those things?"

"I'm sure you can come up with an excuse—say I'm busy. Meet him at the complex's business center. It's a public enough space and should be safe."

I needed a way to make Derrick come to my neighborhood. He might want to help me out just because of a desire to share his expertise, but if I sweetened the pot, I'd be able to guarantee his arrival.

───────◖═══════◗───────

I called Derrick using the landline, and he agreed to meet me at midmorning. He had a free schedule because Pho You and Me didn't open until later in the evening anyway.

At the arranged time, I stood near the entrance to the community clubhouse, which also held the business center. The extra amenities fee I paid on top of the rent meant I had access to its myriad luxuries. If I wanted to, I could swim in the huge outdoor pool, hold an event in the fancy party room, or work out in the fitness area. I came to the clubhouse rarely and only to utilize the computers and printer.

The fact that I had never owned a computer in my life probably lent some veracity to my dilemma when Derrick showed up.

"I'm here to save the day," Derrick said as I led him over to the bank of computers.

"Thanks for coming. I try to use the least amount of tech possible."

"Not hard to believe, given your dad's flip phone," he said. "I was intrigued by your phone call, Yale, when you said we could both help each other. You with your computer problems, and me with the unfair AAROA hierarchy."

I picked an unoccupied seat. Actually, I had my choice of computers. Nobody ever seemed to use the business center except for me.

Derrick scooted over a swivel desk chair and sat close by.

"Here's my issue," I said, launching into my cover story. "You know the night market is happening again on Friday, and I want to bring extra attention to our booth. Celine set up a photo shoot area for Instagram last weekend, but I figured some glossy flyers advertising it would bring even more customers."

"I like your marketing initiative," Derrick said. "Do you have any images you know you want to use for the flyer?"

"Er, not really."

"Why isn't your social media influencer cousin helping you out again?" he asked.

"She thought it was a simple task that I could easily

figure out myself. Plus"—I pointed out the window at the sunny day—"she wanted to take advantage of the great weather and go shopping."

"Isn't it always nice here? But that sounds about right," Derrick said, maybe recalling all the fashionable outfits he'd seen Celine wear.

"So what do I do?" I moved around the computer mouse without clicking on anything.

"We'd better switch spots," he said. Derrick swapped chairs with me. "I can whip something up on Canva in five minutes flat."

He stuck to his promise, and a poster highlighting the photo booth soon appeared onscreen. I made a few comments about what colors and fonts to use, and he finished it all in record time.

"Wow," I said. "That's amazing."

"How many copies will you need?"

"Ten should do. I'll post them around the neighborhood, maybe even on the bulletin board in this clubhouse."

He pressed a button, and colorful flyers came spitting out of the printer. Then he angled his chair toward me. "Now it's my turn. What were you thinking about regarding AAROA?"

"I've given a lot of thought to it. I grew up with Nik, so I'd like to think I know him pretty well. He's book smart but . . ."

"Agreed, Yale. A fancy degree isn't everything," Derrick said, rubbing his hands together. The backs of them were roughened from years of cooking.

"I could maybe talk to Nik about my doubts," I said. "Serving as president, that's a huge role. Maybe he needs a little more kitchen experience before leading a restaurant owners' organization."

"You're absolutely right," Derrick said. "There's a

proper way for things to be done. I told Trisha the same thing after she became an official member. I said there's a process to gaining experience and leadership positions within the association. Co-owning a restaurant isn't the same as actually running one."

"Yeah," I said. "Nik's mother doesn't even let him cook. Mainly, he does the register and serves food."

Derrick stood up and retrieved the flyers from the printer. He tapped their edges on the table to align the papers. "Yale, what made you think of approaching me in the first place about the presidency? I know Nik's a friend of yours from school."

"Frenemy," I corrected. "An old school rival. Actually, this online post made me rethink things." I pulled up the *Eastwood Village Connection* blog on the computer and pointed out the "veep" comment to Derrick. I watched his face carefully.

If I'd blinked, I would've missed the slight shifting of his eyes.

"I think there's some sound advice there," he said.

"Yeah, I agree."

"It's a little too late now, though," Derrick said with sorrow in his voice. "Everybody already put in their votes."

"There may not be a reversal of the decision from the group," I said, grabbing the posters from Derrick, "but perhaps Nik can be talked into resigning."

Derrick seemed to stare at the glamour shot of Nik onscreen. "Do you really think he'll step down?"

Admittedly, Nik looked like he was gloating in the picture. A gleaming smile was pasted across his face.

"I don't know, but I can talk to him about it."

"Can't hurt to try," Derrick said.

He shook my hand, and it felt like I'd made some sort of sleazy deal. I clutched the colorful flyers in my hands, almost giving myself a paper cut, as I watched him exit the business center.

After Derrick left, I pinned one of the posters onto the community bulletin board in the clubhouse. Then I strolled back to the apartment and thought about my new tidbit of knowledge. Derrick had shifted his gaze when I'd shown him the blog comment, a sure sign of discomfort. It seemed likely that he'd been the one trolling the site.

I returned home to find Celine in a celebratory mood. In the living room, she beamed at me and wiggled her phone in the air.

"What? Did you hear some good news?" I said.

"Yes, Detective Strauss called back."

"I can't believe it," I said, sinking onto the settee with mock shock. "He actually listened to us."

"Not really," Celine said. "But I badgered him again about it, so much so that he said he'd stop by India Snack Mart. It probably helped that I described the delicious chai to him so vividly."

"You used a drink incentive to get him to investigate further?"

"Beverage and food bribes," she said. "They work."

I stood up. "Speaking of food and drinks, I want to go over the ingredients list for dinner tonight."

Celine's mood dampened. "I can't believe my parents are actually flying in."

"We should have everything available at Wing Fat, but can I double-check with you once more?"

She nodded, and I proceeded to list the ingredients I thought I needed.

She held up her hand and said, "Wait a minute. You'll be using organic oil and sauces, right?"

"You're kidding me." I checked her face for a hint of joking.

"No, Ma Mi and De Di are totally into what they call

'fresh eating' now. I guess some HK movie star got them into it."

"Then I have my shopping cut out for me," I said.

After a quick lunch, the afternoon disappeared for me in a round of search and discovery at the grocery store. When I finally finished running errands, I found Celine in the apartment suffering from a wardrobe crisis.

She dragged me into her fashion dilemma. Celine re-created runway walks with various outfits, asking after each clothing choice, "Does this signal independence to you? How about success?"

She finally settled on a gray ruffled blazer paired with a camisole and sleek black slacks. "Ready or not, Ma Mi and De Di, here I come."

I n the kitchen at Wing Fat, I mentally prepared myself for the cooking endeavor. I entered the walk-in fridge and was able to march back out with all the needed ingredients . . . except for chives. I'd saved the dark green herbs, tainted with their negative association, for last.

I never cooked chives anymore in any of my meals. Not since my mom's accident. Even when shopping at the local Asian grocery store, I avoided their spot in the re-frigerated area.

I stepped into Wing Fat's fridge, and the fluorescent bar lighting the extensive cooler flickered above me. I'd have to tell Ba about that and have him fix it sometime. It gave me the creeps as I inched toward the container with the chives in it. The long stalks stuck out of a card-board box next to a tub of chili oil with a metal ladle. People really loved the spicy sauce for eating with their dim sum.

I tried holding my breath as I reached for a bunch of *gow choy* chives, but I couldn't last. I'd need to work on my lung capacity.

Inhaling, I sucked in the stink. Chives gave off a clinging kind of funk. The odor of death, I now believed. Images of my mom, stuck in her car and dying all alone, flooded my brain.

My breathing became rushed. I inhaled even more noxious fumes from the herbs and started to feel faint. Air, I needed air. I rushed at the inner handle of the refrigerator.

It slipped out of my chilled fingers. I finally managed to push it open and stumbled into the warm, familiar kitchen.

I decided to switch the chives with scallions. Maybe Celine's parents wouldn't even notice if I added enough soy sauce to the egg dish. Scallions also grew in long green stalks and had a similar look to chives.

After prepping the necessary ingredients, I moved on to the stove. I turned on the giant exhaust fan and let it thrum above me. I spent a few moments under it, gathering my resolve, and hoping the loud hum would drown out any doubts I had about cooking again at Wing Fat.

Then I attacked the dishes. With my spatula, I shoved the food around in the wok until I stir-fried my way through the meat and vegetables. I cooked the chicken chow mein and the choy sum leafy greens with ease.

For the remaining dish, I broke the multiple eggs into the wok and pushed them around, watching them sizzle. The difference between fluffy eggs and overly crisped ones was a slim sliver of time. I tossed the sliced scallions into the wok and watched them curl up.

I'd been so focused in the moment that I'd forgotten about my surroundings. Now I remembered them. I was standing in front of the stove, cooking again in a wok, at the family restaurant. A series of giggles bubbled out of me. I slid the finished eggs dish onto a ceramic platter.

Reaching over to the silver bell behind me, I rang it with a decisive tap. Celine hurried into the kitchen.

"Everything finished?" she said.

"It is now."

The two of us carried the food out together to Ba and Celine's parents. I wondered how our dinner would go. It'd been two decades since I'd last seen my aunt and uncle.

EIGHTEEN

CELINE'S PARENTS LOOKED LESS POWERFUL SIT-
ting down at the table in the present than they did in
my childhood memories. It was in the way that her father
had a more stooped posture in his chair, or how he'd ac-
quired an extensive spread of gray hair. Celine's mother
sat with a stiff, straight posture. My aunt's jet-black hair,
in contrast to her husband's, drew even more attention to
its unnatural, dyed origin.

As we set down the platters of food on the lazy Susan,
I noticed my aunt scrutinize not our faces but what Celine and I were wearing. Based on the slight upturn of her
nose, neither outfit must have passed muster. I almost
wished that a splash of oyster sauce might end up on her
white silk blouse by the end of the meal.

I shook away the uncharitable thought and smiled at
Celine's parents. "Auntie and Uncle, it's so good to see
you." I stumbled on my words, halting in the beginning
both because of my lack of sincerity and also since I
wasn't sure if I should append a name to the "aunt" and

"uncle" titles. It felt awkward and too formal to use our same last name, making them "Auntie and Uncle Yee," but to use their chosen English names seemed unthinkable. Besides, I didn't think I could say "Sunny and Cher" without a hint of laughter in my voice.

Once we'd all sat down at the round table, I made sure to pour the tea for my aunt and uncle with both hands as a sign of respect to my elders.

We began filling our plates with food, and Celine's parents started off with small talk. They asked my dad and me to share about the developments they'd missed over the years. Ba gushed with pride about the expansion to his restaurant, and I mentioned running the food stall at the local night market. I made sure to compliment Celine and her social media prowess, including how she'd boosted Canai and Chai through her powerful Instagram account.

In response, my uncle gave a head bob. My aunt flicked her fingertips at my cousin and had a steely expression. I lapsed into silence, and Celine's cheeks grew pink.

We ate for a few minutes without conversation, the sounds of our chewing and swallowing amplified in the quiet. Ba steered the talk toward a common ground: Celine.

"I've been telling everyone I know here about my wonderful niece and how she's visiting from Hong Kong," he said.

I added, "I've been showing Celine around town. We've already gone to the Korean Friendship Bell, the Venice Canals—"

Celine's mother sniffed at that last location. I bet she'd already seen the more authentic canals in Italy during her travels.

"Anyway," I said, "it's been so nice having someone my own age around."

We continued eating. When Celine's mother took a bite of the egg dish, though, she wrinkled her nose.

"What did you add to the eggs? Scallions?"

My cousin glanced at me, confused.

Her mother fixed a dark stare at Celine. "I thought we were going to eat our favorite foods. You don't even remember the right dish? A month on vacation, and you've forgotten what you know about your parents."

"That's not true," she said.

I fidgeted in my chair. "Auntie, actually I—"

Celine's mother spoke over me. "You don't have to cover for your cousin, Yale. Besides, the less talk, the better. We should eat before the food gets cold."

In silence, we ate our fill. After my uncle had scraped his plate clean, he glanced toward the kitchen. Could he still be hungry? But there was food remaining on the serving platters.

"Will there be any dessert tonight?" he asked.

I hadn't realized I needed to provide anything beyond the main meal.

"Red bean soup is my absolute favorite," he added.

"I'm sorry," I said. "We don't happen to have any on hand tonight. Maybe I could slice up some oranges? Or we have plenty of fortune cookies."

That earned me an eyebrow raise from Celine's mother. She turned to her husband and said, "Anyway, too many sweets aren't good for your blood sugar."

We'd come to the end of the meal. My uncle rested his napkin by his plate in conclusion.

He leaned toward Ba and stared into his brother's eyes. "Do you need anything, Sing?" he said. "We have many influential connections in the States. They could help smooth out your judicial problems."

Ba stiffened his shoulders. "I'm innocent of any wrongdoing."

"Of course you are, *dai dai*"—my uncle used the term

for "little brother" in such a patronizing tone, I almost expected him to pat Ba on the shoulder or ruffle his hair.

Ba spluttered. "Have I ever asked for even a single coin from you? You didn't have to fly all the way here to rescue me. As you can see, I'm doing fine." My dad gestured around the large banquet room. "No, I'm doing well. My business here is thriving."

My uncle clenched his hands into fists. "Oh, I know, Sing. You couldn't wait to show it off. Instead of inviting us to your home for dinner, you wanted to parade your restaurant—"

I raised my voice to speak, but my uncle shushed me.

He continued. "Wanted to throw your precious business in my face. The one that you built up all by yourself, unlike me."

"Come on," Ba said, "you love Hong Kong. Even if given the chance, you wouldn't have moved."

"I didn't have any say in the matter. Someone had to continue the family business, not run off to another continent for studies. You chose—no, wanted—to leave us."

My uncle and Ba frowned at each other. I sprang up to pour some more tea for the two brothers as a distraction. Neither of them noticed, and they didn't raise their teacups to their lips afterward.

A few tense moments stretched out before Ba spoke in a level tone. "I'm sorry we didn't have dinner at the house. You're welcome to stay in my home tonight."

Celine's mother responded in a tight voice. "We already have arrangements at the Four Seasons."

I saw my cousin cringe in her seat, and I wanted to flee from this awkward scene. Standing up, I started collecting the dirty dishes. Celine followed suit and helped me. We both moved toward the more serene kitchen.

After Celine and I had washed everything and returned to the banquet room, tension still remained in the air.

My aunt turned toward my cousin. "You'll help us settle in at the hotel, Celine."

"Of course, Ma Mi."

Celine leaned over and whispered to me, "Can you pick me up later? I'll call you."

I nodded, understanding that part of her request for pickup was code to dissect her parents' discussion later on tonight.

My cousin shuffled behind her parents as they issued polite but aloof farewells to my dad and me. After the front door to the restaurant shut, Ba rubbed at his forehead with his palm.

"That wasn't the happy reunion I'd planned on," he said.

I touched his arm. "There's still the rest of the visit to make things better."

"If it doesn't go even more downhill from here," he said. "I can't believe Sunny wanted to interfere on my behalf with the cops. He always thinks he knows what's best for me. Stay in HK, he said before. Don't open up a restaurant. Now, rely on his influential connections."

Ba's resentment seemed to stem from pent-up irritation over the decades. I, though, could only help him out in the present.

"About that fake check," I said. "It looks like Misty forged your signature."

"What? How do you know that?"

"Detective Strauss is looking into things, and her name cropped up." I didn't inform Ba that Celine and I had done some investigating on the sly to place the detective on the correct path.

Ba seemed to cheer up a little after my revelation, and we finished tidying up together. After turning the lights off at the restaurant, we said goodbye to each other.

When I got home, the answering machine light was

blinking in the spare room. I pressed the playback button to find a message from Detective Strauss.

"I just left a voicemail on Celine's cell," he said, "but I'm leaving a message here as well. Give me a call when you get this."

I checked the timestamp of the recording. He'd left it recently, but I bet my cousin hadn't responded yet because she was occupied with dealing with her parents.

Detective Strauss picked up on the first ring.

"Do you have good news for us?" I asked.

"Well, I did speak with Misty Patil—"

"And she confessed to you."

"Partially. She said she was only the messenger," he said. "A go-between."

"For whom?"

"Nik. But it took her a while to come up with his name." Detective Strauss cleared his throat. "I admit I may have come on too strong earlier with your father. I'll have to research this check situation more."

"Wow," I said. "Are you admitting that you were wrong?"

It took him a moment to reply, and he said, "I'll make sure to buy a chai from you this weekend at the night market."

"Uh-huh." It *was* an apology.

He hung up, and I grinned at the phone. With his resources, it wouldn't take too long for Detective Strauss to verify that my dad hadn't written that check at all.

About an hour later, Celine called me to get picked up from the Four Seasons. I pulled up into the driveway of the hotel, where she already stood waiting for me beneath the overhang of the elegant building.

She slid into the car, and I noticed she looked stressed.

Celine clenched her jaw, and her eyes remained narrowed.

I drove down the street and said, "I'm afraid to ask how it went with your parents."

My cousin took a deep cleansing breath. "I should have expected a parental ambush."

My grip on the steering wheel tightened. "Do they want you to go back to Hong Kong?" I asked, voicing my fear aloud. I'd gotten used to having Celine around, but it'd sounded tonight like both of her parents didn't think too highly of Los Angeles—or my dad and me.

"They didn't talk to me about that," Celine said.

"Really?" After pulling up to a stoplight, I glanced at her profile.

She stared out the windshield and didn't look at me. "They want me to do something for them. It's concerning the restaurant."

"You mean Wing Fat?" I asked, as we traveled west on Wilshire Boulevard.

"Yeah, they told me that once Uncle is 'put away,' I should make sure to convince him or you to pass it over to our side of the family."

I pressed my foot down on the accelerator, and the car shot forward. "But Ba's innocent."

"That's what I told them." She shook her head. "Not like they ever listen to me. They started throwing out ideas about creating a franchise and expanding the restaurant brand to Hong Kong."

"No offense, Celine, but your dad seemed really upset about Wing Fat," I said. "Like Ba had been trying to one-up him with it."

She swallowed hard. "De Di has always had a competitive streak. I guess it applies not only to strangers but to brothers."

We'd arrived back home by then, and I eased into a

parking spot. "Well, I'm glad we're not our parents. Their problems aren't for us to solve. Or repeat."

Celine turned to face me and offered a thin smile. We walked out together into the apartment building.

Even though I'd ended on a note of harmony between us, I couldn't help but toss and turn in bed that night. Our generation might be unified, but I kept on analyzing and worrying about the rift between Celine's dad and my own.

NINETEEN

I WAS ALREADY ANNOYED BY THE LACK OF SLEEP from the night before, so the clanging of the phone in the morning did little to improve my mood. Bleary-eyed, I wandered to Celine's room to pick up the receiver. I tamped down my irritation at how she'd slept through the ringing when I scrutinized her sleeping form a little closer. She'd prepared for a full night's rest by donning a silk sleeping mask and wearing foam earplugs to block out any noise. Maybe the jarring sound had turned to background noise in the watery depths of her dreams.

I answered the call and found Nik on the other end, his voice frantic.

"Yale, something terrible has happened."

"What? Where?" I asked.

"Ma's in a huge panic and calling everyone she knows."

I could hear sirens wailing over the line. "Is she okay? Are you all right?"

"Yes, but we're at Ho's. It's not good. Come as soon as you can."

I agreed to show up at his restaurant and roused Celine from her sleep. "Nik just called," I said. "We need to get to Ho's. And fast."

When we arrived, I spied a few fire trucks and police cars in the parking lot. My cousin and I hurried to the back of the building, where we could see heavy smoke floating up in the air. An acrid smell hovered over the area. We heard the uproar of many voices as we turned the corner.

Celine scanned the crowd and rushed over to Nik. I sprinted to catch up with her.

"Are you okay?" she asked Nik.

His bedhead hair, paired with tired eyes, seemed even more genuine this morning. "I'm fine. We both are," he added.

I surveyed the back of the restaurant's building. Scorch marks stained the stucco wall. "Was it a grease fire?"

Those could flare up easily in restaurants. Working with hot oil always posed a hazardous risk.

"We hadn't even started cooking yet," Nik said. "Didn't even enter the building."

I searched for his mom among the throng of people and found her surrounded by AAROA members. She seemed shaken but unhurt. I watched as Derrick draped a blanket over her shoulders.

"Where did the fire start?" my cousin asked Nik, and I turned my attention to their conversation.

"Oddly, from the outside. I think maybe a large branch fell off from there." He gestured at a nearby huge tree with leaves hanging over a brick wall. "Then it caught on fire near our back door."

"Good thing it didn't spread to the inside," I said.

"Yeah, we were lucky. The flames looked so intimidating." Nik glanced over at his mother with concern and moved toward her.

We followed suit, joining all the other association members. A call must have gone out to the whole group, and everybody had shown up in support.

Misty and Trisha hung to the side, shaking their heads. Mr. Yamada discussed ways of filing an insurance claim with Nik's mother. My dad watched the comings and goings of the firefighters with intense concentration, seemingly keen that they had extinguished every possible flame.

Nik spoke up, and his voice carried over the general hubbub. "Thanks for coming, everyone. Ma and I really appreciate your kindness and care."

Mrs. Ho nodded at us in turn, a wavering smile on her face.

Nik lowered his voice and inclined his head toward his mother. "Are you okay still opening the restaurant today, Ma? Why don't you take the day off? I can cook instead."

Celine piped up. "Yeah, and I'm willing to work the register again." She nudged me in the shoulder after she'd spoken, as though expecting me to volunteer my services as a waitress again.

I first waited for Mrs. Ho to reply.

"No, Nikola," she said. "It'll be good for me to cook. Get my mind away from all this." She waved her hands around, as though trying to push away the lingering burnt smell.

I sniffed the air once more. Something beyond the charred odor remained in the area. I couldn't quite discern the scent, but it reminded me of something. We lingered on the premises a bit longer, but everything seemed to be taken care of, and I still couldn't place the scent.

On the car ride back home, Celine said to me, "Poor

Nik. He seemed to be in shock, both about the fire and how to best help his mother cope. Should we have offered to stay even longer?"

I shook my head. "Maybe it's better this way. Work is a great distraction. I know from experience." After all, focusing on Wing Fat had helped my dad and me cope after the loss of my mom.

"Still, I wish we could help more," my cousin said.

I stared out the windshield for a moment and remembered the stained exterior walls. "How about this?" I said. "We can help with the physical cleanup of soot on the building."

"What a great idea, Yale." Before I could retract my words, Celine had dialed up Nik. She used her speakerphone and offered our assistance.

"We can scrub the marks off the walls," she told him. "I won't take no for an answer."

"Thanks. Actually, I probably will need help with that," Nik said. "Later, though. Right now I'm trying to juggle opening up Ho's, calming down Ma, and connecting with the insurance company."

"No problem," Celine said. "Yale and I have some free time. We're already set for tomorrow's night market. Got all the food and everything ready to go."

That actually reminded me of an unfinished task. I still needed to post the remaining flyers advertising our new Insta-worthy backdrop. It shouldn't take too long, though.

"I'll text you later and give you a time to come by," Nik said.

Celine agreed and hung up the phone.

Since we'd now committed to the task, Celine and I had to conduct research about how to clean soot off walls. In the end, we decided to rent a pressure washer from a local hardware store. While there, we also stocked up on washing supplies.

After we finished getting the equipment, I reminded my cousin about the night market flyers. We strolled around Eastwood Village, tacking our flyers to utility poles. By the time Nik texted Celine back, we had posted all except for one.

Her fingers flew over her phone's tiny screen to answer him, but a frown spread across her face.

"What's the matter?" I asked.

"Nik's saying that the insurance won't cover any of the fire damage."

"Why not? It's an act of nature. Shouldn't that be covered?"

"That was Nik's theory. It sounds like it wasn't so natural," she said. "They're saying it was arson."

"But how can that be?"

Celine finished typing and leaned against the utility pole near us. "He didn't give me many details, but he did say we could come by at three to wash the walls."

That was a good hour to drop by a restaurant. The time corresponded with the afternoon lull, a break between the lunch and dinner crowds. Maybe we could extract more information from him during that quiet period.

"Arson," my cousin said, putting her phone away. "I can't believe someone would set a building on fire."

"Weird what people do for kicks," I said. "Thankfully, the restaurant is freestanding. At least no other shops got damaged."

Celine continued. "If Ma Mi found out about the arson, she'd go ballistic. She's already warning me about the danger of gangs and guns in the States."

I tuned out my cousin for a moment. What if the fire hadn't been randomly set? Could someone have targeted Ho's?

Perhaps the perpetrator had been someone who actually knew Nik and Mrs. Ho. An extreme emotion, like anger or fear, might propel a person to commit arson. In fact, I knew of one such individual whom a detective had recently interrogated.

Plus, we still had a single lucky flyer left to hang up before night market.

"I think we should pay a visit to Misty at her store," I said. "That'll be a great spot for this last poster."

"Huh. Okay," Celine said. "I'm craving samosas anyway."

On our way to India Snack Mart, I filled in my cousin about my suspicions. She took in my theory without any pushback.

"That's a bold claim, but maybe we can find out more when we talk to her face-to-face," Celine said.

At the store, we waved to Misty, who stood near the counter.

I showed her the flyer. "Do you have a place to hang this up? We'd love to tap into your customer base, especially since I'm offering chai at our stall."

Misty played with the end of her braid. "We don't have a bulletin board in here."

Celine pointed at the large glass front of the store. "Maybe we could tape it on that huge window."

"Sure. Why not?" Misty said and accompanied Celine to put the poster up.

After they finished, I said, "But we're not here to just mooch from you. We also wanted to get some of your amazing food. Right, Celine?"

Misty returned behind the counter. "Anything special you'd like?"

"Some samosas and mango lassi smoothies would hit the spot," my cousin said.

"Okay. Coming right up."

Misty gathered the mango lassi ingredients and mixed together the yogurt, milk, and mango pulp. After the whirring from the blender subsided, I said to her, "What a tragedy this morning, huh? The blaze at Ho's."

She started pouring the mango smoothie into two cups. "Yeah, agreed. It's a good thing those fire trucks put everything out so quickly."

Misty didn't spill a single drop. She seemed calm and collected. I also didn't detect any anger from her as she passed over our food and drinks.

After Celine paid for our lunch, I leaned far over the counter. I wanted to enter Misty's personal space for a moment.

"So," I said. "We're going over to Ho's to clean up the walls this afternoon. Care to join us?"

"Sorry." She flipped her braid over her shoulder. "I'm too busy. I gotta run the shop."

I checked out the store. Only two customers milled about the aisles, examining bags of rice and packets of Parle-G biscuits. And I spotted an employee in the recesses of the kitchen.

Had she offered a flimsy excuse to get out of helping us? I couldn't tell if her quick negation was due to her lack of interest in helping out Nik or because of her constraints with the business.

"Thanks again for letting us put up the flyer on the window," I said.

"No prob," she mumbled, her gaze already swiveling to the customer who had lined up behind us, ready to pay.

Celine and I exited the store with our food and drinks.

Back in the car, I asked my cousin, "What'd you think about Misty?"

"She seemed very relaxed. Not guilty or angry or anything."

"You don't think she set the fire?" I said. Could Misty have been calm because she'd already gotten out her rage by trying to burn down Ho's? "I think we should search around the restaurant when we clean it. Look for some extra clues."

* * *

At three in the afternoon, we showed up at Ho's with the requisite equipment for cleaning. Nik stood in the alley, ready and waiting for us.

His mother popped her head out of the kitchen to give us a quick hello. Then she rushed right back inside after the short acknowledgment.

"Oh, do you have customers?" I asked. Maybe that was why Mrs. Ho had been in a hurry. "You should go and take care of them."

"Nobody's dining right now," Nik said.

I gave a pointed look at the kitchen.

He said, "I just don't think Ma's too comfortable with being out here and seeing the damage again."

"Can't blame her," Celine said, connecting a hose from the water supply to the pressure washer. "Those black marks on the walls are downright ugly."

As I added fuel to the machine, I studied the scorch pattern. "What I don't get, Nik, is why your insurance wouldn't cover the damage."

"Come and take a look." He walked me over to a large tree limb lying against the back wall. The wood was charred.

"This is the branch that was involved?"

"Yep. The firefighters spotted it early on and thought maybe it'd fallen and gotten stuck near the back door. Later on, they changed their minds. See the end of the branch, how it broke off?"

I crouched down and studied the break. A clean cut. "It's almost as if someone sliced through it," I said.

"Exactly. Like it was from the work of a saw," Nik said. "A deliberate cut."

"How odd."

"That's not all," he said. "The insurance person asked me what I thought had set off the sparks."

"The wind?" I said, although I knew that the weather over the past few days had been quiet.

"An old power line?" Celine added.

I couldn't spot any electricity poles around.

"Maybe the sun's rays?" I said.

Nik squinted into the sky and grunted. Like me, he knew that the temperatures this past week had been mild and not searing hot.

"It was a match that sparked things," Nik said. "The insurance rep even thought we'd tried to con the company. Wondered if we might have set the fire ourselves."

"That's ridiculous. I'm not going to waste any more time talking about that absurd theory," I said, grabbing the nozzle from the machine and aiming it straight at the wall. "Give it some juice, Celine."

She complied, and we spent our time spraying off the ash from the walls. I think the washing workout was a great way to relieve our stress.

Nik whistled with pleasure when the walls returned to their original beige color. We shut off the machine and gave each other high fives.

"Good thing you caught the blaze early and alerted the fire department," I said to Nik. "At least all the damage was only on the outside."

"Nuh-uh," Nik said. "I didn't even see the flames."

"You didn't?"

"When Ma and I got here, the fire trucks had already arrived. Somebody must have seen the smoke beforehand and called it in."

"That was nice of them," Celine said as she disconnected the hose and coiled it up.

"I'm glad your mother wasn't inside when it happened, Nik," I said.

"Me too." He nodded at the kitchen. "She's not as fast as she used to be and might have gotten hurt if the fire had started while she was cooking."

Celine moved over to the back door, opened it a crack, and called inside to Nik's mother. "All done, Auntie Ai. We cleaned everything so that it looks like new."

I heard a murmured thanks from Mrs. Ho. "Hope the rest of your day is uneventful," I told her through the doorway.

"Thank you both again," Nik said.

We nodded and watched him join his mother in the kitchen. He pulled the door shut behind him.

I studied the wooden frame for a few minutes in confusion. A question arose in my mind, and I wanted to conduct some research about it.

TWENTY

I ASKED CELINE IF WE COULD STOP BY THE EAST-wood Village Public Library. Once there, I claimed one of the glossy wooden tables and piled numerous books about fire on the polished surface.

"Bleh," Celine said, gesturing to the stack I'd piled on the table. "Aren't you tired of thinking about fires?"

I passed one of the nonfiction books over to her. "Why don't you read as well? Double the brain power might mean we find the answer faster."

She flipped open the cover. "What are we looking for exactly?"

"Do you think there was something strange about that fire? The flames ended up scorching the wall of the building, but the door and its wooden frame remained untouched."

"So what?" Celine did a half-hearted flip through the pages. "Maybe the firefighters got there really quickly and put it out before the flames spread."

"Yes, but then how come the scorch marks were on the walls all around the entrance but not on the door itself?"

"Hmm. I could google it, but I might need more specifics." Celine scooted her chair back and stood up. "I'm going to ask the reference librarian."

"But I already pulled out all these books." I waved my hands over the stacks.

"The librarian can use a *dihn nouh* to speed things up," Celine said. My cousin had used the Cantonese word for "computer": an electronic brain. I think she just didn't want to be stuck by my side poring over textbooks, but I watched as she stalked toward the repurposed card catalog desk.

I'd trust my own mind, not an electronic one, to unravel this puzzle. There must have been some kind of fire-resistant material on the door. I browsed through the books before me and soon discovered that there was a special paint that could be used on wood to protect it. Could Nik and his mom have painted the door a long time ago as a sort of preventative measure?

Celine shuffled her way back to the table. "I got an answer," she said. My cousin proceeded to explain the exact thing I'd uncovered.

I tapped my forehead with my finger. "My brain worked faster than the electronic one."

"Well, I also asked the librarian another question."

"About the fire?"

"No." She smoothed down her blouse. "I wanted to know if there were any good clothing stores around."

"Really? Now probably isn't exactly the best time to go shopping."

She gathered up the books from the table. "Why not? We have to go return the pressure washer anyway. Might as well make it a fun trip."

We dropped off the research materials on the shelving cart and exited the library.

I hated shopping, but I agreed on one condition. "Only if you send Nik a quick text."

She pulled out her phone.

"Ask him if he's ever painted a special coating on the back door of the restaurant."

Celine showed me her phone after Nik responded.

No, the message read. We haven't done a single thing to this place, inside or out.

If Nik and his mother hadn't improved, or even changed up, the restaurant's exterior, how had the door been protected from a fire?

———

An hour into Celine's shopping spree, and her phone rang. Thank goodness, because apparently my sole role on the trip was to act as a human clothes hanger. My cousin pulled me behind a rack filled with clothing and answered the call.

From her end of the conversation, I could tell that Ba had called Celine. My cousin quickly agreed to whatever he asked. After she hung up, she turned to me.

"Good thing I went shopping," she said. "Turns out that we're planning a surprise dinner for Nik."

"What do you mean?" I almost stumbled into the clothes rack.

"Uncle said to convince Nik to have a late dinner with us at Pho You and Me tonight."

"Why?"

"To do something nice for Nik and his mom. Getting him to come will be a cinch." She used her phone to text.

A few moments later, she grinned. "There. All done. Nik needed a food distraction and agreed right away."

"Who can say no to great Vietnamese cuisine?" I said.

"How about I find you an outfit while we're here?"

I'd seen the price tags hanging off the fancy clothes in this boutique shop. "No, thanks."

"Your loss," Celine said, moving to the register to pay for her luxurious selections.

* * *

She wore one of her new dresses to dinner that night, a dark navy piece with long sleeves and a keyhole cutout in the front.

"Fancy outfit for a late-night-eats place," I teased her.

"What's the point of buying new clothes if you don't use them?"

Celine and I entered the restaurant, looking for Nik. Not surprisingly, he hadn't shown up yet. Even in high school, Nik had exhibited a tendency to rush into the classroom after the tardy bell had already rung.

We selected a table for four, all part of Ba's game plan. Celine texted him that we'd made it to the restaurant.

Finally, Nik arrived and sat down across from us. Celine and he ordered matching bowls of chicken pho, but I opted for the shredded pork over broken rice.

"It sure was a rough day," Nik said, grabbing some disposable chopsticks enclosed in a paper sleeve. He took them out, snapping the glued wood in half to create the separate sticks. Then he rubbed them against each other to get rid of any splinters.

"Glad you made it through," Celine said as she passed out paper napkins from the metal dispenser.

"Yeah," I said. "And how's your mom doing with everything?"

"She won't talk about it and is at home resting."

"At least she worked today. Maintained some semblance of routine," I said.

Nik folded his discarded paper sheath and fashioned it into a holder. He rested his chopsticks on top of his creation. "I guess," he said. "Too bad we didn't have a lot of customers. The few who did come in complained about the smoke in the air."

"Wow," Celine said. "The fire got into the restaurant somehow?"

"The burnt smell did," Nik said. "Maybe through the gap under the back door."

At that point, Ba came out of the kitchen and hurried over to our table.

"Mr. Yee?" Nik said. "What are you doing here?"

"Making a quick delivery." Ba stood before us, his hands hidden behind his back. "I took some time off from Wing Fat to be here for this."

"You're joining us for dinner?" Nik said, glancing at Celine and me for further explanation. "What's really going on right now?"

"Wait just a little longer," Ba said.

In another minute, Derrick arrived tableside, balancing our bowls on a tray. He distributed the food to us. "Dinner is on the house tonight," Derrick said. "Plus, we've got a special surprise for you, Nik."

Ba grinned, taking his hands from behind his back and presenting Nik with a check.

Nik didn't take it. "What's this?"

"A little something from AAROA," Ba said. "To help you and your mother out."

Derrick nodded. "In that thick binder of association rules, there's a provision for an emergency fund for members in need. I made an executive decision, getting Sing here"—he patted my dad on the shoulder—"to sign the check."

Ba twisted his hands together. "We heard from your mother that insurance won't cover the fire damage, and she told us about the recent slowdown of customers at the restaurant."

Nik reached out for the check and swallowed hard. To even reach for it, he'd needed to put away his pride. Ho's really must not be doing well.

I turned to my dad. "How did you get your hands on

the checkbook again? I thought you handed it over after the election."

The kitchen door swung open, revealing Nik's mother. She joined us at the table.

"You said you wanted to rest," Nik said in an accusatory tone.

"That, and to get the opportunity to pass the checkbook to Sing," she said.

Nik rose, looking both Ba and Derrick in the eyes, and thanked them. "You don't know what this means to both my mother and me."

Derrick ducked his head and mumbled, "Yeah, yeah. Anyway, I have another bowl of piping pho in the kitchen I need to get."

"Jeffery would've wanted to help you out, too," Ba said after Derrick left. He gave Nik a quick squeeze on the shoulder. Then he excused himself to return to Wing Fat.

Nik pulled out a chair for his mother to sit in, and Derrick soon returned with a pho for her. We all ate in contentment since the surprise financial gift had put us in a good mood.

After a satisfying meal, Celine and I lingered together at the table. Nik and his mother, though, said goodbye, maybe weary from their long day. Nevertheless, they strode out of the restaurant with matching smiles on their faces.

I pulled out my wallet at the same time my cousin dug into her purse.

"Are we thinking the same thing?" I asked.

"Derrick can't just give us a meal on the house," Celine said. "Especially for four people. That's not fair."

"But you always treat me, Celine," I said, placing some cash on the table. "I've got it this time."

Celine hesitated but then hung her purse on the back of the chair. "Fine. We don't need to fight over the check like our aunts and uncles." She looked toward the exit. "You know, I'm glad that Auntie Ai and Nik are feeling more positive. It's about time they had some good luck."

I wasn't sure that it'd exactly been ill fortune that had plagued the Hos. Having two alarming incidents occur at their restaurant seemed mean-spirited and deliberate on someone's part. "Do you think the fatal hot pot wiring and the fire are somehow related?"

Celine brushed some crumbs off her sleeve. "Well, the cord involved Jeffery, but now he's gone. So what could the connection be?"

"If Jeffery's death *was* intentional, what if the killer set their sights on Nik's mother next?"

My cousin shuddered. "Like if the person's a deranged serial killer?"

I stared into her shocked eyes. "Nothing as gruesome as that. What if Mrs. Ho saw something incriminating? The fire could have been a warning for her not to talk to the authorities."

"Wouldn't she have already told the police everything?"

"To the best of her ability, though maybe the police are overlooking something. They're so focused on the wrong suspects. Like Ba."

"You're right," Celine said. "We could ask Auntie Ai some more pointed questions."

"Definitely," I said. "Plus, she's got a sweet spot for you, Celine. Especially when it comes to pairing you and Nik together."

My cousin blushed. "Come on," she said and focused on gathering her purse. "We already paid for our meal. Let's go and leave this table for someone else."

TWENTY-ONE

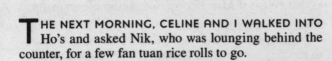

THE NEXT MORNING, CELINE AND I WALKED INTO Ho's and asked Nik, who was lounging behind the counter, for a few fan tuan rice rolls to go.

"Sure," he said. "I already wrapped some. I'll just need to pop them into the microwave to get them warm again."

"Do you think we could go into the kitchen ourselves?" Celine asked. She lifted the gift bag in her hands. "We got something for Auntie Ai."

His brow wrinkled as he tried to peer into the opaque bag. "All these gifts we're getting recently. What'd you bring?"

"Something for the restaurant. It's no biggie." I sniffed the air, which still held traces of smoke. "It'll help clear out the remaining odor."

Nik looked around the empty restaurant. "Okay, go on in, but it's only because nobody is around to see you do so."

We thanked Nik and walked through the swinging kitchen door.

Mrs. Ho stood at a deep fryer but glanced over her shoulder when she heard our footsteps. "Yale, Celine. It's nice to see you two again," she said. "Let me finish up with these *youtiao*, and I'll be right with you."

We waited while Nik's mother pulled the golden crisped crullers out of the fryer and laid them with care on a paper towel–lined platter.

"Those look perfect," Celine said. "Can I get a few shots for my Instagram?"

Mrs. Ho nodded, and my cousin proceeded to take a few pictures with her phone.

"Now, are you here for breakfast?" Mrs. Ho asked, happy laugh lines crinkling near her eyes.

"We *are* getting a few rice rolls," I said, "but Celine also brought you a present."

My cousin placed the gift bag on one of the prep tables. "It's a deodorizer spray. I heard Nik complaining about the smoke yesterday."

"That's very kind of you." Nik's mother made her way to the sink and washed her hands. Then she wandered over to the gift bag and plucked out the spray. "Enzyme powered," she read.

"It's pretty good," Celine said. "If you need something more long-term, though, I can recommend a few air purifier models. My parents use those to get rid of the cigarette odor in our casinos."

"Thank you." Mrs. Ho placed the deodorizer back into the bag. "I think this should do for now."

I glanced over at the sink that Nik's mother had vacated. "Wow. I can't believe it's been a little over a week since our hot pot, and poor Jeffery's case is still unsolved."

Mrs. Ho's lips tightened. "That's because it's *not* a homicide. Detectives see things because of their job. Every dead person becomes a victim. It's like us cooks, Yale. Every plant turns into a potential ingredient."

Not a homicide? "Do you think it was simply a terrible accident, Mrs. Ho?"

She nodded and then gestured at a platter of stacked rice rolls. "There are the fan tuan. Help yourself to as many as you'd like, and warm them up over there."

"Thanks, Auntie," Celine said, grabbing a few and putting them into the microwave.

Mrs. Ho turned toward the stove, effectively ending our conversation.

How could Mrs. Ho think Jeffery's death had been an accident? What had she witnessed that night? She seemed tight-lipped about the whole affair, and I wondered whom she was protecting. Nik was the first person who came to mind.

The microwave dinged. Celine retrieved the rice rolls.

When we went out to the front, Celine approached Nik at the register while I hung back and evaluated him. I could understand if Mrs. Ho wanted to stay silent for the sake of Nik, but the puzzle pieces of the two cases didn't fit together. If the fire was connected to the hot pot murder, then Nik *couldn't* be the culprit. There'd be no need to give himself a warning, and fire damage would only drive away much-needed business.

While I reassured myself of Nik's innocence, the front door flew open. Misty marched in from outside, her braid swinging against her back. She went right up to the counter, almost budging Celine out of the way.

Misty wagged her finger at Nik. "I can't believe it. I got the email this morning about the association's money going to you."

Even from across the counter, Nik took a step backward to distance himself. "Whoa there, Misty. It wasn't my idea."

"Yeah, Mr. President? Then whose was it?"

"Derrick thought of it first, and I didn't put him up to

it. You know I don't have that kind of influence over Derrick. We're not exactly buddies."

Misty withdrew her hand from Nik. "Still, isn't it unethical as the association president for you to accept it?"

Nik scratched the back of his neck. "I guess there's an emergency fund for members that Derrick discovered in our bylaws. And what with the fire . . ."

Her eyes narrowed at him.

"Besides, it got approved by another association officer as well." Nik jerked his thumb at me. "Yale's dad had to sign the check, after all."

She aimed her wrath at me. "To think that I shared my chai recipe with you. That money should go to people who actually need help, like my check did for The Human Connection."

"Nik did nothing wrong," I said. "It's all aboveboard."

Misty didn't respond but turned on her heel and strode out of the restaurant.

"Did you hear what she said?" I asked.

Celine whistled. "Yeah, she sure was mad."

"I thought she might even climb over the counter and tackle me," Nik added.

"Concentrate, you two," I said. "Misty talked about *her* check—and how she'd written it out to The Human Connection."

Celine gasped. "The forgery. She confessed to it."

"You both heard it," I said.

I couldn't wait to see Detective Strauss tonight at the night market and let him know what Misty had admitted to out of anger.

Celine and I spent the next few hours gearing up for the night market. My cousin obsessed over setting up the perfect playlist. She wanted to stream holiday music while attendees took pictures at her photo display.

"The tunes will boost their endorphins and then people will be happy to buy from us," she said.

"That's not why they'll come to our stand," I said. "It'll be because of the great food."

She flashed me a brilliant smile. "Whichever makes them show up."

As it turned out, the first customer didn't arrive because of the photo opportunity or my cooking. He came because of a promise he'd made.

Detective Strauss strolled our way like a man on a mission.

"Here to get your chai?" I asked.

"That's right." He pulled out his wallet, a fine specimen of weathered leather.

I brewed his tea while Celine collected his payment.

After I filled his to-go cup with the steaming beverage, I said, "By the way, Misty dropped by Ho's earlier."

"You won't believe the drama she caused," Celine added, jumping into the conversation and regaling the detective with details of the visit.

"In conclusion," I said, "she basically confessed to writing that check, and you've got three eyewitnesses who were there. We can give statements or whatever it is you might need." I really wanted to make sure Ba got off the hook for that forged check.

Detective Strauss blew on his chai, making the steam swirl my way. "You and Celine are reliable, but I'm not too trusting of Nik."

Celine turned her head toward the booth next door. Thankfully, I didn't think Ho's Small Eats was close enough to us for Nik to overhear.

"What makes you think that about Nik?" I asked.

Detective Strauss sipped his tea for a moment. "I heard about the fire at his family restaurant."

"So unfortunate," Celine said, her attention once again trained on our conversation.

"Horrible, yes," the detective said, "but sources tell me it was arson and not an accident."

Since he'd started down this track, I outlined my suspicions about how Jeffery's murderer might have been warning Nik's mother by deliberately setting the fire. "Otherwise, doesn't it seem weird that someone would try to burn down the restaurant?"

"Yeah," Celine said. "Someone is definitely trying to threaten Mrs. Ho. Or maybe Nik."

The detective replied, "Could be. Or perhaps somebody wants to cast suspicion off himself."

What did that mean? "Are you saying . . ."

"There was only cosmetic damage done to the building," Detective Strauss said.

My cousin spluttered while I stared at him, unable to form coherent words.

He saluted us with his cup. "Thanks for the chai, ladies."

Detective Strauss left, and I could hear the sturdy beat of his confident stride as he walked away.

How could the same fire have led us to such opposing conclusions? While I'd seen the arson incident as a mark of Nik's innocence, he'd labeled the same act as indicative of my friend's guilt.

Celine gasped all of a sudden and brought me out of my reverie. What had I missed? I glanced to my side, automatically checking Ho's Small Eats, worried that the detective would confront Nik right then. But Nik seemed fine as he chatted away with a happy customer.

I followed my cousin's wide-eyed stare and registered two formidable figures walking our way: her parents. Celine's mother reached us first. She eyed our matching bedazzled chef jackets with distaste and then picked at a strand of sparkling lights at the photo display.

Her mouth screwed up. "Is this how you're using your college degree, Celine?"

Celine's father joined us at that moment, so I greeted them both with a fake smile and an overly hearty tone.

My cousin sidled up to her mother and said, "I'll have you know that this is a Gram-worthy backdrop. My media smarts are helping Yale get more customers."

They held a whispered conversation while her father distracted me by asking about the portable kitchen for the night market. "Can you give me a tour? How do you even manage to cook in such a small space?"

"Yes, I can show you around. But it'll be done pretty quickly," I said, motioning to the compact back area.

"And this food stall is actually profitable?" Celine's father asked.

"Yes, Uncle. We do quite well here." I gestured to my nearby cart of supplies. "Sometimes we even sell out of our food and drinks."

"Really?" Celine's father stroked his chin, and I wondered if he was calculating the value of money for both the food stall and Ba's restaurant put together.

I led him back to the front. Although I didn't divulge my recent conversation with the detective, I said, "Rest assured, Uncle. Ba and I are doing fine all on our own." I stressed that last part of the sentence.

"We'll see," my uncle said.

"Excuse me, but it looks like we have a few customers waiting."

People had started lining up, but he didn't budge. Would it be rude of me to ask him to leave? I bit my lip, but Mrs. Ho saved me from my quandary.

She hurried over from the neighboring booth and addressed my uncle. "Are you Celine's father?" she asked.

He nodded.

"Perfect," she said. "We have a lot to talk about in private."

Celine's father trailed behind Mrs. Ho and called out

for his wife to come as well. My aunt, apparently finished with all her criticism, followed them. Then I noticed Celine, framed in the photo display. The merry twinkling lights of the backdrop contrasted heavily with her unhappy face.

TWENTY-TWO

CELINE WANTED TO FOLLOW HER PARENTS OVER
to the food stall, Ho's Small Eats. Maybe she hoped
to overhear the conversation happening between them
and Nik's mother. However, the line of customers before
our own booth had grown large in size by this time.

Besides, someone admiring her photo backdrop display proceeded to ask her questions about her snapwor-
thy setting, and she couldn't slink away. We ended up
serving customers for an hour before a lull happened.
Then the next customer we encountered was Trisha.

"Good to see you here," Celine said. "Enjoying the
night market?"

Trisha dipped her head in the direction of the La Pupusería de Reyes stall. "I'm hanging out with Blake tonight."

"Oh, are you two serious?"

"Nah. It's all for fun." She leaned toward Celine and
whispered, "What about you and Nik?"

"What? We're just friends," my cousin said, although

splotches of color started appearing on her cheeks. "Anyway, do you know what you want to order?"

Trisha peered at our menu. "An aloe vera drink. And the cucumber salad, I guess."

Celine glanced at me, and I moved toward the cooler to extract the two items.

Trisha continued with their conversation. "How is Nik holding up after the fire? Is he okay?"

"He's doing better," Celine said. "Now that there's some funding to help with the restaurant."

I walked over with the order and watched Trisha tug her wallet out of a stuffed purse. "Nik and his mother got extra money?" she said.

"Yeah, from AAROA. Misty didn't tell you? She was in a huff about it earlier."

Trisha shook her head.

"And you didn't check your email? AAROA sent out the news."

"I get a weekly digest," she said.

Celine peered over Trisha's shoulder, at the new customers in line, and stated the amount due for the food.

Trisha paid, and I handed her the items.

She seemed stuck at the counter, hoping to ask us more questions, but the man behind her started grumbling about the wait. Trisha took her items and moved away.

The man bent down and came back up holding a fistful of slips. "Litterbug. She even dropped these."

Celine reached for them and tucked them into the pocket of her chef jacket. Then she concentrated on taking his order.

We continued serving a steady flow of customers until near closing time. Once the last customer was served, though, Celine practically sprinted over to Nik's booth.

I made quick work of cleaning up our area because I'd already sold out of everything. Since my cousin appeared occupied, I copied how I'd seen Celine pack up the photo display. I carefully took down her impressive backdrop and its accessories.

After I finished, I glanced over at Celine. She was still deep in conversation with Mrs. Ho. What else could I do while she talked? Maybe I should chat with my fellow foodie neighbors.

Looking over to one side, I noticed that the Below Freezing ice cream truck had already left. At the other end of the aisle, Blake still had the tent up for their food stall. Although Trisha had dropped by to see him earlier, she no longer remained in sight.

Trisha. She'd dropped those pieces of paper. Maybe I could take this time to give them to Blake. I bet he'd see her again sooner than me.

I tapped Celine on the shoulder at Ho's Small Eats and asked for her chef's jacket. Immersed in conversation, she didn't make eye contact, but slipped off the coat and handed it over to me.

Draping it over my arm, I approached Blake. His grandmother stood in the back area, cleaning a pot. I waved to her, and she smiled at me.

I started off with small talk with him. "Hey, Blake. How was business tonight?"

"Pretty good. It must be the holiday mood. The festive eating that happens after Thanksgiving. What about Canai and Chai?"

"Can't complain," I said. "We sold out of everything tonight."

He gave a low whistle. "That's impressive."

"Actually, Trisha was one of our customers this evening," I said. "She told me she was hanging out with you earlier."

Blake nodded. "We've gone out a few times now. Even cooked for each other. And I've passed on some tips about running a food stall to her."

"She wants to be at the night market, too?"

"Ambitious woman," he said with a smile. "I admire that."

"Since you two hang out with each other a lot, you'll probably see her before me. She left some stuff at our booth." Without looking, I stuck my hand inside the pocket of Celine's jacket and handed over the paper.

"Uh, I don't think she'll need these back. They're just trash from some Chinese takeout place."

I examined the familiar-looking pieces of paper. "Wait a minute. These are from Wing Fat." Ba stocked our restaurant with customized fortune cookies. The Wing Fat name was printed at the bottom of the fortunes to remind people of where they'd eaten.

"How'd you end up with them again?" he asked.

"They fell out of her purse while she was paying."

He chuckled. "Go figure. She has, like, the black hole of all bags. I bet she won't even notice. You can toss them."

"Oh, okay." I thanked him for our chat and located the nearest garbage receptacle. Before I tossed the papers in, though, I unfolded them. I liked reading fortunes for fun.

As I did so, I noticed that one of the pieces had writing on the back. The stark black ink against the white background caught my eye, and I also did a double take when I saw the four strokes written on the paper.

I knew that simple Chinese character. Disturbed, I stuffed all the fortune slips into my pocket and ran to find my cousin.

Celine stood in front of our now dismantled food stall, leaning against the utility cart of supplies. Thankfully, I'd locked the wheels, or else she might have tumbled down. She seemed quite dazed and stared off into the middle distance with unfocused eyes.

"Hey," I said. "Is everything okay?"

She didn't respond.

"What's the matter, Celine?"

Her head turned toward me. "Auntie Ai spoke with

my parents. She, of course, wanted to share with them all about Nik's accomplishments and how we'd make a great couple.

"A little awkward, but my parents flat out told her no." She straightened and bunched her hands into fists at her sides. "I don't know why they always try to run my life for me. Can't people let me make my own decisions in my own time?"

I shook my head in commiseration and motioned to the night sky. "It's getting late, Celine. Maybe we should continue talking on our way back home."

Celine nodded and gathered her box of photo supplies. I placed her jacket on the top shelf of the utility cart and started pushing it across the empty plaza.

"I thought coming to the States was an excellent idea," my cousin said. "That way I could get a break. And I figured maybe my parents would have less influence from across an ocean."

A few thoughts flitted across my mind: *They just care about you, in a smothering sort of way* or *At least you have both of your parents alive and invested in you.* Saying these out loud, though, might make the situation worse. In the end, I simply said, "I'm sorry, Celine."

We'd made it past the fountain when I noticed my cousin shivering. "Oh," I said. "You should put on your jacket."

I retrieved it from the cart and handed it over.

As she put it on, Celine asked, "Why did you want it in the first place?"

"You put those scraps of paper in it," I said and started pushing the cart again.

"Right. The slips that Trisha dropped."

"I wanted to give them back to Blake because he might see Trisha sooner, but he said they were trash." We reached the front of our apartment complex. "Actually, they were fortune cookie slips from Wing Fat."

"They must have been from the meeting when everyone voted."

"I think so too," I said. "I counted out seven slips. That's one for each member."

We entered the lobby and got into the elevator.

"So you threw them away?" Celine said.

"Well, I was about to when I noticed writing on the back of one of them. A Chinese character," I said.

"Huh." Celine and I made our way out of the elevator and to our apartment.

Before the door, I pulled out the fortune cookie slip in question and said, "Do you recognize this character?"

"Of course I do. It's the word for 'fire,'" she said. As she spoke, she almost dropped her box with the photo display.

"I don't think it's a coincidence. Do you?"

My cousin shook her head.

"Could someone have made a plan to set Ho's on fire? Maybe even back at that meeting, someone had already been plotting arson."

"But who?" she asked in a small voice.

In the apartment, we deliberated some more. "It just doesn't make any sense," I said. "It'd have to be someone who knows Chinese, which only leaves . . ."

"You, me, Uncle, Nik, and Auntie Ai," Celine said. She slowly unpacked her photography accessories and stored them in the hall closet.

I put away the cart while mulling over the detective's earlier suspicions. Could he have been right? Had Nik and his mother been driven to starting a fire to get some extra money to float their flailing business?

My cousin and I wound up on the settee next to each other. "It couldn't be Nik, right?"

Celine held her hand out, palm up. "May I see the fortune?"

I passed the slip of paper over to her.

She read it out loud: "As the purse is emptied, the heart is filled."

I laughed. "Gee, that's an interesting fortune."

"And on point," my cousin said.

"For some folks," I said. "Anyway, do you remember what fortune each person got? Oh, wait. I passed out the cookies at the meeting."

"Yeah," Celine said. "I was already sitting down at another table, ready to count the votes." That's right. The fortune cookies were to lighten the association members' moods and to keep them occupied while they waited for the tallying to be done.

"Hmm. So we need to ask someone who was at the table about all the fortunes," I said. "A trustworthy person."

"How about Uncle?" Celine said.

My dad would definitely be honest with us. "Good idea."

Celine glanced at the wall clock, squinting at the Roman numerals. "Is it too late to call now?"

"We could try. If he's already asleep, he won't pick up."

My cousin bit her lip. "A ringing phone won't wake him?"

"No, he's out like a light whenever he falls asleep." It might have been because he worked so hard that he passed out if given the chance to rest.

Celine and I headed to her room, where I picked up the landline and dialed.

Ba answered on the second ring. His voice didn't sound groggy at all, and I put him on speakerphone for both of us to listen.

"What's wrong?" he said. "Is it something to do with Celine's parents?"

My cousin piped up. "No, Uncle. They're fine." In a lower voice, she mumbled, "Or as fine as usual."

"We just saw them at the night market," I added. "They're doing great."

I heard Ba exhale over the phone. He did care about his brother and sister-in-law despite their tangled and contentious history.

"I'm calling about something else," I said. "Do you remember the association meeting at Wing Fat? I passed out fortune cookies while we were counting the votes for president. Everyone was chatting and sharing what they got. Do you recall what fortunes people had?"

"Um," Ba said.

"Anything you remember could help. This might turn out to be very important," I said.

"I'm sorry. I really don't know."

Recalling the fortune with the fire character on the back, I said, "There's a specific one I have in mind. It was about emptying your purse and filling your heart."

My dad chuckled. "Oh, yes."

I hoped the fortune had jogged his memory further. "Who had it?"

"I can't remember," Ba said. "But it was very funny. Why is it so important anyway?"

"Something was written on the back of the slip, but I'm still working on how everything connects. I'll let you know once I figure it out."

Ba's voice filled with concern. "You're not doing anything dangerous, are you?"

Tracking down an arsonist? It might not be the wisest choice. And I wasn't about to tell him over the phone.

My cousin spoke up with confidence. "No, Uncle, nothing dangerous. Besides, Yale and I are always together."

"Yes," my dad said. "It's good that you look out for each other. I'm sorry I can't remember, Yale."

"Well, thanks for trying to help," I said.

"You know what?" Ba said, "I don't know if this is

useful or not, but I do remember who laughed the hardest. Derrick. He was doubled over with tears sprouting from his eyes."

I thanked my dad and hung up. That last piece of information might prove helpful. Maybe Derrick would be the right person to ask about the fortune.

TWENTY-THREE

IN THE MORNING, WE GOT A CALL FROM THE SECU-
rity guard downstairs. "Sunny and Cher," he said, without a hint of mirth, "are waiting for you in the lobby."

Celine turned to me with a panicked look on her face.
"I don't want to handle my parents by myself. Can you
come with?"

I glanced down at the clothes I was wearing. A casual
outfit of slouchy cardigan and trousers would have to do.

In the lobby, we found Celine's parents seated in the
corner of the room with the fake library. Its books were
hollowed-out copies meant to give a sophisticated air to
the place.

Celine's parents greeted us politely, but then my aunt
said, "Do you mind, Yale? We need to have a family
discussion in private."

I took a few steps backward, but Celine grabbed
my arm.

"Yale is my cousin," she said. "She is family."

My aunt frowned and looked to her husband for support, but Celine also stared at her father with pleading eyes.

"It's okay," my uncle said. "Yale can stay."

"Good," Celine said and plopped down into an over-stuffed chair.

I took a seat right beside her.

"As you know," my uncle said, "we're not staying very long here in the States. In fact, we've already booked a flight for tomorrow night."

My aunt picked up the conversation. "We came here to figure out what was going on with Sing and now we know the full extent of it. Our job is done. After some reflection, we want you to come home with us, Celine."

My cousin leaned back in her chair, away from her parents. "I can't. I'm still on vacation."

Celine's father cleared his throat. "We're glad you got the chance to take this trip, a breather of sorts for you. Now you must return—and just in time for the opening of a new casino."

"De Di"—Celine crossed her legs—"I'm sure there are plenty of other young women who would jump at the chance to model new clothes and cut the ribbon."

"Celine, you're not just anybody," he said. "You're our daughter and represent the Yee name."

"But I still have time left on my visa," my cousin said.

My aunt smoothed her long black A-line skirt. "You know that's the maximum. You don't have to stay *that* long, Celine."

"I like it here, Ma Mi." She glanced over at me. "With Yale."

My aunt tilted her chin up. "Your cousin has been dragging you into trouble ever since you arrived. First, it was that brutal boba nonsense. And now it's your uncle's spiraling reputation."

I gripped the sides of my armchair. "Ba is not a criminal. He wouldn't hurt a soul. Besides, the detective has another suspect in mind." Poor Nik.

I might have mumbled his name because my aunt's eyes narrowed. "Nikola Ho . . . and his scheming mother? She wants to tie you down in the States, never to come back home, Celine."

My cousin shook her head. "Ma Mi, I'm an independent woman. I can make my own choices."

My aunt continued as though she hadn't heard my cousin speak. "I can't believe Ai wanted to connect our two families together. A poor widow with a failing business. And doing even worse after that fire."

Celine's father hemmed. "Dangerous stuff there. In fact, you might even get into trouble if you continue to be around the Hos."

My aunt's voice softened. "Leave with us tomorrow, Celine."

"Come back home," my uncle added.

Celine hesitated. I could see her edge closer to them in her chair.

"We're letting you know now," her mother said, "so you can have plenty of time to start packing."

"Wait a minute," my cousin said. "I need to think about this some more."

My aunt began to protest, but her husband put his hand over hers, and she stopped.

"That's understandable," he said. "You have until midnight to make up your mind. We'll come by the night market for your answer."

"Thank you, De Di," Celine said.

My aunt and uncle stood up from their seats and bade us goodbye. When we returned to the apartment, Celine immediately started pacing around the living room.

I worried that she'd damage the fluffy fibers of my floor rug with all her stomping.

"What should I do?" Celine asked.

"Well, do you *want* to go?" I stood still while she paraded to and fro.

"No, not yet," she said. "And definitely not like this, in a rush. But then again . . ."

My cousin stalked over to her bedroom, and I followed. She took one of her matching purple suitcases from its tidy stack. Celine laid it on her bed. "My parents asked me to go."

Celine had first come to the States after some media trouble in Hong Kong, and she'd followed her parents' advice then. I wondered if she felt duty bound to heed their suggestions now, even while wanting to be more independent.

She unzipped the suitcase and let it flop open. "If only Auntie Ai hadn't approached them."

I wasn't sure which thought had alarmed Celine's parents more—my cousin settling down in America with a romantic prospect in sight, or the recent physical danger from the fire.

However, I could only work on one of those facets. "If we could determine who set the fire, maybe they'd feel more at ease with you staying."

"Perhaps," Celine said, zipping up the suitcase.

I reflected on the fortune cookie slip with the character inked on it. "We have a lead, remember."

"You're right. Derrick Tran," she said, restacking the suitcase on top of the others. "Let's go."

I called Derrick to arrange a quick meeting. Since we hadn't eaten breakfast yet, Celine recommended a new eatery she'd found on Yelp. Derrick easily agreed when we called him up.

Celine and I pulled up to the plainly named Bubble Waffle Place, where I knew I'd be in for a treat.

"Aren't bubble waffles meant for dessert?" I said to Celine.

She shrugged. "Only if you add ice cream to your order." The hexagonal waffles, with centers of puffy rounded bubbles, were usually wrapped around ice cream like a cone, but I guessed you could eat them plain.

The scent of batter sizzling on a griddle rose to meet us as we entered the tiny shop. We found Derrick already there, waiting. The three of us decided to split up the small menu of their classic three flavors among us: chocolate, vanilla, and strawberry.

While an employee whipped up the batter, we chose to sit down at a tall round chrome table with matching stools.

Celine placed her hands open before her. "Derrick," she said, "we want to be honest with you. Yale and I are here to talk about a serious matter."

His eyes sought mine, and panic flashed through them.

My cousin remained silent, letting me pick up the conversation. I wondered how to phrase things delicately because it might involve a potential accusation. "Reputation," I finally said, "is important. I don't want to smear anyone's good name unless I have to."

Derrick tilted his stool back, almost falling over. "Please don't tell the association," he said.

My cousin faltered for words, and I raised an eyebrow at him.

"I bet you figured out my identity from the cookies on your blog, right? My old email address must have cropped up."

He had to be referring to the *Eastwood Village Connection*. The trolling that had been done on the blog. "You left those snide comments about Nik," I said.

"But it was all done in jest. Can't you see that? No real ill will. I even proposed the funding to cover the fire damage at Ho's."

Our bubble waffles got delivered right then and allowed us some time to scrounge up a reply.

My cousin spoke first. "It's fine," Celine said. "But no more trolling, Derrick."

He nodded and sliced into his chocolate waffle topped with whipped cream.

I concentrated on my vanilla treat, with its spread of ripe strawberries and banana slices, drizzled with chocolate syrup. Delicious and I was glad we'd resolved the trolling situation.

After taking a few more heavenly bites, I addressed Derrick. "I also wanted to ask you about the AAROA meeting where everyone voted in a new president. Do you remember those fortune cookies I passed around?"

"Uh, okay." He continued chewing. "What about them?"

"Who got the fortune about having to empty their purse?"

He paused eating, his fork in the air. "I'm supposed to remember that?"

"Ba said you were doubled over with laughter."

Derrick's eyes crinkled. "Oh yeah, Roy got this funny fortune about emptying his purse to fill his heart."

I leaned forward. "It was Mr. Yamada? Are you sure?"

Derrick let out a chuckle. "Definitely. But why are you asking me this? What's a fortune got to do with anything?"

Maybe everything. I pushed my half-eaten waffle away from me. "It's just something I was curious about," I said.

He didn't like my nonanswer, but Derrick let it slide.

In the end, Celine still managed to finish her breakfast, while I asked for a to-go container. We all left the Bubble Waffle Place in a subdued mood.

As we walked over to the car, I told my cousin, "We need to visit Yamada Ramen."

Celine and I arrived at the restaurant just shy of opening hours. In the parking lot, I watched as Mr. Yamada arrived and unlocked the door to his business. He took his time turning on the lights and flipping over the sign.

I'd needed to see him in person. I wanted to reconcile this flesh-and-blood version of the man with a potential arsonist and maybe murderer.

Mr. Yamada pulled out a bottle of window cleaner and a microfiber rag. He sprayed the clear door and rubbed at it until the glass shone.

How could Mr. Yamada have set the fire? Especially since he was an old friend of Nik's mother. Mrs. Ho, my dad, and he made up the venerable trio of elders in AAROA.

The seat belt holding me felt constraining all of a sudden, and I tugged at it. "I don't understand. Why would he start a fire?"

My cousin turned to face me and blinked. "Do you think we got the wrong person? But Derrick was certain it was Roy's fortune cookie."

"I know," I said, my eyes locked on Mr. Yamada's figure. "But even though it was Mr. Yamada's piece of paper, couldn't someone else have written on it instead?"

"Hmm. Everyone did have the same type of pen to write down their vote," Celine said.

"Exactly. And would Mr. Yamada know how to write in Chinese?"

"Wait a moment. Let me check something," Celine said, pulling out her phone.

After doing a quick search, she said, "It's not Chinese."

"What do you mean? I recognized the character."

"I mean, it's not specific to the Chinese language. It's the same symbol for 'fire' in Japanese. In kanji."

"Oh." I watched Mr. Yamada bustle around his restaurant, preparing it to open.

"A hardworking man," Celine said, as he wiped down the wooden tables in the restaurant.

"That's what I don't get," I said. "Mr. Yamada knows

what it's like to build up a business. How could he destroy someone else's, particularly that of a close friend?"

A sudden thought surfaced in my mind. The damage done to Ho's hadn't been too much. In fact, when we'd cleaned the walls, hadn't I noticed that the door had remained untouched by the flames?

I saw Mr. Yamada line up some bottles of sake on a shelf, and I twitched my nose in reaction. The leftover scent from the fire. I knew it'd seemed familiar but couldn't place it at the time.

There had been a hint of rice in the air. I corrected myself. I knew now that it had been the smell of fermented rice. I imagined Mr. Yamada pouring his sake around the walls of Nik's family restaurant, placing a tree branch in the right position, and then lighting a match.

"Oh no," I said. "I think we need to call the police."

TWENTY-FOUR

At the Eastwood Village Police Station, I asked for Detective Strauss. Within five minutes, he walked into the lobby through the side door.

"Yale and Celine," he said, his mouth quirking up. "At least you're interrupting some tedious paperwork today. Why don't you come on back?"

The detective led us through the hallway and into the inner lair of the police station. His standard-issue metal desk was right under a sign marked "Homicide." The entire open room was split into various sections and labeled by department.

My cousin and I placed two cobalt-blue visitor chairs next to each other and sat down facing him.

"We've uncovered a key piece of evidence," I said, brandishing the slip of paper and handing it over to him.

He straightened out the tiny rectangle and peered at it. "Am I seeing this right? Because it's a printed fortune."

I made a turning motion with my hand. "The writing's on the back."

He stared at the strokes of ink and then rotated the fortune ninety degrees. "Is this some sort of drawing?"

"No." Celine stuck out her phone at him, having already opened up the translator app. "It's the character for 'fire.'"

"Uh-huh." Detective Strauss placed the slip on his desk. "And?"

"We asked around," I said. "This was definitely Roy Yamada's fortune."

"So Roy must have written that," Celine said. "We think he was involved in setting the fire at Ho's."

"You're telling me I should incriminate Roy Yamada based on a fortune cookie slip?" The detective stared at us with disbelief.

I shuffled in my seat, and Celine blushed.

My cousin leaned back in her seat and crossed her arms. "It's forward progress on the arson at least. Maybe if you used your authority, you could question him further and find out more."

"My cousin means you could have a friendly chat with him," I said. "Like you did with Misty."

"Speaking of which," the detective said, pulling out some papers. "Do you want to give your statements now about what you heard Misty say about the check?"

"Not a problem," Celine said, slipping her phone back into her purse.

We took some time to reiterate what we'd heard from Misty. When we'd finished with our statements, I asked, "What's going to happen to her?"

"We'll handle it accordingly," the detective said. "And I still need to get Nikola Ho in here to give his version of the events."

"Oh, you believe him now," I said. "Does that mean you're crossing Nik off the suspects list?"

The detective pulled out his notepad and pencil. "Not exactly. I'm just following proper protocol." He flipped through the pages, which I assumed had details about the investigation into Jeffery's death. "But your new wild theory about Roy Yamada setting the fire does open up interesting possibilities."

I bit the tip of my thumb. Could Detective Strauss be thinking that Mr. Yamada was the culprit for both the fire and the murder? I knew I'd voiced something like that in the past, but now that we had a tenuous connection between the arson and Mr. Yamada, I wasn't so sure. He didn't seem like a coldhearted killer, especially since he'd tempered the fire somehow and stopped it from spreading inside the restaurant. What could have been his reason for creating the blaze in the first place?

"Well, thanks for your help," Detective Strauss said. He nodded at a pile of paperwork near him. "If that's all, I need to get back to those."

We nodded, and the detective walked us out.

After he left us in the lobby, I asked Celine, "Do you think Mr. Yamada was actually involved in Jeffery's death?"

"Who knows? My memory of that hot pot dinner is getting murkier by the minute," she said.

"Maybe we should go to Ho's to jog our minds. We could sit at the same booth and go through the whole timeline."

"Good idea," she said.

We found a trickle of customers at Ho's. Thankfully, it seemed that business had picked up somewhat after our gift of the deodorizer spray. I sniffed the air and couldn't even detect a hint of smoke.

Nik didn't greet us as we entered, and we didn't see him by the counter. Perhaps he'd stepped into the kitchen for a moment.

"The booth we sat in before is over there," Celine said, pointing.

I nodded and followed her.

We passed a couple sitting together, and I heard one whisper to the other, "No wonder a fire started here. Look at all their ungrounded sockets. This place needs renovation work."

"I don't agree," the other said. "I like the retro chic atmosphere here."

I sat down at the booth with Celine and reflected on the customers' remarks about the electric sockets. Could the fire have been misidentified as arson? Maybe it'd been the building's faulty wiring all along. But no, I remembered the blackened walls of the building. The fire had definitely originated from an outside source.

Across the table from me, Celine used her finger to trace a circle in the center of the table. "Imagine that there's a hot pot before us."

Huh. Could the hot pot murder have happened because of faulty wiring? Muddled, I shook my head. No, it couldn't have been. There'd been evidence of tampering, and Detective Strauss was involved in an open homicide case.

Celine tapped on the table with her fist. "Come on, Yale, concentrate."

I closed my eyes and pretended I heard the sound of broth bubbling and smelled the savory fragrance of vegetables cooking.

"Who was sitting around the table?" Celine asked.

"Us," I said. "And the supposed next generation of restaurant owners. What do you recall, Celine?"

"The same," she said. "Except I also remember thinking that our cord couldn't quite reach the socket. That's why we had to share one hot pot among everybody."

My mind backtracked to her sentence about the

socket, which had been ungrounded. I opened my eyes and reached for her hand. "Celine, do you remember who brought out the burners and hot pots to the tables?"

"It was Uncle who brought out a burner," my cousin said, "along with Roy Yamada."

I let go of her hand and tugged at a hangnail on my thumb. Mr. Yamada again. Had he known about the poor electrical situation already, biding his time until the fatal spark?

During my pondering, Nik showed up at our booth.

"Hey, you two," he said. "Are you dropping by for an early lunch?"

I waved at Nik while Celine smiled up at him. "Why not? Do you have any new dishes I can post on IG?"

He came closer and braced his hands at the edge of our table. "You're in for a treat. Since we haven't had too many customers, Ma actually allowed me to cook something new in the kitchen."

"Ooh. What is it?" Celine said. She already had her phone in her hand, ready.

"*Poh pia*," he said. "It's like a fresh spring roll, but elevated by a sprinkle of sugar and chopped peanuts."

"That sounds amazing," Celine said. "Give us two orders right away."

"Sure thing."

I watched Nik retreat into the kitchen, and my mind flashed back to the hot pot dinner. The murderer must have gone back there to mess with the extension cord. Who had had the opportunity to do so?

"Celine," I said, interrupting her as she fiddled with her phone settings. I bet she was setting up the lighting for her food photo shoot. "Let's go through the list of people who spent time in the kitchen that night, where the extension cord was kept."

She put down her phone. "Um, wasn't that mostly you

food preppers? I was on decoration duty so I didn't go into the kitchen at all."

I counted on four fingers. "Food prep. That was me, Ba, Nik's mother, and Mr. Yamada. But I don't see how anything could've been done while we were all in the kitchen. Every one of us was working hard on preparing the raw meats and veggies. Someone would've noticed if anyone in the group had taken a break."

Celine tapped a finger against her lip. "Where was Roy Yamada after the food prep part? When we were all figuring out the best way to get the cooking started? It was kind of chaotic then."

"People were all over the place," I said. "But Mr. Yamada seems so harmless. I mean, wasn't he taking a nap at this very booth before we began eating?"

"You're right," Celine said. "He stayed at the booth and only left to go wash up for dinner. We'd better think through this again."

"Yes," I said. "He went to the restrooms." I looked in their direction. "And the interior hallway there connects to the kitchen."

"Really?" Celine said. "Because nobody would be the wiser if he'd made a detour while washing his hands."

Nik dropped by with our plates of poh pia then. They looked like giant crepes filled with stir-fried vegetables and smelled fabulous.

Nonetheless, I asked Nik for a takeout container. "I'm not very hungry all of a sudden," I said.

"Are you feeling okay?" he asked.

"Let's just say it's been a rough morning."

"Well, I hope you get better by tonight," he said.

Once he disappeared, Celine said, "Is the stuff about Roy getting you down? We could be wrong about him."

I wasn't a detective, but everything seemed to add up to place Mr. Yamada at the heart of the crime. He had insider knowledge about Ho's and its faulty wiring by virtue of being friends with Nik's mother. He'd also carried the tampered burner to the table. Moreover, he'd had hidden access to the kitchen right before Jeffery's death.

"Oh, Mr. Yamada," I said, "what have you done?" How could I have read him so wrong? Even after Celine finished her foodstagramming and we'd paid for the meal, I remained mired in gloom.

Celine offered to drive, and after we got in the car, I continued to think about Mr. Yamada's potentially dark side. He'd always been kind to me, but maybe not to others around him? I remembered how the Tanaka sisters had known him for a long time. They'd even gone to school together.

Celine started driving, but I told her, "Let's not go home right away. I want to drop by The Literary Narnia first."

"Sure, we can do that," she said, making a left at the next light. Although she hadn't been here long, she was already familiar with the route back to Eastwood Village.

―――――

Both Kelly and Dawn were behind the counter when I arrived. A few customers browsed the aisles, Celine adding to their number, while I stayed at the front and chatted with the sisters.

"I'd love to pick your brains about Mr. Yamada," I said to them.

"What about Roy?" Dawn asked, straightening the books in the spinning rack.

"You went to school with him. Didn't you say he was a prankster?" I said.

Kelly piped up. "You bet."

"Aww, but my sister has a grudge against him," Dawn said.

"He was always making trouble." Kelly shook her head. "For the teacher and all the other students."

"People deserve second chances, don't you think?" Dawn said.

"Only some folks," Kelly answered.

A customer approached asking for reference material on crochet patterns, and Dawn left us to help him.

"Before, you said Mr. Yamada would hide the teacher's erasers, small stuff like that," I said. "Did he ever get into bigger trouble?"

Kelly adjusted her wire-rimmed glasses and peered at me. "Why do you ask, Yale?"

I tapped my fingers against the desk as I gathered up my thoughts. "Did you hear about the death that happened at Ho's on Thanksgiving night?"

She nodded. "Yeah, I read some article that said the police were conducting further investigation into the matter."

I glanced around me and made sure no one else was in earshot. "Celine and I were there when it happened. We were having hot pot dinner together when Jeffery Vue passed away from a sudden electrical shock."

"Oh, I'm so sorry," she said, her hands fluttering in dismay.

"The thing is, we weren't the only ones there. A group of us from an association of restaurant owners was around, including Mr. Yamada." I paused. "The police later discovered a tampered electrical cord on-site."

Kelly's face turned pale. "And you think . . ."

"Could Mr. Yamada have done it?" I asked.

She glanced somewhere in the distance beyond me. "I don't know, Yale. There's no doubt that he's a jokester. Roy was always an opportunist when it came to pranks."

"Never caught for anything more?"

"Not that I know of," Kelly said. "And I know he's done quite well for himself with that ramen joint."

Her voice shrank as she continued. "Sometimes, though, the path is already set in your youth . . ."

I wondered if childish pranks could morph into larger devious deeds. Could Mr. Yamada's prankster ways as a kid have turned into darker acts of crime as an adult?

TWENTY-FIVE

A FTER A HURRIED LUNCH OF LEFTOVER BUBBLE
waffle, I spent my afternoon cooking. I had to prepare for the night market and replenish our entire menu
of food and drinks. In the meantime, Celine locked herself in her room. Behind the closed door, I could hear
exasperated muttering.

I only got to peek inside her bedroom when I called her
out for dinner. She hadn't moved a single item from the
space, and I saw that her suitcases were still stacked up.

"You decided then?" I said, as I split the huge poh pia
I'd gotten from Ho's.

She nibbled on her spring roll and nodded. "Yes, I'm
staying."

"I won't lie. I'm happy you'll be my roomie for a little
while longer."

She grinned. "Me too."

Then I bit into the poh pia and lost all sense of time.
It was as good as Nik had advertised, even after being
reheated. For a moment, I wondered if he might pass the

recipe along to me, but he probably wanted to keep it secret. I bet it'd be a staple item at his family restaurant soon. Maybe he'd even showcase it this evening at the night market.

The thought of tonight's event returned me to the present moment. "Your parents will be okay with you not going to Hong Kong?" I asked my cousin.

"They'll have to be," Celine said, but I noticed she'd stopped eating. "Anyway, we'd better get ready for night market. I'm going to change now."

I didn't know what Celine would be wearing, but I opted for a simple black turtleneck and fitted pants. After a round of primping, my cousin turned out in a belted sweater dress over tights, paired with combat boots.

"Going into battle tonight with my parents," she said, pointing at her footwear.

"I'll be right there beside you," I said as I pulled on my fancy chef's jacket. She draped her matching coat over her arm, and we marched out with our supplies.

It took us little time to set up the Canai and Chai food booth since we'd done it so many times by now. At the top of opening hour, Misty showed up at our stall.

Again, she appeared frustrated. Her voice grew louder with every word as she said, "I know you talked to the police."

Thankfully, the sound of an electric guitar playing on the performance stage drowned out her rising anger.

"We just repeated your own words to the police," I said.

"I can't believe you'd throw me under the bus like that. After what I did for you, Yale."

"Which was?"

"You got the recipe for my chai." She jabbed a finger at our menu's signboard.

But selling drinks was legal, unlike forging checks.

"I've been nothing but honest with you. I asked you straight out for a recipe, and you willingly gave it."

Celine stood next to me and said, "My cousin and I only spoke to the police to share the truth."

Misty tugged at the end of her braid. "I was trying to give money to people who really need it. Steer association funds to a good cause for once. Why don't you understand?"

"Because it involved a fake check and smearing my dad's name," I said, crossing my arms over my chest.

"Can't you see the bigger picture?" Misty said and threw her hands up in the air. She walked away without waiting for a response, pulling her phone out and tapping on it.

"What do you bet that she's badmouthing us right this second?" I said.

Celine shrugged. "Who cares?"

Actually, I hated it when people thought badly of me. Within five minutes, though, I'd forgotten all about Misty's irritation—because Detective Strauss had arrived at our booth.

The detective strode up to us with a spring in his step. "Hello, Yale. Celine. Let me have your infamous brutal boba drink."

"That's not the real name. It's grapefruit green tea with regular tapioca pearls," I said. "In a light bulb glass."

"Right. I'll have an order of that."

"What's the occasion, Detective?" Celine asked as she rang him up. She tilted her head toward the photo area. "Also, want to take a picture against the backdrop I created while Yale makes your drink?"

The detective stared at the display with twinkling lights. "No, thanks. Getting my photo taken isn't really my kind of thing." He pulled out his wallet and paid for his drink.

In the meantime, I moved to the back and pulled out the container of green tea.

"The brutal boba is in honor of me closing another case," he said to Celine. "Fitting, don't you think?"

I paused in my efforts, turned in his direction, and asked, "Is this about the fire?"

He brushed the lapel of his suit jacket. "Yes. You two ladies actually were instrumental by pointing me to Roy Yamada. The man was very cooperative with us at the station earlier."

I dumped the black tapioca balls into his drink, and they stuck to the bottom of the container. Then I concentrated on adding the fresh grapefruit and green tea. Maybe if I focused on simple tasks, I could avoid reading too much into the detective's words.

"Did Roy confess to starting the fire?" Celine said.

"Bingo," the detective said.

"But why would he want to ruin Ho's?" my cousin asked.

"Seems like he had it all planned. Heard that Ho's business was suffering, so he thought a little fire might result in a nice insurance payout." Poor Mr. Yamada. He'd had good intentions, even if his method had been questionable.

"But Roy Yamada didn't stop talking after that," Detective Strauss said. "He also confessed to Jeffery Vue's death."

I sloshed some tea over the edge of the light bulb glass.

"He did?" Celine said.

"That one wasn't deliberate," Detective Strauss said. "Roy Yamada admitted to placing the extension cord near the wet sink. Only he didn't think it'd be quite that dangerous, but live wires and water don't mix well."

I wiped down the light bulb glass and handed it to the detective. "Congrats on closing the case, I guess."

"All in a good day's work," he said, straightening the lapel of his suit jacket and taking the filled light bulb container. "Now I'm off to enjoy the night."

He headed toward the games section.

"Wow. I can't believe it," Celine said.

"Me either."

"But it's good news for Nik." Celine draped her chef's jacket on the back of a folding chair. "I gotta tell him that he's off the hook for both crimes."

She sprinted over to the booth next door and found Nik. Celine spoke with animation, waving her hands around as she talked with him.

Nik seemed happy upon hearing the information—or maybe he just enjoyed my cousin's company. However, I still felt sorry for Mr. Yamada.

I sighed. At least justice was served. Celine returned to our food stall, and I concentrated on running Canai and Chai.

After half an hour of doling out cucumber salad and bubble tea, Trisha showed up. Her pretty face looked pinched. "Can I talk to you guys for a minute?"

I looked behind her, but there didn't seem to be a rush for Canai and Chai's fare just yet. "Sure, there's no line."

"Perfect timing, then," she said. "It's about Misty. She's really upset."

I remembered Misty's furious typing after she left our booth. She must have let off steam to Trisha.

My cousin frowned. "Yeah, but forging a check is a crime."

"I know, and she should face the consequences," Trisha said. "But that doesn't mean she shouldn't have anybody on her side."

"You get what you dish out," Celine said, moving to her photo display and adjusting its twinkling lights.

Trisha widened her dark brown eyes at me. "Yale, you

understand, right? I think she made a wrong choice coming here and getting mad at you two. Burned bridges she
shouldn't have."

"We were just sharing what we heard from her own
mouth with the police," I said.

Trisha gestured to our food stall. "I know, and I feel
like I need to step in and mediate. It's hard to make it in
this business without any friends. There's not too many
young Asian women running local restaurants."

She had a point. Maybe Trisha could see me softening
because she said, "Misty is a good person deep down."

"If she's so interested in making amends, why isn't
she here talking to us?" I asked.

Trisha fluttered her long lashes at me. "Misty needs
some time to cool her heels. A good night's rest will give
her better perspective."

"Maybe," I said. "What do you have in mind?"

"Misty and I could meet you somewhere in the morning. A place that would be convenient to you . . . How
about Wing Fat?"

"The tables get packed during the dim sum rush."

"We'd have to meet in the early morning anyway,"
Trisha said. "Misty has to manage India Snack Mart, after all. How about before both of you have to open up?"

"That could work," I said.

"What time do you go in?"

"My dad arrives around nine," I said. "And the other
workers show up shortly after."

"How about eight, then? That should give us an hour
to talk, and we won't be in their way."

I called over to Celine. "Are you free at eight tomorrow morning?"

"Of course," she said. "My calendar's open."

"Sounds good to us," I told Trisha.

"Great," she said and ordered a soy sauce egg to go.

* * *

Time flew by as Celine and I handled the growing number of customers who came through as the evening grew later. Close to midnight, my aunt and uncle also got in the line. Their deadline had arrived.

When they came to the counter, they didn't order a single item. Instead, they asked Celine to step aside to the photo display area. My cousin and her parents were framed in an Instagram-worthy post that I might have titled, "Family Discord."

I, on the other hand, busied myself with running back and forth between the register and the kitchen, taking orders and doling out food. The rush didn't appear to be letting up, although I was short-staffed. It was a good thing I'd stocked up on disposable gloves because I kept swapping between taking money and preparing food.

In between the various tasks, though, I still caught snippets of Celine's heated discussion with her parents. Their words carried toward me through the still night.

While I brewed some chai for a waiting customer, I heard Celine announce, "I said I don't want to go back."

"Be reasonable, Celine," her mother said.

"My visa hasn't expired yet."

With a hint of worry, my uncle said, "It's really not safe here. What with the fire and everything else going on."

"About that . . ." my cousin said.

I tended to the growing crowd while I assumed Celine was informing her parents about how Nik had been cleared by the police. I wondered if she also told them about the murder case Detective Strauss was on the verge of closing. Her parents would either be relieved that there was no longer a walking murderer and arsonist wandering around, or they'd be upset that we'd stuck our noses into a police investigation.

The line dwindled as I served up several orders of scallion pancakes to a waiting family. In the pause, I caught some more of the conversation happening to my side.

Celine seemed to be standing her ground. Her parents appeared both flummoxed and irritated.

I heard my aunt frostily say to her husband, "Your daughter. She takes after you, just as stubborn."

My uncle cleared his throat. "I think she just wants a little more freedom."

"Well, if it's independence you want, you can have it," my aunt said to Celine. "But I bet you'll change your mind in a few days."

Celine's parents left soon after that remark. My aunt gave a slight shake of her head when she saw me. However, my uncle waved goodbye with a hesitant wiggle of his fingers. My aunt moved away from the booth without a hitch in her step, but my uncle glanced back at Celine as he trailed behind his wife.

TWENTY-SIX

M Y COUSIN HAD HER ARMS CROSSED, BUT WHEN her parents left our sight, she relaxed and slunk over to the booth.

"Are you all right?" I asked her.

She yanked her chef's coat off the back of the chair. "I'm fine."

"We can take a break if you want. Close up the stall for a little bit and talk."

"No, we have to keep working. I don't want you to lose any business while we chat."

I squeezed her hand. "You're more important than a million customers, Celine."

Her voice shook as she said, "I can't believe I refused my parents. Actually said no to them. Repeatedly."

"I think you need to get this all out. Why don't we sit down?" I pivoted our two chairs to face each other. "How do you feel about standing up to them?"

She took a deep breath in and exhaled in a rush. "I'm not too sure. Maybe I'm in shock."

"Sounded like your parents were shocked by your reaction too, from what I gathered."

"At least they let me make the decision in the end."

"What was your mom talking about when she left? About how you'll change your mind soon enough?"

"Beats me," she said.

I looked my cousin in the eye. "Thanks for staying in the States a little longer." Celine's presence had changed me in positive ways, and I selfishly wanted to spend more time with her.

"Well, who else will make things pretty around here?" she said, gesturing to her elegant photo display.

"Exactly. I don't know what I'd do without you," I said, half in earnest and half in jest.

Someone cleared their throat and said, "Excuse me." I turned my head to find a teenager lurking a few feet from the counter. "Are you free now? I'd like to order."

Celine sprang up from her chair and stood behind the register. "Yeah, I'm free," she said. "Finally."

People kept streaming in after that. Business was brisk, and we had to shut down early, fifteen minutes before closing time. We had to turn customers away because we'd sold out of everything.

Celine and I packed up our stall. After we'd finished, she wiped her hand across her forehead in a dramatic display.

"I'm beat," she said.

"We did serve a lot of people tonight."

"Sure did, and I deserve some ice cream after all that hard work." She slung her purse over her shoulder and headed toward the silver truck in our food stall aisle.

Below Freezing still seemed to be open, and I could see the owner, Lindsey Caine, in her lab coat, ready to serve her nitrogen-cold dessert.

My cousin and I strolled over to the truck. Celine did

a quick read of the menu and proceeded to order coffee ice cream.

"Cash or card?" Lindsey asked.

Celine plucked out a MasterCard and handed it over.

When Lindsey tried to run it, she frowned. "Do you have another you could use?"

Celine tried two other cards.

"I'm sorry," Lindsey said, "but these just aren't going through."

"Maybe something's wrong with your machine," Celine said, pointing to the credit card reader.

Lindsey tapped the unit. "Huh. It was working earlier this evening."

"Never mind," Celine said, "I'll use cash instead."

She pulled out a crisp bill and paid for the ice cream. Lindsey concocted Celine's ice cream by using a mixing bowl, cream, coffee, and squirts of liquid nitrogen. Gooseflesh rose on my arms as I watched her make it; I was reliving memories from my first investigative case.

As soon as Celine received the ice cream, she dug into it with her spoon and licked her lips. "This is exactly what I needed tonight."

"Thank you, Lindsey," I said as we walked away. We left her frowning and studying the credit card reader.

Celine and I gathered up our supplies and took our time walking back to the apartment with everything. Besides, she told me she wanted to savor the ice cream in the cool night air.

We'd passed the fountain in the plaza when I decided to ask, "Do you think it's weird that Lindsey's machine couldn't read your cards?"

My cousin spooned some more ice cream into her mouth. "Why? What are you thinking happened?"

"It's just that Lindsey said the machine had been working before. Maybe it's not the card reader that's at fault."

She raised an eyebrow at me. "You think there might be something wrong with my credit? Can't be."

I shoved the utility cart along the path toward our apartment. "I don't know. Your mom seemed pretty smug when she left us tonight."

"Are you saying my parents might have something to do with this?" She scraped the bottom of the cup with her spoon.

"Just throwing out a guess. Are the credit cards in your name?"

"I was made an authorized user on them."

We entered the lobby of our apartment building. "Doesn't that mean they're still the primary holders on the credit cards?"

"Yes." She dumped her ice cream cup away. It landed with a hard thud inside the trash can. "Do you think they froze my accounts?"

"What's your take? You know your parents better than me."

As we got into the elevator, Celine mumbled, "I wouldn't put it past them if they're mad at me for disobeying."

Restricting my cousin's access to money would be a smart move on their part. Celine often used her financial resources to overcome obstacles—and she did enjoy shopping. A vacation would be a whole lot less enjoyable without free-flowing money.

"Anyway, credit cards not working aren't going to change my mind about staying longer," Celine said as we got off on the third floor.

She unlocked the door to the apartment. As she watched me push the utility cart into the living room, she said, "I've got cash to spare anyway. I don't even need to touch the cards for the remainder of my time here."

As I tidied up the apartment, a notification dinged on

Celine's phone. She checked it and sank down into the settee.

"I can't believe it," she said.

I moved to her side. "What's happening now?"

She let me glance at an email she'd just received from her cell phone provider.

"Did I read that right?" I said. "The phone company is asking you to reconsider *closing* your account."

"It's my parents," she said. "Needling me again."

Now, Celine's phone being cut off would be a big deal for her. My cousin did everything on that thing. Plus, she loved going on her social media accounts at all hours. It was a lifeline to her art, influence, and even well-being.

"You can email the phone company, say there's been a mistake," I said.

"No, I don't really need to," Celine said. "The bill is already prepaid for the month."

"Then why would your parents even try to stop your phone service?"

"It's a warning from Ma Mi and De Di. A reminder of their power. Like virtually grounding me. But I'm not a child anymore and can make my own choices without their interference."

I perched next to her, sitting only a few inches apart. "I agree," I said. "I'm curious, though. What *are* your plans for the future?"

I asked not only because of the aggressiveness of her parents' actions but because I wanted to know what my cousin would choose and how to best stay in touch with her later on. "I love having you here, Celine, but I know you'll be gone soon. What will you do then?"

She tucked the blue chunky knit blanket around us. "Well, social media can really be done anywhere."

"Wait a minute." I touched a soft loop on the blanket. "Are you thinking about extending your stay somehow?"

"Yeah, maybe."

"Your home, though, is back in Hong Kong," I said, trying to maintain neutrality.

"My parents are over there, for sure."

"And your friends, right?" I'd never asked, but I imagined Celine would have tons of people flocking around her.

"I have people I know, but we mainly hang out because our parents are friends."

That sounded more like a business connection than a true pal. Could Celine also have felt lonely, like me, while growing up?

My cousin continued. "I know Ma Mi and De Di would like me back, if only to show my face at galas and casino openings. They always want me in the spotlight to bring attention to their business ventures."

"At least you get to glam up for exciting events," I said.

She let out a strangled laugh. "Sometimes I feel like I'm the family mascot."

I couldn't imagine her luxurious life in Hong Kong, but it must have its perks. "Is it a big contrast to being here? In this small apartment and with our humble restaurant?"

"It's nice here," she said. "And I really like Wing Fat. It's relaxing to have a steady schedule to your day."

I imagined my cousin flitting about Hong Kong, without a care in the world and shopping to her heart's content. Would she really prefer order over that? "Honestly," I said. "I think Ba works too hard. We used to make sure to take a day off once a week. But after my mom died, he threw himself into work without stopping." If Celine stayed for a while in the States, I wondered if Ba would reconsider his schedule.

"Also, the night market is fun," Celine said. "And the Eastwood Village community is great."

Now that she mentioned it, I had grown closer to our neighbors over the many weekends we'd worked together.

I didn't quite consider them family, but I enjoyed seeing our close group of vendors on a weekly basis. "I didn't think about that before. I guess you're right."

Celine continued. "Even Uncle has a group of friends with that restaurant owner association of his."

Ba did rely on and connect with those in AAROA. I wondered if I could salvage the ties in that group now what with everything that had happened. At least I could revive some harmony again by having a heart-to-heart talk with Misty tomorrow.

TWENTY-SEVEN

I N THE MORNING, I ATE A RUSHED BREAKFAST OF toast while Celine munched on some granola. I changed my outfit a few times, finally settling on a silk blouse with pants. I thought the soft material might make me seem more sensitive to Misty, even more approachable for negotiations.

Right before we headed out the door, Celine's phone rang. Who could be calling my cousin so early? Perhaps it was her parents, trying to talk her into catching the flight meant for tonight.

After glancing at the caller ID, she answered with a hesitant hello.

I heard the cadence of the speaker on the other end. The fast-paced talking didn't sound like either my uncle or my aunt.

Could it be someone she knew from Hong Kong? The place was sixteen hours ahead of Los Angeles, so maybe it was a night owl friend of hers . . . but hadn't she just told me about her lack of community over there?

"Who is this again?" Celine said. The phone wobbled in her hand. "The Department of Homeland Security?"

Yikes. That sounded serious.

She gripped the phone tighter and nodded. "USCIS. Okay. How can I help you?"

Celine seemed more relaxed after hearing that acronym, but I paced the floor before the front door. I wasn't sure what the initials stood for, and with the unexpected phone call, we were now running late to our morning appointment. I stared at the wall clock, studying the Roman numerals and wishing the second hand might move slower.

My cousin caught me looking and whispered, "Go on, Yale. I'll catch up to you when I'm done."

———

When I arrived at Wing Fat, I noticed a solitary figure wearing a parka standing in front of the restaurant and examining the building's roofline. Why was only one person standing around outside? I'd arrived late, after all.

I bustled out of the car and hurried over. "Who's there?" I said.

Trisha turned to face me and tapped her watch. "Misty apologizes, but she's running a little late."

That was understandable. "Oh, okay. So is Celine," I said, unlocking the restaurant door with my spare key.

I flicked on the lights as we entered.

Trisha paused before the hostess podium and looked around the space. "Did your family do a lot of renovating?"

"Yep. Ba modernized everything. Of course, we kept some of the Chinese décor." I pointed out the folding screens and lacquered cabinets.

"It's a nice-looking restaurant," she said.

"Thanks." I gestured to the dining area. "Want to sit

out here and wait? We don't need the banquet room for only the four of us, and we can keep an eye on the front door for Celine and Misty."

"Sounds like a plan," Trisha said. "But could I take a peek at your kitchen? We still have time before Misty comes, and I like seeing other restaurants' layouts."

"Oh, that's right. You're probably looking for inspiration," I said. "Congrats, by the way."

"For what?" She blinked at me.

"Your AAROA application went through, so I figured you must be opening up that new branch of your family restaurant."

"Yes. We're hoping to move in soon," Trisha said.

"And where is the new branch located?" I asked, but Trisha had already gone ahead of me through the swinging door.

In the kitchen, she looked like a kid in a candy store. She oohed at the industrial dishwashing machine, touched the shiny handle of a wok, and widened her eyes at a rolling cart stacked with towering bamboo steamer baskets.

I admitted that we had a great kitchen layout and cooking equipment.

She headed over to the range. "Wow. This is all so professional."

"Ba loves the classic gas burners with the heavy-duty range hood overhead." Stir-frying created a lot of splattering oil, and the powerful fan did an excellent job of capturing the grease.

"This would be an amazing stove for barbecue," she whispered.

"Huh?" I leaned closer. She must mean for the expansion of her Koreatown restaurant. "But don't you use those flat grills at the customers' tables for your KBBQ?"

She turned back to me, as though remembering I was

there, and thought for a moment. "Yeah, but we also have the option for you to get other cooked dishes from the kitchen."

"I guess some people don't like getting their hands dirty," I said. Or maybe they preferred not having the smell of smoke seep into their clothes. I personally thought the trade-off was worth it. "Hey, if we're all done in here, maybe we should go see if Misty has turned up."

"Hmm, I think my phone vibrated a moment ago. It might be her." Trisha located her cell and checked her messages. "Misty should be here in about five minutes, but she's wondering . . ."

"What?"

Trisha looked down at the floor and seemed embarrassed. "Uh, she had to skip breakfast. Misty wondered if she could eat something here."

"Tell her not to worry," I said. "Let me just check the fridge real quick."

"Great. I'll let her know." Trisha started typing away while I entered the walk-in fridge.

I'd forgotten how cold the chamber was as I shivered in the frigid air. The temperature was kept at a crisp thirty-five degrees, and I regretted wearing my thin silk shirt.

I rummaged through the various boxes of produce, wondering if I should cook something instead. That could be an olive branch to her. Celine and I had given our statements to Detective Strauss, and once he had Nik's account, she'd probably need to serve time.

What would be a quick breakfast dish? I could throw together an eggs-and-scallions combo. Ha. Maybe Misty would appreciate it more than my aunt and uncle had.

I heard noises coming from beyond the fridge door. Had Misty arrived while I'd been looking in here? Maybe I no longer had the time to cook something, but I could reheat something from the freezer. Custard buns might hit the mark.

I edged into the ice-cold territory and took a few moments to locate them. Maybe I could parallel task and steam them while we talked.

I darted out of the frostland and shut the freezer door. My teeth chattered, and I wished I had on a warm sweater. And a nice mug of hot cocoa. Or better yet, a huge bowl of soup.

Like the yummy broth Mrs. Ho had made for Thanksgiving hot pot. My thoughts strayed from there to the burner. And who'd really had access to that burner's dial. Nik, Celine, Misty, me, and . . .

A realization chillier than the current cool temperature hit me. Uh-oh. I had to get out of the fridge fast.

I pushed against the door handle, but it didn't open. It wouldn't budge an inch. I was stuck.

"Trisha," I shouted through the thick door. "Are you there? Let's talk. I know you must have had good reasons for doing what you did."

I didn't believe my own words, but I figured this wouldn't be the best time to rile Trisha up. She'd already trapped me inside this huge cooler.

I shoved against the handle again, this time putting my weight into it. It still didn't move. She must have blocked it on the other side with something heavy.

My breathing grew fast. "Let me out!"

Trisha didn't reply. Had she gone away and left me in here?

Or maybe the thick metal had muffled my words. I banged against the door. Again, no response. How much oxygen was in here anyway?

I gulped in the air—and a sudden stench assaulted me. It was the stink of the dreaded chives.

Skirting the herbs, I checked the other shelves for anything useful. I kicked at a cardboard box of broccoli resting on the floor of the walk-in fridge. How would all these vegetables help me open the door?

If only I could appeal to Trisha. She must still be around. It hadn't been that long, right?

I called her name several more times, until my voice grew hoarse. Then I sank down to the cold floor.

I sniffled, and the funk of the chives seemed to grow even stronger around me. Had it been like this for my mom? Had she known the end was near and cursed the chives she'd gone out to buy for me? Was her heart beating then like mine was now, with a racing rhythm so intense she couldn't take it any longer?

I lost sense of time as I started crying, unleashing a grief I'd stuffed inside for years. Perhaps I should give up here and grow cold until I slumped over in the fridge. It'd be kind of a fitting payback for my role in my mom's death.

But then I thought of Ba, and how devastated he'd be. I shivered in the chilly air. It brought me back to the present. I refocused.

Here I was in Wing Fat. The chives I smelled weren't from years ago but right now in the walk-in fridge of my dad's restaurant. For him, I needed to get over my fear and continue fighting.

Moving closer to the chives, I took in a few measured breaths. I focused on their long green stems in the dim, flickering light, bringing my face up close to them. They were nothing more than herbs, ingredients that would shrivel up in a wok under my skilled cooking.

I thought I heard "Yale" being shouted through the door. Trisha called my name several more times, but I didn't answer her.

The fridge wasn't that small. It should have enough oxygen to sustain me for hours, particularly since Ba would be opening the restaurant soon. Since my dad would be coming, I bet Trisha would have to come in and finish the job herself.

I again scanned the space around me to find a weapon. Beyond the door, I heard scraping, like something being moved.

It was time. And I knew what I had to do. I lunged for the tub of chili oil.

TWENTY-EIGHT

WHEN TRISHA OPENED THE DOOR TO THE walk-in fridge, I was sitting next to the tub of chili oil, holding the slippery metal ladle in my hand. She laughed at me, long and hard. Trisha herself held a huge wok in her steady grip.

"You're funny, Yale," she said. "So weak you can't even stand."

I rose to defy her.

"I know you're really cold," she said. "You're shivering."

I envied her then for the thick jacket she wore. She'd come prepared for the cold and dealing with a walk-in fridge. Trisha had planned things out, even from the very first death at Ho's. "It was you all along," I said.

I'd been so focused on the tampered extension cord that I'd forgotten that nothing fatal would've happened on Thanksgiving if no one had turned on the burner. The only person who would have had access to the hot pot would have been sitting at our booth of next-generation restaurant owners. With my cousin, Nik, and me innocent, that left only Misty and Trisha as suspects.

"Of course it was me," she said. "I'd already arrived at Ho's that night with a special purpose in mind."

"Why Jeffery Vue, though?" I asked. "What did that man ever do to you?"

"I didn't mean for *him* to get a shock," she said.

I gasped. "You mean you were aiming for Nik or his mother?" After all, the dinner had been held at their restaurant. It'd be logical that one of them would set up the cooking equipment.

She nodded. "Except Jeffery volunteered to get the cord."

"But when were you ever in the kitchen long enough to tamper with it?" I said, but even as I asked the question, I knew. "You went in there to get the noodles for the hot pot."

"And it was oh so convenient that the extension cord lay near the sink already," she said. "I wasn't sure up until then how to create the perfect injury. Seeing the cord there literally sparked my imagination."

Mr. Yamada had left it on the sink as a prank, but Trisha had taken advantage of its location.

She gave me a wicked grin. "After that, it was only too easy to find the Swiss Army knife in the cabinet. And I didn't leave any fingerprints on it, what with those kitchen gloves lying around."

I remembered the sponge and thick gloves in the sink area, ready for use. Except Trisha had used them not to clean but to cover her tracks.

"Poor Mr. Yamada," I said. "He really thought putting the cord near the sink and having it accidentally splashed on had killed his friend."

Trisha pulled the fridge door shut behind her to seal us in. "I think my dunking the cord into water might have had more to do with that."

"Do you know that he confessed to the murder?" I said. "And the arson, which you must have had a hand in as well."

She batted her long eyelashes. "Who, me? I merely gave him a tiny nudge. Let him know that some fire insurance money might come in handy for the Hos."

Trisha had definitely planted the seed in Mr. Yamada's head, even though he'd carried out the task. "You gave him the idea, and he wrote it down on his fortune cookie slip."

"Yes, and I kept the paper for leverage in case the fire wasn't ruled an accident. That way I could shift the blame and pin everything on Roy," she said.

"How could you?" I said.

"The beauty of the thing is I didn't have to lift a finger. You, Yale, did all the work for me."

She was right. What had I done to poor Mr. Yamada? I'd gotten him charged with both murder and arson. I leaned against a metal shelf for support. "By the way, you failed with the fire."

"How so?" she asked.

"Mr. Yamada is a family friend. He made sure not to set the fire when Nik and his mother would be inside. I think he even put some resistant coating on the back door."

"That all went according to my plan."

"But I thought you wanted Nik and his mother harmed, out of the picture."

"Oh, Yale, I just need to scare them away. I don't really have it in for the Hos, but for their building."

"You want the restaurant damaged?"

"Only slightly. I knew Roy wouldn't have the heart to burn it down. Besides, I needed that property mostly intact."

I gave her a blank stare.

"For a restaurant," she said. "The new branch to extend my family's business."

"Don't you already have a building in mind? You're an approved member of AAROA."

"I'm like Nik, a co-owner. Of my family's Koreatown establishment." Her eyes locked on mine. "You know, a fire from faulty wiring is how my folks got our original building for super cheap. That's the way to do it."

"But why Ho's?"

"The atmosphere, Yale. All the original diner artifacts," she said. "Perfect for my family's famous burgers and brisket."

"Wait. What?" But then I thought back to Blake's comments. He'd never said what kind of food Trisha had cooked for him. And Trisha herself had recently talked about barbecue but not Korean BBQ. I'd just assumed because of the location of her family's restaurant. "You want the Ho's restaurant site for your expansion," I repeated, the idea finally sticking in my head.

"Ho's would have been perfect."

"But not anymore?"

She sighed. "There's too much hassle involved. A lot of questions because of the hot pot fiasco and now the fire. I had to move on, and you have nice cooking equipment here at Wing Fat. It'll do, even though I'll have to redecorate the dining area."

I recalled the way she'd inspected the building when I'd arrived at Wing Fat. How she'd scrutinized the dining space and the kitchen's amenities. "I don't like where you're going with this."

She jerked her thumb behind her. "Too bad you were cooking here this morning and had a horrible accident. I didn't realize until it was too late."

"What kind of accident?" I asked.

"No need to worry about that," Trisha said. "You'll be knocked out before then and won't feel a thing."

I straightened up and raised my metal ladle high.

"Don't come any closer." Chili oil snaked down the handle and onto my fingers.

"Your lips are turning blue, Yale," she said. The flickering fluorescent light cast shadows across her pretty face, turning it sinister.

"We can find a different solution," I said. "A mutually agreeable one."

"I already made a solid plan."

I cowered back.

She stepped forward with the wok held high—and slipped on the floor I'd completely covered with chili oil. Arms flailing, she dropped the wok and lost her balance. As she fell, the side of her head thudded against the edge of a hard metal shelf. She lay on the floor in an unmoving heap.

I trembled but not from the cold this time. How long would she be out? I didn't know if I could confront her again in my weakened state. Edging around Trisha, I made a quick escape.

Right outside the walk-in fridge, I noticed a utility cart piled high with a mishmash of equipment. She'd placed steaming baskets, porcelain platters, anything she could get ahold of to weigh it down. I used the same cart to block the fridge and keep her in there.

I rubbed at my arms, thankful for the warmth of the room. Actually, it was unnaturally warm. I heard a sizzling noise and looked over at the range.

A wok sat on the burner. High flames were leaping out of it. A grease fire.

That must have been the accident she'd been planning. I rushed toward the stove as someone burst through the kitchen door. Celine. She looked frazzled.

"I smelled smoke," my cousin said. "Are you okay?"

Not trusting my voice, I pointed to the flaming wok.

"Where's the extinguisher?" Celine looked around the room, her breathing growing ragged.

The back door swung open. Ba peered in.

"Yale? Celine?" His eyes widened at the grease fire. "Get out of there. Right now."

I wasn't about to let our family restaurant go down in flames. That would mean Trisha would win.

Celine wasn't having any luck finding an extinguisher, but my eyes landed on a bag on the counter. Perfect.

I rushed over and grabbed it. To snuff out the flames, I poured a mountain of salt on top of the wok. After putting out the fire, I finally heard the blare of sirens approaching.

Ba rushed in and inspected me at arm's length. Satisfied I was fine, he hugged me.

Within minutes, the cops also showed up. They were led by Detective Strauss, who strode through the back door to assess the situation.

Not seeing any clear danger, he relaxed his hand near his holster and moved toward us three. "Is everyone okay?"

We each gave him our reassurances.

"Who called for you?" I asked after he seemed satisfied with our responses.

"I did," my cousin said. "Since I was running late, I texted Misty to let her know. That's when she told me she wasn't aware of a meeting set up by Trisha."

Detective Strauss paced the kitchen. "Where is Trisha Kim right now?"

I pointed to the fridge with the cart blocking the door. "In there."

"Interesting," he said. "Yale, I can tell there's a good story behind all this."

The police informed Ba it might take time to settle everything, so he called his staff to let them know. He decided to shut down Wing Fat for the day because of the unexpected emergency.

Several hours passed by me in a blur due to my shocked state. Paramedics came, pulling out Trisha's unconscious body and reviving her to a drowsy state. They also evaluated the health of Ba, Celine, and me.

The police also made sure to take down our statements, recording every word and tracking the exact details and timing.

By the time we were released, morning had dissolved into the afternoon. Despite not being a hugging kind of man, Ba embraced both Celine and me after the ordeal. We all agreed we needed some downtime and returned to our respective homes.

TWENTY-NINE

BACK IN THE APARTMENT, WE TOOK A MUCH DE-served lunch break. I made an easy meal of "doll" noodles, or ramen. Quick comfort food for the both of us.

As we slurped down our noodles, we rehashed the harrowing details and processed our emotions.

"When I saw those leaping flames," Celine said, her eyes widening, "I was afraid for you."

"Unintentional grease fires happen, especially around kitchens," I said. "I'm grateful the salt trick worked." I'd never personally set off any flames whenever I had cooked, but I'd heard stories about them, along with the different methods of snuffing them out.

"I'm super glad you're safe," Celine said. "That was some quick thinking on your part. With both the salt and the chili oil."

"It was pure luck that Trisha hit her head like that when she slipped. I was just planning on making a run for it while her balance was unsteady." I put down my chopsticks. "I have to give props to you, for putting two and two together and getting the cops on the scene so quickly."

My cousin shook her head. "If only I'd done it sooner. Or gotten off that annoying call earlier so I could come help you."

"You didn't know." I continued eating and drank the remaining broth. "What was that call in the morning about anyway?"

She played with the rim of her bowl. "It was someone from USCIS—U.S. Citizenship and Immigration Services."

"That sounds important. What did they want?" I wiped my mouth with a napkin and placed my bowl to the side.

"The caller was concerned about my stay. Said they'd heard I wasn't following visa rules."

"How? You're here on vacation."

"Someone reported that I was working and abusing my tourist visa."

I raised my eyebrows. "But you don't even have a job here."

"A witness claimed I'd been seen working the register at both the Eastwood Village Night Market and Ho's."

I opened my mouth and closed it again. She *had* been helping out with the food stall and at Nik's restaurant. Did those duties count as working?

Celine pulled back her shoulders. "Of course, I told them that I'd bring my lawyer in to dispute these false claims."

"Can you do that?"

"Of course," she said. "They can't accuse me of having a job. I wasn't in violation of anything. All the stuff I've done hasn't been for pay. I was just helping out friends and family."

"How did the representative react to what you said?"

"The worker sounded nervous to me. I even asked to

speak to their manager right then." My cousin fiddled with her chopsticks. "That might have been why I arrived even later to Wing Fat. I made sure to give the manager a piece of my mind."

"Wow," I said. "You're bold."

"Thanks," Celine said, but she frowned. "I'm still mad at *them* for bringing immigration officials into the picture, though."

"Who are you angry at again?"

She sighed and pushed her bowl away. "My parents. I mean, who else could have reported me?"

"Why would they do something like that?"

"To get me to go on that flight with them tonight."

"Oh." I hadn't thought of that. Would my uncle and aunt really have stooped so low to report their own daughter to the government?

I wanted to defend her parents, but I really didn't know them that well. She could be right, after all.

We'd finished with our lunch, so I cleared away the dishes and started washing them. While I was at the sink, Celine's cell phone rang.

My cousin first took the call in the living room but then scurried over to my side. "Hold on a moment," she said. "I'm going to put you on speakerphone, Misty. That way Yale can join in the conversation."

I stopped in the middle of washing and followed Celine to the settee for the call.

We sat down next to each other as Misty asked, "So what was that fake meeting with Trisha all about?"

"Hmph. How much time do you have?" Celine said.

"A ten-minute break."

"Might not be enough." My cousin proceeded to talk about my showdown with Trisha at Wing Fat. She managed to paint me as the heroine.

I shook my head vigorously to deny it even though Misty couldn't see me. "I wasn't half as brave as Celine makes me out to be," I said. "It was scary, but I managed to pull through."

"I recently started suspecting that Trisha was trouble," Misty said.

"But weren't you texting her last night after you confronted us at the food stall?" I said.

"Uh, no. I was using Line to message my sister."

When she spoke again, her tone sounded frosty. "Anyway, once I put some distance between us, Trisha started moving in on Blake even more."

Maybe that's how Trisha had known there had been trouble between us and Misty. She'd seen our interaction while hanging out at Blake's stall.

My cousin continued talking to Misty. "Aren't Trisha and Blake a couple?" Celine said. "I saw his Facebook posts."

"He might have thought so, but Trisha was using him. She pumped him for info. Contacts in the area, that sort of thing."

Celine played with a strand of her honeyed hair. "She sure is ambitious."

"Well, the middle part of that word kind of matches what I'm thinking," Misty said.

Gabbing together like this made me feel closer to Misty, but I needed to ask her outright. I leaned closer to the phone. "So, Misty, are things okay between us?"

"Yeah," she said. "Sorry I blew up like that at you. It actually all worked out in the end."

"How so?" Celine asked.

"One of my uncles is a lawyer, and he got them to lower the consequences for the check fraud."

"Good to hear," I said, relaxing back into the settee.

"Based on my clean record, all I got was community service."

"That's great. I think?" Celine said.

"It sure is. I got to choose the nonprofit to work with,

and of course I selected The Human Connection." Misty's smile came through even over the phone.

I was happy for Misty that she didn't get punished too harshly for trying to help out a nonprofit. Speaking of organizations, I said, "Misty, I know AAROA hasn't been very welcoming to you, but I think you could add a lot to it. Plus, now that Nik's president, he can change things for the better. I'll talk to him."

"Maybe Celine might be more of an influence," Misty said with a lilt to her voice.

My cousin's grip on the phone slipped, but she corrected it. "I don't know what you're going on about."

"Uh-huh," Misty said. "Keep telling yourself that."

We said goodbye, and I teased Celine a little about Nik, but then she got distracted by a notification from her phone.

"More of your social media fans?" I said.

"No, it's an email from your father to a bunch of us."

"Huh." I peered at her screen. Ba had sent out a message to Celine, her parents, and me, inviting us for a Yee family meal together. He called it a well-wishes dinner for good luck before the Hong Kong flight for my uncle and aunt.

It wasn't held at any slapdash location, either. Ba had invited everyone over to our old family house in Palms for the get-together.

I felt the breath get knocked out of me. Were we really having dinner at my childhood home? Sure, I'd won a small victory over a bunch of chives today, but I didn't know if I could handle the onslaught of grief at my old house.

Feeling torn, I called up my dad to talk it over with him. He'd decided on the dinner location as a symbol of reconciliation with his brother, he told me. Ba quoted his favorite saying: "Relationships are the essential heartbeats of life, and family should be together."

However, he knew about my reservations and had decided to host the dinner outside on the patio. He assured me that he understood if I needed to back out of the meal, though.

I went back and forth, but finally decided that sacrifice for my current family circle was worth it. It also helped knowing that Ba had totally redone the backyard since my mom's death. He'd pulled out the entire lawn where I used to do teetering cartwheels and replaced it with smooth concrete.

When Celine and I showed up at my old Palms neighborhood, I avoided glancing at the house. Instead, I made my way directly through the side gate and into the backyard. Thankfully, it looked totally transformed from my childhood memories.

On the new extended patio, Ba had sectioned off the wide space into two comfortable areas. One was a cozy spot with two outdoor couches facing each other across a wicker table. The other side held a large patio table with chairs. Tiny lights hung down from a pergola placed above the table, adding soft mood lighting.

My cousin and I greeted my dad, proceeding to compliment him on the backyard. If I didn't look behind me, I could've imagined myself being at a stranger's house.

Soon, we heard car doors closing from the street out front and knew Celine's parents had arrived. My cousin smoothed the T-shirt she wore underneath her blazer. She'd gone with a casual look, telling me she didn't want to bother with impressing her mother anymore. The fact that she wanted to work out any creases, though, told me a different story.

My aunt stepped through the side gate first. She wore a long-sleeve green lace dress with a matching shawl draped around her shoulders. Even while wearing high heels, she managed to glide toward us with elegance. She clasped her hands around Celine's in greeting.

Then my uncle ambled in. He hovered near his wife and daughter, patting Celine on the shoulder a few times.

Then they turned to me and said hello. Both of them had sincere smiles on their faces.

After we got seated, Celine whispered, "Why don't they look mad at me?"

Their actions seemed to be ones of happiness at seeing Celine. I suspected that Ba had told them about the grease fire at the restaurant, and they were relieved that nobody had been hurt.

My cousin, however, didn't want to settle for peace that easily. Celine looked at her parents, both seated across from her, and said, "So, which one of you called USCIS on me?"

"Who?" my aunt asked.

"Like you don't know. The immigration agency," Celine said.

My dad leaned toward me with a confused expression on his face.

I whispered to him, "Tell you about it later."

Meanwhile, Celine said, "Guess what? Your trick didn't work. I still have a valid visa to stay here."

My mind traveled back to Celine's comments about her phone interview. She'd been accused of two places of employment: the food stall and Ho's. *Wait a minute.* Celine's parents hadn't known she'd pitched in for Nik during his time of need.

I grabbed Celine's arm to stop her accusations. "I don't think it was them," I said.

"What do you mean?" My cousin shook off my hand.

"They never knew about Ho's." Only the customers at the restaurant that day had seen her helping out at the register. Who knew beyond that? The AAROA members. Those who'd been around when the firefighters had doused out the flames at Nik's family restaurant. Celine had talked then about helping at Ho's. "I think it was Trisha," I said. "Working behind the scenes."

Celine started to shake her head but stopped after a moment. Maybe she was thinking about the same detail I was: the timing of the USCIS call.

It'd been placed just before we were both supposed to go to Wing Fat. It would be a clever way of separating us.

"Never mind," Celine muttered. "I may have been mistaken."

My uncle spoke up in a loud voice. "Sing, I really like these patio lights. They're so, um, very nicely lit."

"Thank you," my dad said. "Since we're here to have dinner, let me go ahead and serve the food."

Ba darted inside the house and brought out some wonderful dishes to eat. He'd cooked up a scrumptious meal of clams with black beans and chili sauce, braised abalone in oyster sauce, stir-fried snow pea leaves, and wonton noodle soup.

We dove into the food and spent time savoring the bursts of flavor on our tongues.

Celine's mother broke the eating stretch first. She dabbed at her mouth with a napkin and said, "It's all very delicious, Sing."

My uncle added, "I can see why you called your place Wing Fat."

The restaurant's name sounded like "always prosperous" in Cantonese. This was high praise coming from my uncle.

Ba grinned and said, "And I wanted to make a special dinner for you. To send you off with good and hopeful wishes on your journey."

My aunt blinked hard, as though trying to ward off tears. "Thank you," she said, "for the kind thoughts about the flight for . . . only Sunny and me."

Celine dropped her chopsticks, and they clattered

against her plate. Did this mean they had accepted her decision to stay for sure?

My uncle looked at the profile of his wife with an admiring glance. "It'll be good to spend more time as a couple in this new life stage. What you call empty nesting."

"Maybe we can even take a short vacation or two," my aunt said, readjusting the shawl around her shoulders.

"Step away from the hustle and bustle," my uncle said.

My dad sipped water from his glass and said, "Actually, I've been thinking the same thing. After having to close the shop today because of the fire . . ."

Aha. I'd been right. He *had* told Celine's parents about it.

Ba continued. "It's been refreshing to take a break from work. And I know I'm not getting any younger as time goes by."

"What are you trying to say, Sing? You're younger than me," my uncle said, but there didn't seem to be much vinegar in his words.

"It'll be good to reprioritize. Spend more time with family," Ba said, looking at my cousin and me, his eyes filled with warmth. "Maybe I'll go back to a schedule of six days a week."

Ba had made a huge concession. I lifted my glass of water to him in a toast, and he smiled back at me.

"Are you sure you're okay with this?" Celine asked her parents.

I wasn't certain if my cousin was asking for their permission to not go with them on their flight tonight or for something more nebulous, like her independence. In either case, my aunt and uncle nodded in unison.

I suppose I'd misjudged them. At the dinner table, I discovered their true dim sum personalities. My uncle was like a stuffed pepper; he appeared unassuming but contained hearty, down-to-earth qualities. My aunt was like mango pudding. She looked delicate and almost unapproachable in her elegance, but then surprised you with her flexible interior.

Ba looked at all of us in turn around his patio table and said, "I want to share that I'm thankful for every one of you. For my whole family."

"Yes," I said, raising my glass again.

"Hear, hear," Celine added.

My aunt nodded, and my uncle beamed at my dad.

It could have been the hum of a nearby cricket, but I swore I also heard the whisper of my mother's voice. "Agreed," she said.

THIRTY

AFTER THE EVENTFUL TIME WE'D HAD, IT WAS NO surprise we were both exhausted and slept in the next day. Celine and I lounged around the apartment because we didn't have anything planned except for a relaxed outing in the afternoon to visit a Los Angeles hidden gem. I was losing myself in a few chapters of *Wuthering Heights* when I got a call from the security guard in the complex's lobby.

Nik was downstairs asking for us. Interesting because I didn't expect company. I hadn't bothered to brush my hair earlier, although that would be fine. I'd only match his bedhead style.

My cousin, though, looked alarmed when I told her about Nik's sudden appearance.

"I have to go change," she said. "He can't see me like this."

"Fine. I'll go first and keep him busy," I said. Nik wouldn't care that I wore an old high school shirt and sweatpants. I took the elevator down and saw him right away, pacing around in the polished lobby.

"Yale," he said once he noticed me. "Are you okay?"

"I'm fine. Why?"

"I heard that Wing Fat closed down yesterday due to an emergency. Then Ma got ahold of your dad early this morning, and we got the inside scoop about the fire." He peered across the way toward the elevators.

"Don't worry. Celine's okay," I said. "She'll be coming down soon. Why don't we sit?"

Nik followed me as I led him to the library area.

"How's your restaurant been doing?" I asked.

"Good, actually." Nik ran a hand through his hair. "Business is picking up, and the funds AAROA gave us made a big difference."

"Speaking of the association," I said, "Misty has been feeling kind of unwelcome. Do you think you can make an extra effort to help her fit in?"

"For sure." He twisted his hands. "There's so much I want to do as the new president, including making certain we have the next generation involved. How about you?"

"What do you mean?" I scooted my chair away from him.

"You could join the association, Yale."

"I'm not a restaurant owner like the rest of you," I said.

He waved his hand in the direction of The Shops at Eastwood Village. "You're at the night market every weekend running a business."

"Food stalls aren't restaurants," I said. "And I'm not the co-owner of Wing Fat."

"Rules are meant to be improved, and I am the president, aren't I?" He gave me the cocky grin he'd perfected in high school.

"Anyway, Canai and Chai is an offshoot of Wing Fat," I said. "So everything ties back to my dad."

"Is it, though? The two places have even got different names. And the food stall is basically operated by you."

I rubbed my chin. "Well, let me think about it."

"Make sure that you do."

I got saved from Nik trying to increase his membership numbers for AAROA when Celine arrived.

His gaze slid from my face and moved over to hers when she took a chair next to mine. Celine had dressed in a vibrant ruched-sleeve top.

She said hello to Nik and added, "It's good to see you, but what are you doing here?"

"I came, uh, because of the blog." He nodded twice as though to infuse some truth into his words. I bet he'd come running to check on Celine, although he was embarrassed about it and had a cover story ready.

"What about the *Eastwood Village Connection*?" my cousin asked.

He pulled out his phone. "Well, I've been getting emails. A lot of people want to advertise with us."

"Really?" Celine pulled her chair closer to him.

"The blog is getting popular. I bet we could monetize it."

My cousin seemed to have influencer stars in her eyes, like when the heart count took off on her Instagram posts. "That's great news, Nik."

He seemed speechless, enraptured by her dreamy look.

"Er, I realize I need to go do something," I said, excusing myself and leaving them to chat or dream or whatever.

I returned to the comfort of my home, launching back into the novel's Yorkshire moors. Unfortunately, I didn't get to linger there long.

The phone trilled, and I answered it to find Detective Strauss on the other end.

Without preamble, he said, "Yale, I'm glad you're safe."

"Thank you, Detective Strauss."

His deep voice rumbled on. "And you're sure you're fine?"

"Absolutely." Actually, doing quite well considering I'd been locked with a killer inside a giant fridge. "Do you have an update?"

The detective was usually direct, but he didn't answer right away. He hemmed a bit before forcing out his next words. "Even though what you did wasn't standard procedure, Yale, I'm grateful for your help in capturing Trisha Kim."

I gave myself a mental pat on the back. "Did she end up saying anything incriminating to you?"

"She admitted to everything, including a call to US-CIS to try and sabotage your cousin's visa."

"Wow." I sat down on Celine's bed with a thud. "Trisha doesn't seem like the type to crack under pressure."

"It's funny how being on the edge of death can encourage someone to tell the truth," the detective said.

Trisha had sustained a major bump to her head. It'd either taken down her guard or scared her enough to share. "So you can definitely tie Trisha to Jeffery's death now?"

"Yes on that count. She also planted the seed for starting the fire at Ho's, but . . ."

I sighed. "I know. Mr. Yamada is still actually responsible for setting it."

"But given the circumstances and the fact that he'd put some fire retardant on the building as a preventative, I think he might get off with a steep fine."

I was glad to hear it. Mr. Yamada was older, and I wouldn't want him to waste away in jail.

Detective Strauss continued. "Since Trisha Kim confessed to Jeffery Vue's death, along with your attempted murder and the deliberate fire at Wing Fat, you can rest assured that she'll be locked away for a long time. Justice will be served."

I thanked the detective. Before hanging up, he wished Celine and me well. I couldn't wait to tell my cousin the good news.

C eline came back from her time with Nik as though floating on a cloud. I rose from the settee, where I'd been reading, and said, "Looks like your talk with Nik went well."

"Perfectly," she said. "We got a business plan in place and brainstormed more blog ideas."

"I've got more good news," I said. "We got a call from Detective Strauss."

Once I summarized the conversation, Celine said, "This is cause for celebration."

"And our upcoming outing will be loads of fun, I guarantee it."

Her lips quirked. "Honestly, Yale, it doesn't sound that exciting."

"Excuse me?" I clutched *Wuthering Heights* in front of me like a shield. "You know, I had to set an appointment to get a private tour."

"I mean, the International Printing Museum?" she said. "It sounds kind of dull."

"You'll change your tune when you see it." I grabbed her arm and gave it a gentle tug. "Come on, it's about time to get going."

Once we arrived in Carson and explored the museum, she seemed more impressed. The whole space was a massive warehouse that contained impressive antique printing machines. My cousin admired the print works on the walls and their high quality.

The pinnacle of the tour, though, was the Linotype printing press.

I gestured to the machine and said, "You can make a customized stamp with your name on it and even a tagline."

"Neat." Celine thought for a moment and then whispered what she wanted to print to our docent. He assembled the keys and cranked the machine. Soon it issued a metal slug.

"We can stamp it on a piece of paper so you can see how it'll look."

Celine put her palms together. "I'd love that."

Once he'd done so, Celine showed the paper to me. She'd embellished her name and turned it into: CELINE YEE, INFLUENCER EXTRAORDINAIRE. "What do you think?" she asked.

Really, Celine had and continued to influence those around her for the better, including Ba and me. "I think it's perfect," I said.

She tossed her hair and beamed. "Guess I'm influential not only in Hong Kong but also in America. In fact, I kind of like it here. Maybe Ma Mi and De Di can pull some strings to help me stay indefinitely."

My voice rose in pitch with excitement. "Really? Do you think that could happen?"

"Sure. Why not? I'm young and free." She patted my arm. "Besides, what would you do without me? I'm like the *C* part of Canai and Chai."

"Both of the words in the food stall start with the letter *C*."

"Exactly," she said.

"You might have a point, though. It'd be weird being at the night market without you."

"Yeah, and who would take all those #LAeats shots of your cooking?" she said, miming taking a picture with her phone.

"I know, right?" I clasped my hands in an exaggerated begging motion. "Celine, say you'll be my foodie partner in crime."

"Of course I will, cuz." She jostled the purse on her shoulder. "Now, where is a good restaurant around here?"

"Oh, I know the perfect place," I said, and we walked out of the museum arm in arm.

Acknowledgments

First, I'm grateful to all the readers, librarians, and book-sellers who've approached me and shared about how much they're enjoying this tasty new series. Special shout-out to John McDougall for selecting *Death by Bubble Tea* for the Murder By The Box subscription, to Alpha Park Public Library for featuring the novel as Book of the Day, and to local bookstore owner Jhoanna Belfer of Bel Canto Books for organizing AAPI author festivals and cheering on Asian American writers.

I'm always happy to connect with people online, so please check out my newsletter offering and find my social media handles at JenniferJChow.com.

Thank you to hardworking bloggers like Dru Ann Love, bookstagrammers (too many to name!), podcasters like Alexia Gordon, and supportive journalists like Elisa Shoenberger. Happy to have been on fun group blogs like *The Wickeds* and *Jungle Red Writers* and reviewed in great magazines like *Kings River Life*.

Sisters in Crime—you all are amazing! Thank you for

allowing me the privilege of serving on the national board as president. Heartfelt thanks to executive director Julie Hennrikus and immediate past president Stephanie Gayle for their wonderful support. Excited to be working with a fabulous board and fantastic volunteers this year!

Crime Writers of Color: You inspire me and allow me to dream bigger. Thank you for the care I feel from everybody. I'm so appreciative of Kellye Garrett, Walter Mosley, and Gigi Pandian for starting this group.

Many heart emojis to my fellow Chicks on the Case bloggers (Becky, Cynthia, Ellen, Kathleen, Kellye, Leslie, Lisa, Marla, and Vickie). I'm happy to call you friends.

To my local writing pals (Lisbeth, Robin, Sherry, and Tracey), thanks for being my cheerleaders. Hugs to you all!

A lot of authors did joint events with me while I was promoting *Death by Bubble Tea*. These include but are not limited to Dale Berry, Vera Chan, Hannah Mary McKinnon, Hank Phillippi Ryan, Alex Segura, Sheila Lowe, Peggy Rothschild, Susan Rowland, Ellen Byron, Nancy Cole Silverman, Daryl Wood Gerber, Jayci Lee, Susan Lee, Suzanne Park, Naomi Hirahara, Tori Eldridge, Julie Tieu, Ed Lin, and Fleur Bradley. Many, many thanks!

A huge thank-you for the invites from organizations, bookstores, and libraries asking me to speak, places like MWA NorCal, SinC NorCal, SinC LA, Long Beach Library, Belmont Books, California Writers Club–OC, Mysterious Galaxy, LAPL Northridge, Vroman's Bookstore, and Torrance Public Library.

Jessica Faust and the BookEnds family: Thanks for constantly believing in me, even when I'm not so sure about my ideas. Also, plenty of pats to Olive the literary dog!

Jane Liu: You've again delivered a vibrant and captivating cover. Thanks for your creative genius! Stephanie

Sheh: Heartfelt gratitude for giving my characters true and engaging voices in the audiobooks.

To the Berkley superstars . . . Angela Kim, thanks for being on my side and always making my words better. So happy to have met in person—bubble tea is on me the next time we see each other! Special thanks to the entire team involved in interior design, copyediting, and proofreading—so very grateful! Stephanie Felty and Kim I: Thank you, thank you, thank you! It's been exhilarating to be featured in the *New York Times Book Review*, *Woman's World*, *Bustle*, BookBub, *Booklist*, Book Riot, CrimeReads, Fresh Fiction, *Mystery Scene*, *Woman's Day*, and more! Also, squee about hitting the SoCal Indie Bestseller List for multiple weeks!

Yay for family and friends, who continue to go to my events and buy my books. Thanks for supporting me! Cheers to the Chows, Laus, Lims, and Ngs!

To my immediate family: I love you more than (gasp!) words can ever express. B and E, thanks for thinking that writing is a cool job and that my books are quirky and fun. As always, I'm indebted to my husband, Steve, who never doubted my abilities and was game enough to go on this writing journey with me. I'm truly blessed to be able to do something I love so dearly.

Recipes

Chai

(SERVES ONE)

1 cardamom pod
2 cloves
1/2-inch slice of peeled ginger
1 cup water
2 teaspoons sugar
2 teaspoons loose leaf black tea (I used
   Brooke Bond Red Label)
1/2 cup 2% milk

Using a mortar and pestle, or even a meat mallet, crush together the cardamom, cloves, and ginger. (Placing the ingredients into a sealed plastic bag may make the crushing less messy if using a meat mallet.)

Boil the water in a small saucepan over high heat and add the crushed spice mixture.

Add the sugar and tea and boil for 1 minute.

Reduce the heat to low and slowly add the milk.

Using a sieve, strain the contents of the pan over a mug.

Enjoy with biscuits dipped in the tea (I prefer the Parle-G brand).

Scallion Pancakes

(SERVES FOUR)

2 cups flour
3/4 cup water plus 2 tablespoons water
2 tablespoons sesame oil
5 scallions, chopped
Sesame seeds, toasted (as desired)
Oil to cook with (I used avocado oil)

Cover a cutting board with clear plastic wrap.

Combine the flour and the 3/4 cup water to form a dough.

Whisk together the 2 tablespoons water and the sesame oil in a small bowl.

Separate the dough into 4 balls. While holding a ball in the palm of your hand, brush it with the oil mixture to coat the ball evenly.

Flatten the ball into a disk on the cutting board.

Flatten the disk into a pancake approximately 6 inches in diameter, and sprinkle on scallions and sesame seeds.

Fold the dough onto itself so the scallions and sesame seeds are on the inside.

Flatten the dough into a pancake again. Repeat for all the dough balls.

Add 1 tablespoon oil to a skillet over medium heat. Cook the pancakes for a few minutes on each side, until golden brown.

Dipping sauce (optional):

1 tablespoon soy sauce
1 tablespoon rice wine vinegar
Pinch of chili pepper flakes

Whisk together the soy sauce, vinegar, and chili pepper flakes until well combined.

Serve in a small bowl with the pancakes.

Ready to find
your next great read?

Let us help.

Visit prh.com/nextread

Penguin
Random
House